Claire,

Your early positive response to my idea of writing this story was a good motivation for me. Thanks for your support & I anticipate your book!

Siddy

UP THE NOTCHED-LOG LADDER

ARTHUR AND EDNA AMONG THE DAYAKS OF BORNEO

BY

SYDWELL MOUW FLYNN

authorHOUSE

1663 LIBERTY DRIVE, SUITE 200
BLOOMINGTON, INDIANA 47403
(800) 839-8640
www.authorhouse.com

First published by AuthorHouse 09/30/04

ISBN: 1-4184-7105-4 (sc)
ISBN: 1-4184-7104-6 (dj)

Library of Congress Control Number: 2004095134

Printed in the United States of America
Bloomington, Indiana

This book is printed on acid-free paper.

For my children, Jim and Erin,
so you will know who you came from.

Table of Contents

INTRODUCTION

"Go ye into all the world and preach the Gospel." These are the words of Jesus recorded in Mark 16:15. In 1931, my parents, Arthur and Edna Mouw, answered this call, going to the Netherlands East Indies, now Indonesia, to become missionaries to the Dayaks, the indigenous people of Borneo.

While I was growing up, I never questioned what my parents taught me. In these early years, I had been surrounded by other Christians. But later I came to realize that, while not all people accept the Christian faith, they are not without their own knowledge of God. My link to God is through Jesus Christ, but I do not judge the path to God chosen by others as long as it exemplifies God's love. I began to question whether we should try to persuade those of other cultures to embrace Christianity. My own trip back to Indonesia forty-one years after our family had left in 1950, and the writing of this book, laid this question to rest.

I spent ten days in Borneo, visiting the people and the places I had known as a child. Everywhere I traveled among the Dayaks, I was joyfully received and surrounded by love. In addition to this warmth encompassing me, I became aware of the depth of feeling they had for my parents and what had been accomplished through their work. My parents are not only loved and revered by those who knew them personally, but this love and reverence has been passed down through generations.

Why are my parents still remembered and revered by the Dayaks? It is not because of a specific theological position; it is because their love of God empowered them and radiated through their lives. They *showed* this love to the Dayaks, as I believe the stories in this book will attest to. And I believe that anyone of whatever place, culture, or time who radiates love is capable of transforming people's lives.

In the twelve years since my visit, my faith in God has grown. And as my faith has grown, so too has my desire to tell the story of what my parents did in the land of Borneo many years ago. (I can hear my father's voice correcting me: "It is not what *we* did but what *God* did.") To assist me in this task, I was fortunate to have 186 of my parents' letters written to friends and family between 1931 and 1950, thirty tapes of my dad's sermons, several photograph albums, and a few annual reports written to the Christian and Missionary Alliance, the denomination under which they served.

This is my parents' story, much of it told in their own words.

1 THE BEGINNING: MEETING, MARRIAGE, AND BIBLE SCHOOL

Arthur Mouw and Edna Stephenson met at Simpson Bible Institute in Seattle, Washington, in 1927. This is my father's account of their meeting and first date: "Because I had been a carpenter, knew a little bit about mechanics, and a little bit about plumbing, they made me the maintenance man. After I'd been at the school for some time, I was out working one morning—I had put in some forms the night before, and some men were going to come and pour the cement—about 8 o'clock, and a certain young lady walked in through the gate. She walked up the sidewalk, and that sidewalk curved awfully close to those forms that I was fixing, and as she passed by she just said, 'Good morning, Mr. Mouw,' and I nodded and said, 'Good morning, Miss Stephenson,' and something went bang inside of me; and my gaze followed her as she walked up that sidewalk, went up the steps and through the door. And I said, 'I'm going to see that young lady just as soon as I can.'

"And one day as she was walking down the hall in one direction, I was walking down the hall in the other direction. It was only three feet wide, and so I stopped her right in the middle and said, 'Miss Stephenson, will it be all right if I come and see you on Friday night?' She said, 'Yes,' just like that. And she looked like she was terribly troubled, half scared to death. And I found out later that she was! She told me the reason she said 'yes' was because if she had said 'no' we would have had a little discussion. And she thought it would be easier to just say 'yes' and then get out of it afterward. But later she thought she'd let me come once and then she'd tell me what was on her mind, and then I'd stay away.

"Well, on that Friday night I was right there in my Model T Ford. We were in her home, and we played the piano for a while. I tried to sing and we went into the kitchen and made fudge. I don't know what young people do now, but we made fudge. Then we came out and sat on the piano bench again, and she played and I sang. Then she told me what was on her mind." (Arthur, taped sermon)

What was on my mother's mind was to tell my father that she was almost two years older than he, because she believed this would make him lose interest in her. But my father already knew this, having talked to one of my mother's best friends to learn all he could about her. So they continued to see each other, and soon he wrote his mother a postcard saying, "As far as I'm concerned, I've met Mrs. Arthur Mouw."

Edna and Arthur, Seattle, 1929

My father, Arthur Mouw, was born in 1903 in Sioux Center, a Holland-Dutch community located forty miles north of Sioux City, Iowa. In 1916 his family moved to California and settled in Arcadia, where he, his brother, and six sisters grew up on ten acres. After graduating from high school, my father worked as a carpenter with his father, making eighty-seven cents an hour, or about seven dollars a day. He also tried his hand at real estate, promising God, "Lord, If you will help me get some money, I'll go to Bible school." Soon he was working on a deal that would pay

3

him a $5,500 commission, but this deal eventually fell through, leaving him $1000 in debt. Later he described the next series of events this way: "And I said, 'Lord, now if you'll help me get out of debt, I'll go to Bible school,' and I thought surely the Lord would help me make another deal. But I couldn't have sold a lot if it'd had gold bricks on it. Finally I gave up and just went back to my hammer, and I pounded with that hammer for twelve hundred hours to pay back my indebtedness, and more hours than that to keep myself alive." With his friend Bob Chrisman, he left for Simpson Bible Institute in Seattle in 1927.

My mother, Edna Stephenson, was born in Montana in 1901 and lived in Stockett and Lehigh until 1917, when the family moved to Seattle. Her father, John Stephenson, was killed in a horse accident in 1912, leaving a family of six children. My mother had hoped to go on to the University of Washington when she graduated from high school, but instead took a job as a secretary to help support her mother. Her strong interest in the church led her to Simpson Bible Institute, where she began her studies by attending at night while working days. Her work schedule required her to drop out for several years, but in 1927, when my father arrived at Simpson, she was again attending half days and working at a department store, Frederick and Nelson's in Seattle.

In 1929 Simpson Bible Institute had to close because of financial difficulties, and my father returned to California to attend the Bible Institute of Los Angeles, only thirteen miles from his parents' home in Pasadena. But he continued to correspond with my mother.

After they had corresponded for some months, my father wrote to my mother asking if she would marry him. She said "yes" and came down to Pasadena on a Greyhound bus, where she was met by her good friend,

4

Stella, with whom she stayed for three days before the wedding. My father picked her up the next day and took her home to meet his family for the first time. In a letter to her own family, my mother described this first meeting: "I certainly love his family. His mother is very sweet and reserved. His dad is tall and quite heavy; he makes up for his wife's quietness, for he is very jolly and full of fun. … The Mouw family take the prize for being affectionate, and I can understand why Arthur is not bashful around girls. There are six [sisters] in his family, and they surely love each other and always kiss when they meet and when they leave." (Edna, letter, January 1930)

My father described the few days before their wedding: "I had to take care of all the details—get the ice cream, buy the cookies, buy the cake and punch and all the rest. And I'll tell you, that was the hardest work I ever did in my life, and I was fit to be tied about the time this was all over. … About 8 o'clock the night that we were to be married, I stood in front of the minister. I was just as nervous as I could be, and I looked over at this young lady and she seemed just as calm as could be." (Arthur, taped sermon)

The marriage ceremony took place at my father's parents' home in Pasadena on January 15, 1930. My mother came in with Stella, her maid of honor, and saw my father waiting in the dining room with his best man. Later my mother described the marriage ceremony in a letter to her mother. "Arthur looked quite white and rather nervous, but I don't think I ever felt calmer in my life, and it sort of tickled me to see my usually bold sweetheart look as he did. Brother Davis [pastor of the local Christian and Missionary Alliance Church] didn't read the service as some ministers do; he has memorized it and looks right at the bride and groom. … When

5

he started, Arthur thought he was praying, which was natural because he didn't bring out the little book. I was quite sure it wasn't customary to pray first and I recognized the beginning, but Arthur closed his eyes and bowed his head for quite a long time until he could tell by what Brother Davis said that he was not praying. This amused me so much that I couldn't feel nervous the rest of the evening had I tried. You may be sure that no one had to tell Arthur to kiss me when we were pronounced man and wife; and then he felt more himself and acted as though he were really happy he was married." (Edna, letter, January 1930)

Marriage, January 1930

After a short honeymoon in Coronado, near San Diego, and a visit to Tijuana, Mexico, the newly married couple returned to their apartment in Los Angeles, which they rented for twenty-two dollars a month. Both attended the Bible Institute of Los Angeles.

Returning from their honeymoon

After they had been married for nine days, Edna wrote her mother, "Arthur is very considerate and thoughtful, Mama. He helps with everything, and he is the greatest 'fixer' you ever met. Every day he fixes something so that it will be handier and less work for me. He told me to tell you just now that he has the sweetest little wife in the world, and that he loves me more than ever. We are head-over-heels in love, all right, and it is hard for us to get anything done. He is more wonderful as a husband than a sweetheart, and we are very happy." (Edna, letter, January 1930)

That summer my father worked as a carpenter, helping to build a Nazarene college in Pasadena. He was foreman of construction, earning eight dollars a day. At the end of the summer, my parents left for Nyack, the missionary training institute of the Christian and Missionary Alliance in Nyack, New York. There they joined the "Island Band," a group of students interested in becoming missionaries in an island country. Near the end of that school year, which was my parents' senior year, they appeared before the school's Foreign Board for an interview. They were told they had been appointed to go to the Netherlands East Indies and would be leaving in September, just three months away. There was one problem, however. In the next three months they needed to raise $3200, a very large sum of money in 1931, and at that point they hadn't even enough money to pay their bill at Nyack. So they stayed on for a little while after the school year had ended to earn some money to pay their school debt.

They needed to get to the West Coast because they were due to sail from Vancouver, Canada, but they had no car. Here my father's exceptional mechanical skills came in handy. For twenty dollars, he bought a 1927 Chevy with an engine that didn't work and, with the help of a friend, towed it away. Then he went to a wrecking place, bought a block for three dollars and replaced the cracked block. Now they were ready to go home to California in this twenty-three-dollar car.

Leaving Nyack in $23 car

On their last Sunday in New York, my father went to teach his Sunday school class of six young boys whom he had been teaching all year. He described them as "little roughnecks who had fourteen muscles to wiggle with and only two to sit still with." When he arrived that day, the boys were hiding behind a bench, but they jumped up and yelled, "Hi, Mr. Mouw!" They walked past him single file, and as they walked, each boy reached into a pocket and came up with a dollar bill, which he put on a table. One said to him, "Here, Mr. Mouw. Here's something to help you get to the mission field with." My father bowed his head, a few tears ran down his cheeks, and he thought, "Lord, if You can lay it upon the hearts of these little boys to give a dollar each, you can take care of that $3200."

10

Arthur's Sunday school class

When my parents got to California, the superintendent of the Christian and Missionary Alliance churches in the area said, "Arthur, every church is open to you. Go wherever you want. Make your own program." This gave them the opportunity to raise the money they needed by speaking at the churches. My father described what happened: "We went to this church, that church, that church, told them about how we wanted to go to the mission field, thinking that we could raise some money to go. We got $1.87 in one church, $2.14 in another, $5.26 in another—just enough to buy gas to get from one church to another." This was, of course, during the depression years.

One Sunday my father was scheduled to preach in his own church, the one he had attended when he lived in Pasadena. Pastor Davis, who had married them, asked the congregation to give an offering. The money collected amounted to a little over $400. The pastor asked the congregation to make it an even $500. The second offering brought the total to a little over $500, which they sent to mission headquarters in New York.

My parents got in their twenty-three-dollar car and started up the coast to Seattle, where my mother's family lived. From there they were to go on to Vancouver, where they were scheduled to set sail for the Netherlands East Indies. But they were still far short of the required $3200, and time was running out. When they got to Seattle, there was a telegram waiting for them saying, "Ignore letter. Proceed to field as planned." They had received no letter and didn't know what they were to ignore, but the next day the letter came. It was from the treasurer of the Christian and Missionary Alliance, who said, "We're sorry. Only $500 has come in for your support and travel, and we won't be able to send you. So you'll just have to stay home until it does come in." But they already had the telegram telling them to ignore this letter. What had happened? Someone had walked into the mission headquarters in New York, gone into the office of the treasury, and said, "How much do the Mouws lack for their transport and all that they need?" That dear person, who wished to remain anonymous, had laid $2700 on the counter and said, "Send them out."

2 A SHORT INTRODUCTION TO INDONESIA

"Send them out," meant sending my parents to the Netherlands East Indies, now called Indonesia, a country little known to most Americans.

Indonesia is a country of over 18,000 islands, 6,000 of which are inhabited, 1,000 of them permanently settled. It stretches 3,000 miles from east to west, its land mass about three times the size of Texas. When my parents went there in 1931, the population was 62 million. Now, with 232 million people, Indonesia is the fourth most populous country in the world, after China, India and the United States. Jakarta, its capital and home to eleven million people, is one of the world's most densely populated cities. Thirty percent of Indonesia's population is under fifteen years of age, and thus the population projection for the year 2050 is 330.5 million people.

It is a country of great cultural differences; more than 300 distinct cultural groups are recognized and over 250 languages are spoken. Predictably, ethnic conflict is a major source of social instability. Over the last few years, as Indonesia's economic problems have worsened, violence has broken out among several of these different cultural groups.

Muslims make up 87 percent of the population, Protestants constitute 6 percent, Catholics 3 percent, Hindus 2 percent, Buddhists 1 percent, and others 1 percent (U.S. Bureau of Public Affairs, 2003). However, Alan Sipress of the *Washington Post* writes that about 80 percent of Indonesia's people are Muslims ("Court Slashes Sentence for Cleric Linked to Terror," March 10, 2004), and I found supporting testimony for this lower percentage (and a higher percentage of Christians) in my talks with Indonesian people during my own trip to Indonesian in February 2004.

The Hindu and Buddhist religions reached Indonesia by the fifth century; the Muslim religion spread along the maritime trade routes and was firmly established in Indonesia during the fifteenth and sixteenth centuries. Indonesia's constitution guarantees a secular government and harmony between the Muslim majority and other religious groups. Indonesia's largest Muslim organizations have condemned the violence and bloodshed that has occurred in recent years and say the small cells of radical Islamists do not reflect the views of Indonesia's Muslim population.

It was European desire for spices and the possible profits to be made from such trade that first pushed Europeans in the fifteenth century to find new trade routes to the East. The Indonesian islands lying in the midst of these trade routes account for the name "Spice Islands" being given to the archipelago. The Dutch replaced the Portuguese as the area's most important trade power in the seventeenth century and had secured territorial control of these islands by 1750. During its three hundred-year rule, the Dutch developed the Netherlands East Indies into one of the world's richest colonial possessions. Following the Japanese occupation during World War II, 1942-1945, a national movement led by Sukarno declared independence in 1945. Four years of war followed before the Netherlands ceded sovereignty on December 27, 1949, with Sukarno as President.

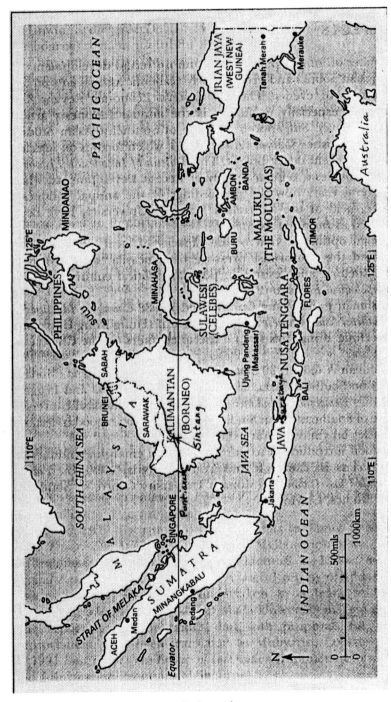

Indonesia

3 FIRST YEARS IN THE NETHERLANDS EAST INDIES

At 4:15 P.M. on September 26, 1931, my parents boarded a little streetcar in Vancouver, British Columbia, which took them to their steamer, the *Empress of Russia.* There, as they approached the gangplank, my father whispered to my mother, "It is not yet too late to turn back, dear." There were tears in her eyes, for she had said good-bye to her mother only a few hours earlier, but she kept right on walking. After surrendering their tickets, they climbed the gangplank and were met by three other missionaries. The five of them made up the Christian and Missionary Alliance (C&MA) party on this boat. Some of their fellow passengers were also missionaries going to China as part of the China Inland Mission.

The group traveled tourist class, which was very comfortable. My father enjoyed eating and was delighted with the ship's menu. It listed twenty-eight choices, and passengers could select as many as they wanted. One evening, my father and a fellow male passenger decided to eat their way down the menu, starting from the top. They managed to get to number seven that night before they were too full to go on.

The ship stopped at Yokohama, Kobe, and Nagasaki in Japan, and my parents were given time to do a lot of sightseeing. In Nagasaki my mother saw what she later described as the sight that fascinated her most: the coaling of their ship by hand. A dozen or so large rowboats drew up alongside the ship; Japanese men and women quickly passing baskets of coal hand-to-hand loaded twenty-four hundred tons of coal in six hours.

They stopped in Shanghai and then Hong Kong, where they said good-bye to the *Empress.* Since their boat to Makassar, Celebes, their final destination, would not leave for several days, they accepted a missionary's invitation to visit Wuchow by boat. When their boat anchored in the middle of a river, dozens of sampans immediately surrounded them. My mother wrote of this event: "Such yelling in connection with selling their wares we have never heard before or since!"

On October 27 they boarded a Dutch steamer bound for Makassar by way of the Philippines, arriving on November 3. As their boat pulled up to the wharf in Makassar, they were met by Dr. Robert A. Jaffray. Dr. Jaffray was from Toronto, Canada, where his father had owned and later sold the *Toronto Globe* for $3 million. The younger Jaffray should have been heir to at least a million dollars, but his father had disowned him when he turned his back upon the wealth of Canada and went as a missionary to China, where he labored for thirty-five years. His father had said in parting, "Robert, if you ever change your mind, just send me a telegram, and I'll send you all the money you want to come home." In all those years, Robert Jaffray never sent the wire. After thirty-five years he could have retired, but instead he went down into the Netherlands East Indies to open that area to missionaries of the Christian and Missionary Alliance. And there he stood on the dock waving to my parents.

My parents remained in Makassar at the mission home for eighteen months. The mission home was a six-room stucco house owned by a Chinese man. Because it was located some distance from the business area, the house was cheap to rent, about thirty-six dollars per month. Six missionaries shared this expense. Because a large number of Dutch people lived in Makassar, there were conveniences such as electric lights, running water, and gas for cooking, which were not available in the interior and on other islands.

In Makassar, the cheapest and most popular mode of travel was the bicycle. My mother described her early attempts at riding a bicycle: "Learning to ride a bicycle seems to me just now more formidable than learning the language! Why didn't I learn when I was a tomboy? There are quite a number of autos here, and these are used as taxis. But it is too expensive to get around this way, so a bicycle is necessary to the missionary."

Nighttime brought new experiences and nightly visitors. My parents slept under mosquito nets, which not only served as protection against mosquitoes but also kept out lizards, bumblebees, other large insects, stray cats, and rats. They were frequently awakened by the noise of rats running over the top of their net. My mother described one visit: "Our room opens out into the backyard, and we always leave our double doors wide open. One night, about 12:30, we were awakened by a noise on our back porch as though someone were prowling around. But after getting up to investigate, we found that it was just a party of rats who were having a gala affair under our wardrobe cupboard and in the halls and porch. They had carried chicken bones, potato peelings, and whatnot into our room from the garbage pail. Even rats have their ideas about suitable times and places."

(Edna, letter, May 1932) The favorite breakfast conversation concerned how each one had fared during the night and who had the biggest rat story. In a later letter, my mother described a new nightly visitor: bats.

In January, at the annual C&MA conference of all missionaries in the Dutch East Indies, my parents were appointed to be in charge of the mission home in Makassar for 1932. My mother was to plan the meals; my father, a jack-of-all-trades, said he managed to keep busy. While my parents were studying the language, my father taught in the Bible school and occasionally preached in one of the churches, and my mother taught a class for women and high-school-age girls. Both needed interpreters for these more formal occasions, but each time they spoke they would say a few sentences in Malay (now called Indonesian) and by March could carry on simple conversations.

In 1932, as the United States remained caught in the middle of an economic depression, the missionaries received only 65 percent of their usual allowance. My mother assured her family that she was not complaining about this, but wrote that their allowance didn't leave anything for extras. Occasionally, they would receive a little money from friends and family, and in their letters they gave thanks for these gifts of one, five, and, rarely, ten dollars or more. My father wrote to his sister, saying, "We need a car here; a secondhand one will do. There are good dirt roads here, not all over this island, but about a third or more [of it], and that's about two hundred miles. I could buy a 1927 Model T for about $50 G [probably Dutch guilders, which would be about twenty dollars], but I don't know whether to or not." (Arthur, letter, July 1932) He didn't buy the Model T, but the head of the mission in Makassar did buy a secondhand car in Singapore, and my father used it to make eight trips into the interior of the island with students from the Bible school.

Arthur with second-hand Hudson

They distributed several thousand gospels and tracts and spoke to the people they met whenever there was an opportunity. My mother visited a nearby village and led a weekly meeting among the women. By this time they no longer needed an interpreter.

Edna's Sunday village meeting

Soon after their arrival in Makassar, my mother became pregnant. My father was already making a bed for the new baby. They had decided against having a bassinet as it would do for only about eight months, and it would be cheaper to spend the money on materials for a bed that would last two or three years. My brother, Robert Burneal, was born in August 1932.

Birth of Robert Burneal

My mother's letter to her family three months later described what I think most people would consider some dated ideas about caring for babies. "I am nursing him. ... I eat spinach every day, drink diluted canned milk three or four times a day, eat peanuts, and drink lots of water. ... Mrs. Brill [another missionary] told me about some of these necessary items in the diet of a nursing mother. It seems sometimes that all I do all day is take care of the baby, eat, drink lots of water and canned milk. It would be a pleasure indeed to just play with the baby all day long, of course, but I know that wouldn't be good for him, and I wouldn't be a missionary." (Edna, letter, November 1932) Of course, she also described what a joy he was and how much she and my father loved him.

At the annual mission conference in early 1933, my parents were appointed to West Borneo. "We are very glad to be on our way," my father wrote, "but we will have to wait another month before leaving. In the meantime we will be able to get packed and buy a few necessary articles. It takes money to travel, and that is something we do not have much of these days. The other day Edna asked me what we would do for the necessary things we needed, and I said the Dear Lord will send us some specials [meaning money contributed by people in American churches, over and above their regular allowance] and behold, the very next day we received two money orders ($13 and $4) ... so you see, the Lord supplies our needs, doesn't He?" (Arthur, letter, February 1933) In this letter he also commented that many of the Dutch people who lived there were going back to Holland because of the depression.

The planned move to Borneo had to be delayed when my brother became very sick and was unable to keep food down. By mid-March he was seven months old and weighed only eleven pounds—down from the thirteen pounds he weighed before he got sick. He was x-rayed at the military hospital but showed no gastronomic obstruction. My mother talked in a letter of how she longed to have her own mother or one of her sisters with her during this difficult time.

4 BORNEO AND ITS PEOPLE

After my parents were appointed to West Borneo, they moved to the town of Sintang in mid-1933 and, later, farther into the interior. This chapter offers a short introduction to Borneo, a land that often conjures up mysterious and exotic images in the Western mind.

Borneo, the largest but least populated of Indonesia's islands (it constitutes 28 percent of the country's area but has only 5 percent of its population), is also the third largest island in the world. North of the Indonesian portion of Borneo, now called Kalimantan, lies Malaysian Borneo, consisting of Sarawak, Sabah, and the Sultanate of Brunei. The interior of the island is occupied by many different tribal groups, collectively referred to as Dayaks. These people are designated as Dayaks in contrast to the Islamic people of Malayic culture, who live along the major rivers and coast, as well as a significant number of ethnic Chinese, many of whom embrace Christianity.

Islam spread into Borneo along with elite Malay families who came to dominate the trade routes along the river systems. Several of these traced their ancestry to Arab traders who brought their religion to the archipelago. By physically controlling the traffic along the larger rivers, they were able to establish Malay rajadoms supported by Dayak commerce. No doubt some of the nearby Dayak peoples were controlled by the Malay rajas and adopted Islam. However, for the most part, Islam did not penetrate far into the interior, where the tribal Dayaks continued to follow their traditional beliefs based on an elaborate folklore detailing the deeds of their ancestors and associated spirits. Their traditional practices included paying homage to sacred rocks and trees, interpreting omens from birds and animals thought to be messengers of good and evil, and placating the numerous spirits they believed inhabited the natural world around them.

The Dayaks are subsistence farmers who practice dry-rice cultivation. They cut down trees and other jungle vegetation by ax and long knife and then, after a period of drying, burn the plot, letting the ash provide some fertilization. This method of rice cultivation is sometimes referred to as "slash and burn," a name that conjures up a negative image but in fact is a method that requires stewardship of the land and environmental sensitivity. The Stanford-trained anthropologist Michael Dove has written extensively about the "ecological wisdom" of Bornean Dayak societies.

Burned fields, ready for planting

Rainfall varies significantly from the wet season to the short dry season, the timing of which is crucial for successful dry-rice cultivation. Determining the end of the dry season and the beginning of the wet season, when planting is begun, is perennially a time of anxiety, as family heads struggle with this fateful decision. After the plot is burned, the farmers use a small, sharp digging stick to make holes, into which they drop rice grains. This occurs in late August and September. Some weeding must be done over the next three months; the rice matures in four to six months. Other crops are also randomly planted in the rice field: cucumbers, onions, beans, spinach, pumpkins, and sweet potatoes.

The key to this type of farming is to leave much of the farmland fallow so the soil can regenerate. If this were not done, the people would eventually have to move their longhouse, because there would be no fertile land nearby. Each rice plot must be abandoned after one to three years and left fallow for up to ten years. The system works because there is sufficient land available, the population density is low, and only a few, simple tools are needed.

Rainfall averages 100 inches per year in most areas, with up to 175 inches in mountainous areas. The average daily temperature in Borneo is eighty degrees Fahrenheit. There is little change in day length, because all of this island lies within eight degrees of latitude of the equator. Humidity is quite high, seldom less than 78 percent.

The Dayaks who live in and exploit the resources of the rain forest are thought to number about four million, less than one-third of the island's population. Historically, the Dayaks collected the products of the forest and sent them downriver with Chinese and Malay traders to the coast, where they were exported. Today the trade in forest products is supplemented by the exported cash crops of rubber and pepper. Because land transportation in Indonesian Borneo remains rudimentary, the larger rivers continue to be the major routes of travel and commerce.

In a 1993 article, the Nature Conservancy says of Indonesia, "In terms of biodiversity, the 3200-mile archipelago bridging Australia and Asia has no equal. With its 17,000 islands of evolution, Indonesia harbors more species of mammals, birds and reptiles combined than any other country" ("Indonesian Island Rescue," *Nature Conservancy*, March–April 1993). Borneo forests are extremely diverse in number of species. In a study conducted in East Kalimantan, nearly 250 plant species were found on five acres. The Dayaks collect forest products for trade—rattan, timber, aromatic woods, and birds' nests prized by gourmets in China and elsewhere in Southeast Asia. However, rubber and pepper are the primary trade goods today.

West Borneo (Kalimantan Barat)

5 A DAYAK VILLAGE

Dayak societies vary widely in character, from very small-scale, egalitarian tribes of a few villages each to large, hierarchical tribes composed of classes, with powerful chiefs whose influence can pervade entire river systems. It is the former kind of tribe that predominates in West Borneo, now called Kalimantan Barat, where our family lived. The Dayaks to whom my parents ministered were mostly of the Mualang tribe.

From outward appearance, the Dayaks would seem to be a communal people. Typically, an entire village, called a *kampung,* lives in one longhouse built on eight-to-twelve-foot-high stilts. The longhouse is elevated primarily because of heavy rainfall, but this type of construction also affords protection from wild animals and, in the past, marauding enemy tribes. The Dayaks climb up a notched-log ladder to get into the longhouse.

Typical Dayak longhouse

Half of the longhouse is composed of a wide, covered veranda that extends the entire length of the building. This wide passageway is the scene of most of the housework, handicraft work of both men women, hulling and winnowing of rice, and public meetings and ceremonies. The social character of Dayak life is very much facilitated by this veranda. The other half of the longhouse is divided into a series of individual, closed apartments, which are accessed through the main room. These individual household apartments are called *bilik;* a traditional longhouse consists of fifteen to thirty family *bilik*.

The *bilik* has one room in which people gather, entertain guests, and sleep on mats that are laid out at night. A second room has a dropped floor of rattan-tied sticks, where cleaning and chopping of food and washing of dishes and utensils is done. Little cleanup is required, as garbage and water all fall through the wide cracks in the floor. Any fallen morsel is immediately devoured by the pigs or chickens that roam the area below the longhouse. A third room is used for cooking and eating.

Each village holds rights to its surrounding territory, and membership in the village entitles each household to land. An average village and its surrounding territory cover 4.7 square miles but can encompass as much as 13 square miles. In addition to land, membership establishes the individual's right to the community's production resources, such as timber, raw forest materials used for handicraft products (baskets, hats, mats, traps, cages, spears, nets), game and gatherable foods, and plots for cultivating rubber trees. Other village resources include a forge, located near the chief's *bilik,* a rubber mangle for processing rubber, and the graveyard, all common property.

Each household either possesses a rubber grove or the right to use one. Rubber is the Dayaks' primary source of cash. Recently there has also been some pepper production. Working for wages is rare and undertaken only as a limited, temporary measure, never as a way to make a living. All the goods the Dayaks buy from the Chinese merchants are nonperishable items, such as sugar, salt, cloth, metal, brass ware, tea, coffee, kerosene, soap, matches, and tobacco.

These egalitarian Dayak societies are a harmonious blend of communal and individualist principles. Despite the marked individualism of most Dayak societies, social accord among the individual families is the consequence of a high regard for a social order based on customary law, the term *law* being used in the loose sense of rules, customs, conventions, manners, and so on. Due to this marked individualism, in most Dayak societies the chief has very little political power. He is essentially a leader among equals. He presides over meetings and ceremonies, but in regard to breaches of customary law that threaten the harmony of the community, he strives to achieve a consensus resolution rather than the enforcement of a strict interpretation. Relations between the sexes and generations flow easily, and any attempt to control others by aggression or domination is considered unacceptable. Men and women enjoy nearly equal status; for example, wives can initiate divorce and own property equally with their husbands.

(I am greatly indebted to anthropologist Dr. Allen Drake for his significant contribution to this and the previous chapter.)

6 LIFE IN SINTANG

My father sailed for Borneo in early April 1933. He traveled third class, which entailed sleeping and eating on the deck. His bed was a camp cot. After stopping first in Java, his boat arrived in Pontianak, the major coastal city in West Borneo. From there, he traveled to Sintang (my parents' Borneo destination) on another boat, which he described as lovely. He wote my mother that when she came "we will just have a second honeymoon coming up this river together."

Traveling to Borneo third class with Dr. Robert Jaffray

By May, missionaries were receiving only 50 percent of their allowance, and their financial situation was made even worse because the exchange rate—U.S. dollars to Dutch guilders—had also decreased. But in spite of these conditions, my mother wrote, "We are glad that our Heavenly Father never changes, and His promises are still the same." (Edna, letter, May 1933)

On May 13 my mother and baby brother, who was better and gaining a little weight, left to join my father in Borneo. "From Makassar we take a steamer to Batavia, Java, changing boats there. From Batavia we sail north past Sumatra and the smaller islands of Banka and Billiton to Pontianak on the west coast of Borneo—opposite Singapore. At Pontianak we leave the steamer and take a riverboat up the Kapuas River, going five days into the interior. Our new home will be in Sintang, Borneo." (Edna, letter, May 1933) My father had found a newly built house for them to rent at six dollars per month and was already busy with his hammer and nails adding a closet in the bedroom, putting up shelves in the kitchen and bathroom, and making the furniture they would need. They took very few things with them from Makassar.

My mother was very happy to have their own home in Sintang after living in a home with other missionaries for eighteen months. The new house in Borneo was unpainted inside and out, with board walls and studs showing, and bare unpainted floors with half-inch cracks that allowed them to see the ground below. She was eager to unpack some of the things they had never been able to use in Makassar and "make the house look cozy." She asked her family to send her a subscription to *Better Homes and Gardens,* and told them, "I'll enjoy a magazine better than anything. I haven't had one of my own since I left home. In Makassar the Standard

Oil lady used to lend us her *McCalls*, but when she left we didn't get any. We don't want you to send us any packages as we haven't enough money these days to pay duty." Later that month my father also advised his family not to send packages, because the duty was very high, 30 to 40 percent. "Don't worry about us going without a Christmas package, and if you think you must send us something, please let it be money, as there is no duty on a dollar bill." (Arthur, letter to his parents, June 1933)

By June my brother weighed only 13 ½ pounds—what he had weighed before he became sick—and he was still unable to sit up on his own. But he was getting stronger each day, and my mother wrote about him quite optimistically. By October he weighed almost twenty pounds, and she described him as having good color, being very active, and acting like "just a plain boy full of pep in every respect." My father had built him a little screen house that he could play in outside, free of mosquito bites. My father had also had a little wicker seat made that he fastened to his bicycle between the handlebars and his own seat. My mother said that all they had to say was "ding-aling-aling," and Burneal would start jumping up and down, so excited to be going off riding with his daddy.

Riding with Daddy

I was born in Sintang in December 1933. I arrived two weeks early because my mother had a bad bout with malaria at the time and suffered from a terrible fever and headaches. The Dutch doctor gave her quinine even though he knew it would make her baby come sooner, but she was in such bad condition that the fever had to be stopped. Her labor was over in two hours, and I emerged a healthy baby. My parents named me Sydwell after my maternal grandmother, but most of the time they called me by my nickname, Siddy.

Birth of Sydwell Donna

During the two and a half years our family lived in Sintang, my father was away quite often. He traveled with Dutch officials on their trips, sometimes overland, sometimes by boat. He also sailed on Chinese boats up the Melawi and Ketungau Rivers, both close to Sintang. On these trips he spoke to the Chinese and Malay people, who lived along these rivers, and to the Dayaks as much as he was able (he knew Malay but little of the Dayak dialect) and gave out tracts written in Chinese and Malay. In 1934 he decided he needed to have his own boat in order to travel farther up into the jungle. He journeyed to Pontianak and hired men to build one. The boat was promised for the first of August, but was still not finished by the end of September—so my father brought it to Sintang and finished it himself. He also installed an engine, a secondhand, one-cylinder motor he bought from a Japanese trader. He named the boat *Kabar Baik,* which means Good News. "I do praise the Lord for my little boat. I can go at will now to the Dayaks and it only costs me sixty cents (U.S.) per day to run it," he wrote to his parents. He was also thankful for the gifts of money from those in American churches that made the purchase of the little boat possible.

The *Kabar Baik*

The new boat also gave us some fun family outings. "Edna, Burneal, Siddy and I went for a three-hour trip up the river to a Dutch rubber plantation. Burneal had a good time. He held a long stick in the water for some time, occasionally patted the boat, and mixing Malay and English said, '*Ini* Daddy's boat, *putt, putt, nyanyi,*' which means 'This is Daddy's boat, *putt, putt* sings.' Little Sydwell enjoyed it too. We stopped before we got to the plantation and had our dinner on the boat. We brought fried chicken, mashed squash, bread and fruit. We ate the chicken with our fingers and threw the bones in the water, and literally thousands of little, tiny fish would come from all directions. Burneal enjoyed watching them. We parked under a big tree, and Edna and Burneal saw monkeys swinging from the trees for the first time in Borneo." (Arthur, letter to his family, December 1934)

My father now motored up and down rivers all around Sintang and was often gone for two weeks at a time. On one of these trips up the Ketungau River, he found people eager to hear the Gospel. In one of her letters, my mother told her family not to worry about her when she was alone. "I am not a bit nervous at night," she wrote. "I have a man and his wife who live here in the room in back of our house. They are Javanese and we like them fine." This couple had been hired to help with the cooking and other chores for sixteen dollars a month.

In December 1933, my mother wrote about starting a Sunday school class for the local neighborhood children. She enticed them into our yard by asking if they wanted to learn how to play some games. After the games, she asked if they would come back on Sunday morning to learn some songs and hear a story. Six children between six and twelve years of age attended the first Sunday; all were from Moslem families. (My mother didn't write of this class again, so I don't know if it grew and continued.)

My brother was old enough to comprehend that, when my father was gone, he was away on a trip, but I didn't understand his absences. My mother told me later that, whenever he left, I would run all over the house, hunting and calling for him, and that I carried his picture around with me when I did. When we heard the *putt-putt-putt* of his engine, our welcoming

41

committee—my mother, my brother, and I—would run as fast as we could down to the place where he docked his boat. On these trips, my father had also begun to look for a home where our family could live and be closer to the Dayaks, who only came to Sintang to trade, but this move was not to happen until almost another year had passed.

In January 1935, our family left Sintang to attend the yearly missionary conference in Makassar. My mother wrote, "We stopped in Singapore on the way, and it seemed something like visiting New York for the first time, after having been in the interior of Borneo for nineteen months."

Our family in Makassar, 1935

After we returned home, my father began a general letter, one sent to my parents' many supporters in churches in the United States: "Home Sweet Home is just as sweet and real in the center of Borneo as any other part of the world, and we were very glad to get back to Sintang and our work again. ...During our absence, something took place which perhaps is too commonplace to mention, but to us seems sublime—namely, the painting of our house inside and out. The bare, brown boards became a light cream." (Arthur, letter, June 1935)

On our return trip to Sintang, we were accompanied by two young Malay preachers, Patty and Adipatty, graduates of the Bible school in Makassar. At the conference, my father had told of the hunger of many of the Dayaks he had met to hear the Gospel, and he pleaded for two native workers to assist him. These two men were not Dayaks but came from the islands of Ambon and Menado. Shortly after they began to work with my father, what he called a "great awakening" took place among the Dayaks. It was an event so powerful that my father and the Dayaks who witnessed it would refer to it for years to come.

7 A GREAT AWAKENING

There were two events that my father described as helping to open up the hearts of the Dayaks to the message of the Gospel. One is the story of a young Chinese man, Lim Hong Lip; the other is about a Dayak named Siga.

Lim Hong Lip

One day when my father was away on a three-week journey traveling through the jungles where the Dayaks lived, two young Chinese men came to our yard in Sintang. They were not residents of Sintang, but were there because one of them, Choen Sen, was being treated in the hospital. They had heard of my parents through another man to whom my father had sold some Christian literature.

Choen Sen and his friend, Lim Hong Lip, came to the gravel path in front of our house and coughed a few times to get someone's attention. When my mother heard them, she walked outside and invited them to come up on the porch. They came somewhat reluctantly, as they had never been invited to a white man's home before. My mother asked them to sit down, which at first they did quite tentatively, using only a few inches of the wicker chairs. She talked with them for a little while and sold them each a New Testament.

The next day, they both came back, eager to know more about Christian teaching. This time they sat a little more easily in their chairs. My mother talked with them, and they prayed together. She invited them to come back again when my father would be home. A week later, my father returned on Christmas Eve. The next day, on Christmas (1934), the two men came to our home, and after spending several hours talking with my parents and listening to portions of Scripture, they received Christ into their hearts.

Choen Sen expressed a desire to go to Bible school. My parents knew he was suffering from a constitutional disease that left his body weak and emaciated, but he was so earnest in his desire to attend school that my parents helped to send him to the Makassar Bible school, where, sadly, he died a week after his arrival.

Lim Hong Lip went back to his home on the Belitang River, close to Dayak villages, where his father had a small trading post. He told all of his extended family about his new faith, and as a result of his witness, many Chinese people became Christians. (One of these Christians, a Chinese man, later offered us his house to live in.) When the Dayaks came to trade and barter with his father, Lim Hong would witness to the people who came and tell them about this "new religion of the Jesus' way." It was through his witness that the people in that area became interested in hearing the Gospel.

Lim Hong Lip

My father told the story of how, at a later time, when he was at Lim Hong's home with his parents, Lim Hong was baptized. "I asked him if he wanted to be baptized, and he said he did. So I told him all about baptism, but I didn't tell him about the mode of baptism. Then he went inside, to another room and put on a white shirt and some black pants and stood there in front of me as if to say, 'Is this all right?' I looked him up and down and I didn't know if it was all right or not; I didn't know why he put them on. Then he walked to the edge of the raft (their home was built on a raft on the river) and jumped in the water which was way over his head. There was a current that carried him down the river a little ways, and he had to swim back. He climbed up on the raft and I asked him,

47

'Lim Hong, what did you do? Why did you do that?'

He said, 'I went out and baptized myself.'

I told him, 'Oh, no, I made a mistake.'

The root word in Dayak for both bathing and baptism is *mandi*, so all the time I was talking to him about baptism, he was thinking about bathing.

I said to him, 'That isn't the way it's done,' and then I took him in the presence of his father and mother and baptized him. And this man was a key man. ... He was the one who made those people up there expectant." (Arthur, taped sermon)

Siga

A few weeks after we had returned to Sintang with the two national workers, Patty and Adipatty, my father took them with him on a trip up the Ketungau River to an area where there were more than ten thousand Dayaks who spoke the same language. These Dayaks had never had contact with any missionaries, Catholic or Protestant. My father's plan was to let the two men work this district by themselves. After three days of getting them settled at this outstation, a two-day journey from Sintang, he returned home. Two months later he wrote in a general letter, "Already the Lord is blessing their efforts and Dayaks are coming from far and near to hear the Good News."

At that time my father knew only a little of the Dayak language although he was fluent in Malay, the commercial language of the Netherlands East Indies. Patty and Adipatty were also just beginning to learn the Dayak language. On one of their trips together they met a man, a Dayak named Siga, who knew Malay. Very few Dayaks knew the Malay language, and my father asked him if he were willing to become their interpreter. Siga responded, "Yes."

How had Siga learned the Malay language? One day this Dayak man went crazy and started slashing with his long knife; before he could be stopped, four people were dead. He was imprisoned in Sintang by some of the national soldiers under the Dutch. By chance, my father happened to walk past that prison. (Of course my father would say it was not by chance; God had him walk past that prison at the proper time.) Siga asked a fellow prisoner who the white man was and was told that he was a man who had come all the way from America to teach the Dayaks a new way of life. This made an impression upon Siga who was not yet in his right mind. A few nights later he had a dream: a man in white appeared to him looking at him with love and sadness and said, "Do not do these wrong things any more."

Because he had no memory of having killed anyone, the prison officials believed that Siga was insane and sent him to Java for treatment. He was placed in an insane asylum and kept there for ten months. It was during this time that he learned the Malay language. As his mind began to clear, a Dutch doctor at the asylum talked to him one day and asked,

"Siga, why did you do these terrible things?"

"I don't know. I don't even know if I did it. I don't remember anything."

"Hasn't any one ever come to the jungles to teach you about God and the right way to live?"

"Not yet."

The doctor unknowingly predicted, "Siga, some day someone is coming to your jungles to teach you the right way to live. When they come, follow their teaching."

But Siga reasoned, "How will I ever be free from this asylum? If I say I didn't kill those people, they will keep me here. If I say I did kill them, they'll put me back in prison. I haven't a chance." And yet, after ten months he was pronounced cured, released and sent back to the same jail where he had been imprisoned in Sintang, because that was the only place they had to keep him. A message was sent to his longhouse and some men from his village came to take him home. As they were going up the river in their sampan, they passed my father who was working on his new boat, putting in an engine. The sampan pulled up alongside my father and the men asked what he was doing. He told them about his boat and the engine and how he would use it to go up the river.

"Where are you going?" they asked.

"I always go to you Dayaks."

"When you get your engine going, come to our area."

Of course my father didn't know who Siga was in the sampan.

When Siga got back to the jungle, people came from far and near to hear his story because he had killed four people, been arrested by soldiers, sent to Java, and now was back to tell about it. Java was only seven hundred miles away, but to these Dayaks it was like the other side of the world. But in telling his story, instead of dwelling on what he had done, Siga told about his dream of the man in white and what the doctor at the asylum had prophesied. While Siga told his story, on the sideline sat a man named Jaban who was from another village. Jaban listened to Siga's story and every time a new crowd came, Jaban would go over to hear it

50

again. Sometimes he came on his own and asked Siga to tell him the story. He heard it again and again, and this made a great impression on Jaban. When he finally went home to his own village, one night he had a dream. He saw two dark-skinned men and a white man, and a voice said to him, "Jaban, these are the men that are coming, and when they come, you do what they say, you follow what they teach." Jaban told many people in the area about his dream.

My father continues the story. "And in the fullness of time, God sent me up that river – at the proper time to a particular people, to a particular person. And here I was on the trail. This didn't happen by accident ... and here was an interpreter ready." (Arthur, taped sermon)

Siga became the interpreter for my father, Patty and Adipatty. Wherever they went, great crowds followed because of what Siga had told the Dayaks and also because of Jaban's dream which most of the Dayaks knew about. With the coming of my father and the two national workers, the picture was complete according to Jaban's dream. Writing in the *Pioneer** in December 1935, my father said, "In all we visited eight longhouses. The people followed us from place to place, drinking in the good news. They had been bound by fears for hundreds of years and now someone had come to tell them of the freedom in Christ Jesus. Is it any wonder they showed us every kindness and insisted upon feeding us chicken, hard and soft-boiled eggs, and fruits of the jungle?"

Siga became a Christian and it was then that my father learned many of the details of his stay in Java, what the doctor had said, and Jaban's dream.

*A publication of the Christian and Missionary Alliance covering missionary work in the Dutch East Indies.

He also told this anecdote about Siga: "Before Siga came to the Lord, he interpreted for us more or less just what we said, but after receiving Christ into his heart, he enlarged on what we said with much joy and enthusiasm. If we gave him a sentence a foot long, he made it a yard long!" Siga's son, Dawan, went to Bible school and became pastor of one of the Dayak churches.

Siga pointing to heaven

8 A GREAT AWAKENING, AN ANTHROPOLOGICAL VIEW

This chapter is based entirely on the research and writing of Dr. Richard Allen Drake, Research Associate, Dept. of Anthropology, at Michigan State University. Dr. Drake did fieldwork among the Mualang people (June 1978 to November 1979) in the same area where my parents, Arthur and Edna Mouw, lived and worked. Dr. Drake's data on the early years of the Dayaks' conversion to Christianity suggested to him parallels with the well-known millenarian movement phenomenon, the expectations of a coming "new age." Casting my father in the role of Kling, the heroic figure of much of Mualang mythology, he was interpreted by them as a "messiah." To tell this story I shall piece together several passages from two of Dr. Drake's publications, cited at the end of this chapter.

"For the Mualang people, one of the Ibanic peoples of the middle Kapuas River in Kalimantan (Indonesian Borneo), the conversion to Christianity has unquestionably been the most important development in their cultural history in the past sixty years." (1,pg.1)

How historical and sociological events contributed to this conversion, is the subject of this chapter.

"The Mualang are a tribe in the sense of a self-conscious socio-cultural entity characterized by common customs and law, a distinguishable language, and a sense of common history and destiny. Like all the Ibanic tribes, their folklore specifies that their ancestral home is the Sai River. ... Here in the gigantic original village of Tampun Juah, all the Dayak tribes lived in harmony until they were bothered by a satanic nation of people. After prolonged struggle...they abandoned the site for points down river with plans to reunite by following signs left along the course of travel, but the signs were altered by the swift current of the flood waters, and the confusion resulted in the various parties getting separated from each other. One of these emigrant parties...became the Mualang." (2,pg.22.)

The Mualang had for a very long time lived on the margins of various riverine Malay state societies. They had avoided Islamization and integration into Malay culture by retreat into the sparsely inhabited interior, but in 1820 the Dutch established a presence in Sintang, and in a system of indirect rule, the Dayak tribes were forcibly incorporated into the Malay Rajadoms of the Kapuas River. Beginning in 1822, they were required to pay taxes (a specified amount of rice per household) to the Rajah. The Dayaks saw this increasing visibility of Dutch power as threatening to their traditional way of life. This led to a series of anti-Dutch rebellions that were always put down by superior Dutch forces and weaponry, with the rebellious leader often exiled to Java and imprisoned. "The brooding Mualang refused to have a school built in their territory by the Dutch and otherwise resisted with suspicion colonial government policies as far as they dared." (2, pg.24)

"If we look within Mualang society and culture itself, we notice that the Dutch suppression of headhunting, while no doubt bringing about an unprecedented peace and security for improved trade opportunities, at the same time foreclosed the opportunity for men to achieve prestige in the traditional way of distinguishing themselves in war raids and emasculated much of the Mualang religious ceremony and worldview. The Mualang were experiencing a shift in power from the Malay Rajas to the Dutch with severe consequences for traditional conceptions of Mualang power and authority." (1, pg.6)

This context of anti-colonial conflict and cultural vulnerability created a heightened religiosity and an atmosphere of expectation among the Mualang people. "The single thread running through all the sacred Mualang folklore is the nostalgia about their separation from their cultural heroes, the Buah Kana, the long lost heroic ancestor spirit deities, and the longing to be once again united with them. A kind of redemption is envisioned for them as living together again with these Buah Kerinduan as they once did in the golden age at the fabled Ur village of Temawai Tampun Juah." (1, pg. 8)

"It was into this aftermath that the missionary Reverend Arthur Mouw and his wife Edna came with another religious movement promising a new vision of salvation, a new vision of redemption for the Mualang. The missionary came on the scene as a change agent of the most profound kind. He came with a messiah, promises of a changed life, rules of righteousness, visions of perfection, victory over the powers of evil, exaltation of the poor and downtrodden, and the confidence of truth. This would be a vocabulary of change and hope welcome to a context of frustrated millenarian expectations." (1, pg. 7) For some, my father was seen as the incarnation of one of the Buah Kana. "Plugged into prophetic history and the folklore of the ancestral heroes, conversion to Christianity proceeded expeditiously from Balai Sepuak where Reverend Mouw took up residence. ..." (2, pg. 25)

How would my father have responded to these conclusions of Dr. Drake? Although he didn't have the opportunity to read his two works cited below, I am certain that he would accept the data of Dr. Drake as simply more evidence of God's spirit working among the Dayaks, preparing their hearts to be receptive to the Gospel story.

1-Drake, Richard Allen, The Christian Conversion of the Mualang as a Phase of a Messianic Movements Cycle, Prepared for Presentation to the Second Extraordinary Session of the Borneo Research Council at Kota Kinabalu, Sabah, Malaysia, July 13-17, 1992.

2- Drake, Richard Allen, The Material Provisioning of Mualang Society in Hinterland Kalimantan Barat, Indonesia, A Dissertation, submitted to Michigan State University in partial fulfillment of the requirements for the degree of Doctor of Philosophy, Dept. of Anthropology, 1982

9 PREACHING TO HUNGRY HEARTS AT MIDNIGHT

(This chapter is entirely Arthur's words, transcribed from a taped sermon given in 1953.)

Nineteen hundred years ago, Jesus said to His disciples, "Say not ye, There are yet four months, and then cometh harvest? Behold, I say unto you, Lift up your eyes and look on the fields for they are white already to harvest." (John 4:35). … It has been my privilege to go to the land of Borneo and there see a harvest gathered.

I want to tell you about one village. I remember walking to it about five o'clock one afternoon. The people begged us to stay. A few of them had heard a little of the message of life in another village, and they wanted us to stay overnight so they could hear more. After I entered the village and remained with them a little while, they pleaded saying, "*Tuan*, [Mr., Sir] stay here." I said, "I wish I could stay with you, but I promised to be in another village." After a while, I had to leave them. As I walked out of that longhouse, my heart was heavy for here were people who wanted to hear more. No one had ever been in this village before to bring them the message of life. All I could do was to promise them I would come back just as soon as I could.

We walked on a couple of hours. It was dark before we got to the longhouse or village for which we were headed. When we got there, we found only one lone man tending one lone fire. I asked him where the people were, and he told me they had been ordered away by a higher chief who was angry that some of the Dayaks were turning to Christianity, and he alone remained to watch the longhouse.

My heart went out to the people of the village we had just left. After about twenty minutes, I made a decision to go back. I asked if those who had brought us down the trail would be willing to take us up the trail again. Two men and one lad from that first longhouse spoke up and said, "*Tuan*, we'll take you." So one of the native workers stayed, and the other native worker and these men who had shown us the way started back up the trail.

We had a lantern for light. There is nothing better than a lantern in the jungles. It gives a nice glow all around the path and gives light in all directions which is needed where there are many snakes. After a while, someone banged the chimney of the lantern against a log, and a gust of wind blew out the light. We used our flashlight, and in about half an hour its batteries were dead. It was very, very dark indeed, with no moon shining. We asked the men who were guiding us how much farther it was. They said, "You are just about half way." Well, if you are only half way, it is just as far back as it is to go ahead. So we said, "Lead on, if you can, and be sure and keep on talking so we will know where you are." So they continued to talk as they walked. Once they said, "*Tuan*, be careful. In about four steps you will go over a log. Don't turn to the right; the curve of the river is there, and you will go in way over you head." I don't know whether you ever played blindman's buff, but this was the real thing in the middle of the jungles in the middle of the night in Borneo.

About 11:30 that night, we stumbled back to the village. A man was walking down the long corridor of the longhouse with a pitch torch in his hand. The reason for this was that dogs were barking and he and the people were afraid. We called out and told him who we were, and he was so relieved he let out a war whoop that awakened everybody in the longhouse. In a little while, we heard the squeaky doors open and close. By the time we got to the longhouse, they had called off the dogs and had let down the notched-log ladder. We walked up into this longhouse which was about fourteen feet off the ground. It is quite a feat to ascend them in the daytime, but at night and so very dark it is really an accomplishment.

We got to the top, all right, and the people were all standing in the doorway to welcome us. They filled the opening so we couldn't get in, and there we were, balancing ourselves in the air. After a while, they moved out of the way, and we entered and sat down on the floor with them. As I looked at them, I wondered if I dared ask them if they would like to hear the Word of God, even that night. Finally, I did, and they said, "Oh, yes, *Tuan*. We don't need to go to sleep. We can stay up all night. Teach us all night if you want to." So I talked to them about forty minutes. Then the native worker stood up and talked to them about half an hour or so. I stood up again and preached for another half-hour. Then I said to the native worker, "You take over." Now it was about 2:30 in the morning.

I recall sitting down on the floor as the native worker began to speak. I leaned against one of the poles that held up the longhouse, and evidently I just kept on leaning until I was in a horizontal position. When the native worker saw that I was sleeping, maybe he heard me too – I don't know – he shooed all the people away and they went through those squeaky doors into their little apartments in the longhouse. In just a minute the native worker was lying beside me fast asleep. Ours was not a Beauty Rest mattress; it was a grass mat, about one sixty-fourth of an inch thick.

At 5:30 in the morning I awakened, and as I blinked my eyes, sure enough, there were all those people sitting on the floor around me! I thought they had been sitting there all night, but they hadn't. They just got up earlier than we did. They had never seen a white man get up in the morning, so I guess they wanted to know what it was like. If you don't like people to stare at you, don't come to Borneo, because they think they are paying you a compliment when they watch everything you are doing. We went to the river to wash our faces, then we had a bite of breakfast, and again we stood before these people, telling them the sweetest story that anyone has every heard – that God so loved them that He sent his son, Jesus, who died for them, and that His precious blood shed on Calvary would wash away their sins.

I want to say, friends, that before two o'clock that day all the people of that village of Rasa Terbang bowed their heads and their hearts to Christ. … And I told you about that young man and how he said that night, "*Tuan*, if no one else will show you down the trail, I'll take you and lead you back to my village." His name was Surah, and some months later my wife had the joy of teaching him how to read and write. He was sent to our Bible school [on the island of Sulawesi, previously called Celebes] and studied for a number of years. Today, Surah is the pastor of the Bethel Church, a church which grew and grew in the jungles until it had a membership of 1,315 people. He is ministering to those people to this day [1953]. That church, however, had to be divided because it got too large, and now there are two churches instead of one.

Yes, Jesus said nineteen hundred years ago, "Say not ye, 'There are yet four months, and then cometh harvest.' Behold, I say unto you, Lift up your eyes and look on the fields, for they are white, already to harvest." We didn't find the only harvest field. There are such harvest fields around the world. God is waiting for someone to go.

10 A NATION BORN IN A DAY

My father had been traveling with the two national workers, Patty and Adipatty, to several longhouses, and as they approached a longhouse

The Dayaks as we first met them with Arthur, Patty, and Adipatty

called Balai Ranjuk to which they had been invited, they had misgivings because it was so quiet.

No babies were crying, no chickens were cackling, no roosters were crowing, not even any dogs were barking. It seemed as though no one could be there, but the chief had asked them to come.

They walked up the notched-log ladder, and as their eyes reached the level of the longhouse floor, there they saw about three hundred people sitting on the floor. The crowd waited until the three visitors had just stepped inside, then they all rose en masse and came to greet them with their hands stuck out in front of them. My father had never had a reception just like this; he nodded at them, they didn't nod back; he smiled at them, they didn't smile back. He asked one of the national workers what was happening, but he didn't know.

Later that evening they found out that when the chief, who had invited them, went back to his village and told the people about his invitation, he had said, "When they come don't offer them rice gin, because they don't drink rice gin. And don't offer them tobacco, because they don't smoke. But we have to make them welcome, so when they come, you go down and shake hands with them."

But shaking hands is not a custom of the Dayaks and so they asked, "What do you do? How do you shake hands?"

And the chief replied, "Well, when I give you the signal, you just go up to them with your hand stuck out, and they'll do the rest."

So they came, with their hands stuck out, waiting for my father to do the rest. But they held their hands up so high that my father and the two other men couldn't get their hands into theirs. They reached up and tried, but it was impossible. Instead, they just reached up and tapped this hand, and tapped that hand, until finally everybody was tapped and they seemed to be satisfied.

After they had been given some coconut water to drink and a few delicacies (usually rice balls that enclosed a little sugar in the center), the people all sat down on the floor and my father began to talk to them for about an hour. Then he turned the teaching over to one of the national workers, then the other national worker, and the people all continued to sit and listen. They were given an opportunity to say something if they wished, but did not. Finally, it was my father's turn to speak again, and when he closed some of the Dayaks said,

"Tuan, aren't you going to eat?"

"Well, I've been waiting for you to invite us to eat."

"Tuan, we've been waiting for you to stop so we could invite you to eat."

The chief announced that everyone was going to eat, but as soon as they were finished, they were going to gather again for another meeting. At this point the Dayaks went into their individual family rooms, called *bilik*, and ate whatever food they had. My father and the two other men sat on the floor, and their meal was served to them on a little tray.

After the people had eaten, my father, Patty and Adipatty again taught them until late at night. "Our message was redemption through the precious blood of the Lord Jesus Christ. Beginning at Genesis and ending with the resurrection of Christ, we told them redemption's story, and oh, how they loved to hear it!" (This and following quotes from Arthur, taped sermon.)

Early in the morning, when they awakened, they went down to the river to bathe; when they returned to the longhouse, the people were all gathered on the floor again, ready to listen. And so my father taught them again and about ten o'clock he bowed his head to pray. He didn't ask the

65

Dayaks to bow their heads with him, but he and the two national workers bowed their heads, closed their eyes and prayed. And the Dayaks could not understand this ritual. Why were they talking with their eyes closed? Could they see someone the Dayaks themselves couldn't see? It made them very afraid, although my father didn't realize this at the time. But much later in the day many of these Dayaks did bow their heads and asked God to come into their hearts.

"Suddenly, en masse, they bowed their heads and they started to cry. And God deigned to come down into that longhouse and visit it with His presence. And these Dayaks knew, they <u>knew</u> that there was Someone there who had never been there before. ... And though I didn't go around and question each one of them, I found out little by little, that there, as they bowed their heads, they had said 'yes' to the Lord Jesus Christ.

"I remember on the second or third night, we were going strong about eleven o'clock at night, and we had been going all day and the day before that, and I said to the two national workers, 'I really am all in. I don't think I can go on any more.' And these two national workers said, 'We're half dead ourselves.' And I said, 'Let's close the meeting,' and we all three agreed to close the meeting. We asked the people to stand up and said that we were going to close the meeting and that tomorrow, again we would teach them. So they all stood up, and we had the prayer, and when we said 'Amen' they all sat down on the floor again where they had been sitting all day long.

"There was nothing to do but put down the mosquito net, unfold the camp cot, and turn down the lantern. I crawled onto that camp cot, under the mosquito net, and the lantern was close by, just giving a little light. And not one of those Dayaks had moved; they just sat there. ... And as I thought about these people coming to know the Lord, it was like a nation being born in a day, the nation being that particular tribe.

"And as I was lying there, just about ready to go to sleep, I could see people all around my camp cot. If I'd lifted the mosquito net, I could have reached out and touched them. And finally some of the bolder ones stuck their face right up against the net and asked,

'Tuan, have you gone to sleep yet or not?'

And I said, 'No, I'm not asleep yet.'

And then they said, 'Oh, Tuan, sing some more, teach us some more. Don't go to sleep. We can stay up all night.'

"I couldn't sleep knowing there were such hungry hearts at my side, so lying in my cot, with my head sticking out of the mosquito net, I sang for them and then taught them some more. Months later, Dayaks would speak to each other of this day and say, 'Do you remember that afternoon at Balai Ranjuk?'"

My father was finally able to sleep for four or five hours. When he awakened, there were the people, still sitting on the floor around him. Those who lived in this longhouse had gone to their own rooms to sleep, but those who were visiting from other villages – and this was about half of the three hundred people present – had slept on the floor in the large corridor room. My father went down to the river to bathe, came back, had something to eat, and then started to teach the people again.

My father had been at this village for several days when one of the Dayaks came to him and asked where he was going when he left this village. He added that he and others had to go as they didn't live in this longhouse and had run out of food. And he asked again,

"We just wondered what you were going to do?"

"What do you mean, what am I going to do?"

"Tuan, we heard of some people in another area where you've gone to teach, and those people became followers of the Lord. And because they were followers, you took them down to the river and you put them under the water and you brought them back up. Are you going to do that to these people who are here? If you are, we don't want to go away. But if you're not going to do that, we'll have to go."

"Oh, we don't baptize people so soon…We want to be sure that those who believe know Jesus Christ as their Lord and Savior, and that they won't go back."

"Tuan, until we die, we won't go back. We didn't know about this before. But for a long, long time, there's been a longing in our hearts for something and we didn't know what it was. And this is it. And, Tuan, until we die, we won't go back."

As these people were getting ready to go back to their own village, my father felt bad because he had said he wouldn't baptize them yet. Then he had what he thought was a bright idea and reached into his pocket for a little notebook. He told those who had to go that he would write their names down in this notebook (none of the Dayaks knew how to read or write at that time), and started to write down their names. As the people crowded around, wanting to make sure their names were written down, the other people who lived in this village and weren't going anywhere wanted to know what was happening. The others answered, "He's writing down our names. And the next time he comes, if we're following the Lord with all our hearts, he's going to take us down to the water and bring us back up." And in a little while the other people said, "We want our name written down too." So my father wrote down their names, but finally he came to the last page of this small notebook, and he didn't have any more pages to write on. "I'm sorry, but I've run out of paper and I can't write down your names anymore; there's no more room," he told them.

A woman sitting quite close to him said, "Tuan, the Chinese merchant that lives down by the river, he has a lot of paper and we can send and get some paper." A young man was immediately delegated to run as fast as he could down to the river, which was some distance, and get some paper. The people who had planned to leave decided to wait, and they had another meeting. About eight o'clock that night the young man returned with a roll of wrapping paper. When the people saw that roll of paper, they gave a collective sigh, because they could see there was enough paper to write down all the names.

The next morning, the first thing on the agenda was to tear up that paper, make a notebook out of it and write down names. As the people came one by one and stated their names, my father and the two national workers asked them a few questions because they wanted them individually to give a testimony to the Lord.

"And I can see some of those people yet, sitting on the floor. And, you know, when somebody's heart is beating – of course you can't see it if you have a necktie on -but these Dayaks were practically all of them nude to the waist, and right here [pointing just below his neck] there's a little pocket, and if people are excited, you just look there at that little pocket, and you can tell the way their heart's beating. And when they came I saw that little pocket and it was just throbbing, and the reason it was throbbing was because they were going to be asked some questions, and they were scared to death they wouldn't be able to answer the questions. They sat there, not in fear of us, but afraid that their name wouldn't be written down in that book, and that they wouldn't be taken down to the water and be brought back up. And that's enough to melt the heart of a stone."

Finally, there were 312 names written down. My father didn't know what to do. The mission policy was that people should be Christians for six months before they were baptized. And here were people who had only been Christians a few hours and they wanted to be baptized. He told the national workers that he was going out by himself into the jungle to pray. Sitting on a fallen tree, he opened his Bible and turned to the book of Acts; "There's never been a better book written about missions." As he read in Acts, he came to the tenth chapter and read these words: "Can any man forbid water, that these should not be baptized, which have received the Holy Ghost as well as we? And he commanded them to be baptized in the name of the Lord." (Acts 10:46-47) The ground where he was sitting became holy ground. He believed this was God's holy word, spoken to him for that particular time.

He went back into the longhouse and told the national workers that he was thinking perhaps they should baptize the people. Without waiting to discuss the issue further, one of the national workers called out, "Everyone whose name is written down can be baptized." Again there was a collective sigh, almost of relief, from the people gathered.

My father, Patty and Adipatty went down to the river and began to baptize the people, but were unable to finish before it became dark. That night they had another meeting and the next day began to baptize again. Because there were so many people, one of the national workers stood with the notebook in his hands and read their names. My father described how "these Dayaks thought we were the cleverest people in the world.

That they could say their name, and we would write it down, and then the next day, we'd look at whatever was written there, and we'd say the name, just like they had said it the day before with their lips! And they really thought we were super-duper!"

Patty or Adipatty read the names of ten people and this group would walk down to the river. Then each of these names would be read again, individually, and that person would walk into the river and my father would baptize him or her. When all ten were baptized, another group of names would be read. My father stood in the water a long time; he became weary and tired, but it was a joyful occasion. (At that time, the Dutch government had stipulated that only my father could baptize people. In later years, the native workers, who were Bible school graduates, were also allowed to baptize.)

Baptizing new believers

71

When there were only thirty people left whose names hadn't been called, and a group of ten had just walked down to the river, my father noticed one man who was the dirtiest Dayak he had ever seen. "He had long, tangled hair to the middle of his back, he only wore a loin cloth, and he had a dry, scaly skin disease from the crown of his head to the sole of his feet. His fingernails were long and black, and from his mouth dripped betel nut; his teeth were black and his lips were red with the juice. And when his name was called, something inside of me – call it culture, call it what you will – something inside of me just rebelled. And I thought, 'How can I take hold of him? He's so dirty, just so dirty.' And I had no more had that feeling, just like that, as though it were a vision, the Lord God showed me that the reason He was willing to look down upon <u>me</u> was not because I washed my hands, or my hair was combed, or I had clothes on my body. The only reason He could look down upon me was because the blood of His Son had been applied to my heart, and I was accepted into the beloved because of the precious blood that was shed. And I bowed my head and said, 'God forgive me, God forgive me for my resentment of that dear man.' And when his name was called, bless his dear heart, I put his left hand in my left hand, I put my right hand on the back of his neck, and I baptized him in the name of the Father, the Son and the Holy Spirit."

After the baptism ceremony, the chief of this village came to my father and said,

"Tuan, we want you to dedicate this longhouse to God."

11 EDNA'S BARN

"Arthur, I would rather live in a barn and be with the Dayaks than stay here in Sintang." This is what my father heard from my mother upon his return to Sintang from one of his many trips up the river, farther into the interior of Borneo. He was gone for weeks, even months at a time as he walked from longhouse to longhouse ministering to the Dayaks. When he came home my mother would ply him with questions. He said she would listen intently, not interrupting as he jumped from mountain top to mountain top in his narrative, telling her the highlights of his trip. And then for the next three days she would ask questions, making him fill in all the valleys.

She did not accompany him on these trips because she had to take care of my brother and me. There was also the question of where we could live in the jungle. Sintang, where our family had moved in May 1933, had a small community of Dutch families and the house my father had rented there provided a modest degree of comfort. Because there were no homes in the jungle, my father expected he would have to build one and wished his own father, a carpenter, could come to Borneo for six months to work with him.

But one day as my father was going down the Belitang River in a sampan (he had temporarily left his motorboat and walked overland to this river) he saw an old house on the bank. And the moment he laid eyes on it he thought, "There's Edna's barn!" He asked Surah, a young Dayak man who was accompanying him, if he knew to whom it belonged. Surah answered that it belonged to Tauke Tua, a Chinese merchant who, with two other Chinese families, ran a small trading post at Balai Sepuak. The Dayak people of this area came here to trade their jungle products for salt, fishhooks and other small necessities they could afford.

My father introduced himself to Tauke Tua who was living in a raft house on the river, just below the bigger house. Tauke Tua explained that for many years he had lived in the big house with his family, but now he was old and found it too difficult to walk back and forth between the house and the river several times a day. My father was delighted when he learned the house was empty and immediately said he would like to rent it. Tauke Tua answered, "Oh, you don't need to rent it; if you want it, you can have it." But my father knew something of the Chinese way of bargaining and insisted that he really wanted to rent it. At this point, Tauke Tua said, "Let's have some tea." After about an hour and a half and thirteen small cups of tea, my father again brought up the subject of renting the house, and they finally settled on a price of fifteen Dutch guilders, about six dollars per month.

Following this negotiation, my father walked up to look at the inside of the house for the first time. There was no ceiling, just the roof, the floor was made of hewn lumber, the walls of bark with no doors hung in the doorways and he thought, "This is surely Edna's barn."

That Sunday afternoon at a service in one of the longhouses, he announced that he had rented Tauke Tua's house and was going to gather his wife and children in Sintang and bring them to Balai Sepuak where the house was located. He asked if any of them would like to go along and help them move, and just about everyone – there were about three hundred people – said they would. My father believed this was because they had never ridden in a motorboat in their lives and because they knew they wouldn't have to paddle. He chose six young, stalwart Dayak men to accompany him and they set out on their journey, a trip the young men found exciting. When they came to the bigger Kapuas River, thirty-six miles away, the men on the boat, who had never been this far in their lives, said, "No fooling! This is a big river!"

In Sintang, my father rented a barge that would hold our furniture and other belongings. In two days everything was loaded on the barge, and that night, our last in Sintang, our family slept together in the empty house on one mattress. On the day we were to leave, in November 1935, only one member of the five Dutch families who lived in Sintang came to say good-bye. This was Dr. Keypers, the doctor who had attended my mother at my birth. When my parents and nine-month-old brother had first moved to Sintang in May 1933, all the Dutch families had been very friendly. But as time went on and they heard of the Dayaks becoming Christians, some came to believe that my parents were fanatics, and, while not hostile, ceased being so friendly. This was probably another reason why my mother wanted to leave Sintang and live closer to the Dayaks.

Our family started up the river in the little Kabar Baik with its one-cylinder engine pulling the larger barge. As we neared Balai Sepuak, my father announced to my mother, "Dear, when we go around this bend, you're going to see your barn." The news that my father had gone to get his family had quickly spread through the jungle, and as we rounded the last curve in the river, we saw not only the house but hundreds of Dayaks standing on the banks of the river ready to greet us. My mother described the occasion in a letter: "There were over five hundred Dayaks to greet us when we arrived at Balai Sepuak. The native drums were going full force and all in all it was quite a gala affair. Eighty percent of the Dayaks here had never seen white women or children, so we were almost mobbed with friendly greetings. Wherever we sat or stood, there were a hundred or more Dayaks in a circle around us. Though it took two days to load, it took just twenty minutes to unload our furniture and baggage as everybody wanted to help, even if it was only a book to be carried." (Edna, letter, March 1936)

Dayaks greeting Edna and children upon arrival at Balai Spuak

A few Dayaks who had traveled as far as Sintang knew that white men shake hands when they met, and they told others about this custom. All five hundred Dayaks wanting to properly welcome my mother stood in line to shake her hand. But when they also wanted to shake hands with my brother and me, she told them it wasn't necessary. My brother and I both had very light, blonde hair, something the Dayaks had never seen before. Some of them even came up and rubbed our arms to see if the "white stuff" would come off.

As is the Dayak custom, the people had gifts for us. They presented my mother, my brother and me with forty chickens (live, of course), about two hundred eggs, stacks of cucumbers, and much of their precious rice, which is the main staple of their diet. Some of the Dayaks got busy and made a chicken coop out of bamboo poles, so we would have a place to keep the chickens.

That evening after the beds and other necessary things were taken care of, there was a meeting. My mother played the pump organ to accompany the Dayaks as they sang some of the choruses they had learned, and there were many oh's and ah's over the organ. The people loved to sing along with it, something entirely new to their experience.

We stayed that night in our new home on the Belitang River, about sixty miles from our previous home. Later, in a letter, my mother described her new house.

Edna's Barn, our home on the Belitang River, and Tauke Tua's raft house

"The building we live in was built eighteen years ago and is very large, having been built to accommodate two or three Chinese families. The boards are hand hewn and so bumpy, that when you look at the floor you would almost think it was the ocean with waves rippling in. There is one immense room in the middle, a long room on the left, which Tauke Tua formerly used as a store, and three small rooms on the right. We use the three small rooms for bedrooms and the long store room for a living and dining room. The large, central room was originally built to provide sleeping accommodations for Dayaks who came to trade with these Chinese merchants. ... All the Dayak women with their babies slept on the floor in that big room. I must confess that the first Saturday and Sunday nights that Dayaks slept in this large room, I had rather a hard time going to sleep since it was a new experience, and we had nothing but curtains for doors. They seem to think that the only reason curtains are

78

put up for doors is to pull them aside and look in, because they do it all the time. I guess I need never be nervous because they love us and we are safer here than in America perhaps, or at least just as safe." (Edna, letter, March 1936)

The next day was Sunday and more people began to arrive. The morning service was to be held behind our house where about nine hundred Dayaks had gathered under the rubber trees. As my father was walking toward the rubber grove, some men stopped him and one of them asked, "Tuan, who is going to speak today?"

My father thought the question a little odd, as he had always done the speaking, and he answered, "I thought I would."

"Tuan, if you don't mind, we would like to hear *Nyonya,*" (Mrs., Madame).

He went back to the house and said to my mother, "Dear, you're it. They want to hear you."

My mother spoke for about twenty minutes using an interpreter (she knew Malay, but not yet the Dayak dialect), and the Dayaks listened intently not wanting to miss a word she said. After my mother finished, my father and a national worker also spoke. And then how the Dayaks did sing! My mother had heard them sing a little when they came to visit our home in Sintang but she later said, "I was not prepared to hear such an outburst as the 906 voices made. They love to sing and will sing for an hour or two and still ask for more. Most of the Dayak Christians know more than forty songs from memory. We feel there is a great ministry in song here for the great majority cannot read; so they are taught the Gospel in song, and it is a great blessing to them." (Edna, letter, March 1936)

After lunch, when there was to be another meeting, the Dayak delegation again came to my father and said they wanted to hear *Nyonya* speak. And my father went back and said, "Dear, you're all right! They want to hear you again."

That evening, because it rains in Borneo almost every night, the meeting had to be held indoors in the large middle room of our house. The Dayaks were packed in so tightly – of course they sat on the floor – that some asked if they could sit up above on the ceiling joists. The remainder who couldn't get in either sat on the porch or went underneath the house and sat on mats. (Because of the rain, all houses in this area are built on stilts and stand about ten feet off the ground.) Again, the same delegation came and asked to hear my mother speak, so she spoke to them for the third time that day.

When they went back to their homes, the Dayaks told others, "*Nyonya* believes the same as Tuan. We heard her with our own ears; we watched her as she spoke." My parents learned later that before my mother came, there was some fear among the Dayaks that perhaps this new Christian message was more for men than for women because my father and the two national workers who had been accompanying him were men. Frequently they had asked my father about his wife, whether he had children and whether his wife believed as he did.

Why did they ask these questions? Why were they so eager to hear my mother speak? For decades the Muslims who lived in Borneo had tried to win the Dayaks over to the Muslim faith. And the Dayak women were the ones who said, "No, we will not become Muslims," because they believed if they did, their husbands would then take three wives. Thus it was very important to them that my father had only one wife, that my mother also believed what my father had been teaching them, and that she had a part in this new faith.

And so, as my father described it, in those early days after our move, "We had Dayaks for breakfast, lunch and supper." They came to visit from all directions, and the arrival of my mother into the jungles had an enormous influence on the Dayaks becoming Christians. If this Gospel had not been for women as well as men, they would not have accepted it because they are family people, and they didn't want any divisions.

12 *LIFE ALONG THE BELITANG RIVER*

Balai Sepuak, where our new home was located, was also a small trading post for the Dayaks. Our house was on the very edge of the river. Three Chinese traders with their families lived in tiny houses built on rafts on the river just sixty feet away from our house. Once we had settled into our home, a constant stream of Dayaks came to visit. Some came for salt, to buy or sell rice, or bring jungle products to trade, and nearly every one of these Dayaks followed the path to our house before they descended to the Chinese store. Others who were sick came to be prayed for or to have a wound treated. Some came just to visit.

On Friday, Dayaks began to come for the Sunday services. By Saturday afternoon there were between one and two hundred already gathered with more coming all the time. On those days our home resembled a beehive. One group was listening with rapt attention to our hand-wound phonograph; always there were groups of women and children waiting for my mother to play the organ and sing with them; on another side of the porch my father was busy listening to some problems or helping sick people. By five and six o'clock there were many cheery little camp fires burning in the grove of rubber trees behind our house. By 7:30, three hundred or more people had gathered in the large, central room, sitting on the floor, ready for the evening service.

Just two months after our move into the jungle, my father wrote his family, "It's not all roses on the mission field, but Dear Loved Ones at home, I'm having the best time of my life. There are three thousand Dayak Christians here now. Christmas we held two meetings a day's journey apart. There were 1,076 at our meeting and 1,008 at our native workers' meeting. On New Years 2,300 gathered at our place in Balai Sepuak." (He wrote this letter January 7, 1936, sitting in the back of his boat. He must not have had any regular paper for it was written on brown wrapping paper, torn off a package that had come from Chicago. The address on the package was simply: John Arthur Mouw, Sintang, West Borneo.)

My mother described this period in a letter. "Within six or eight months we hope to have a church building here in Balai Sepuak. ... As it is, on Friday, Saturday and Sunday nights, Burneal and Sydwell have rather a hard time getting to sleep inasmuch as three hundred or more Dayaks singing for an hour or more in an adjoining room is not exactly conducive to sweet slumber. Burneal, however, does not seem to mind being kept awake at all. In fact, he had just about learned to conduct a meeting in the Malay language by himself. I have been quite amused at times after having put him to bed to hear him sing a few songs in Malay, then hear him say, 'Let us pray.' After praying he made a few attempts to preach a little sermon, but so far his best efforts are along the line of singing and praying." (Edna, letter, March 1936)

Most of the time when my father traveled to the Dayak longhouses, my mother, brother and I stayed at our home. But in March 1936, four

84

months after we moved to Balai Sepuak, the three of us accompanied my father into the jungle. My mother described our trip in a letter to her sister. "I put on my high top boots which I brought from America and I was glad I had them for we waded through mud and water up to our knees. Very often Arthur and the native workers wade through water up to their waist and now and then they have to swim through deep puddles after there has been very heavy rain. We tried to pick out a week when it probably would not rain every day and it didn't, so it was better walking. The children were carried all the way – in native fashion by a sling on the back of our Dayak boys. Burneal and Siddy enjoyed the trip very much.

Burneal and Siddy with Dayak children in front of a Dayak longhouse

"We didn't have to worry much about the sun because the jungle is so dense in most places that the sun didn't bother us. Now and then we walked through open spaces and it was hot, but that wasn't very long. One day I got a bad headache from the heat when there wasn't as much shade as usual.

"We visited four longhouses in all, and the trip took us nearly six days. We had a big crowd with us because a large number of Dayaks from the first longhouse came to get us to carry our stuff. They enjoyed it and I am the first white woman who has gone to any of these longhouses, so it was quite an event to them. Arthur, of course, has been to the Dayak villages before, but I have never gone and so everything was done in honor of myself and the children. Arthur teased the Dayaks and said they all came to get *Nyonya*, that's me, and the children, and that they didn't love him. They tried to explain that this was my first visit and of course they loved him, and they tried so hard to convince him that Arthur had to laugh and tell them he was just teasing. I didn't do any of the preaching. I like to get little groups together and show them a picture and tell them the story of the picture, and I taught them many Gospel songs.

"I tried to give the children their usual food as much as possible but Arthur and I ate what the Dayaks gave us and sometimes it was quite good and other times it was almost impossible. The rice was always good, though, and that means a lot.

"At one of the longhouses a blind man expressed regret that he could not see the children. Burneal sat on the floor near him and he felt him all over and exclaimed over his fat legs! I was tired enough when I got home and had a slight attack of malaria but very slight, so I was glad for that. It was a good trip because we can get much closer to the Dayaks in their longhouses than even here where we live." (Edna, letter, March 1936)

13 *GOING TO SEE THE GOVERNOR*

Two months after our move to Balai Sepuak, a letter came from the Dutch Governor of West Borneo, who resided in Pontianak on the coast. The letter said that my parents were no longer allowed to leave their station in Balai Sepuak, which meant my father was no longer permitted to travel through the jungles visiting the longhouses and churches that had been established. After praying with my mother, my father decided he would go and see the assistant governor in Sintang. This official had previously given orders that the national workers (the ones who had come from neighboring islands) could not go into the villages and teach unless they were accompanied by my father, and had compelled Patty and Adipatty to leave their district for twenty-two days. However, he later rescinded this order.

When my father met this official in Sintang, he showed him the letter from the Governor, and learned that he had already received a copy.

"I'm here to ask you to help me."

"That's absolutely impossible. I can't do a thing. It's in the Governor's hands."

My father left his office, rented a boat from a Chinese merchant, tied it alongside his own boat, and started back to Balai Sepuak. His plan was to use this barge of a boat to take our family down to the coast to see the Governor. After he arrived home, it took a couple of days to get ready and put the necessary provisions in the boat so we could cook, bathe and sleep on the journey to Pontianak, which would take about five days. Because I was still in diapers that needed to be washed, my father made a clothesline on the roof, and as we went down the river there were diapers flying in all directions.

Traveling to Pontiank to see the governor

As they neared Pontianak, my parents prayed for God's help, as they had each day. My mother sensed in my father's prayer that he was discouraged and she said to him, "Arthur, when you meet that Governor tomorrow, don't you kowtow to him at all. You stand up and talk to him and tell him exactly what is on your heart and mind." My father was so surprised, he hardly believed it was his wife speaking, for my mother rarely talked in such a way; she was a very gentle and quiet person.

The next day when they arrived in Pontianak, my father tied the boat to the bank and left us to go to the Governor's mansion. When he got there, there were three policemen who asked what he wanted. He responded that he wanted to see the Governor.

"Do you have an appointment?"

"No."

"Well, he never sees anyone without an appointment."

"But I've come over two hundred miles to see the Governor, and I must see him."

"Well, write your name down on a piece of paper; maybe he can see you after a while."

His name was taken into the Governor who sent back a message that he would see my father when he had finished with his business.

My father waited for two hours. Finally, someone came and said, "The Governor will see you now."

As he entered, the Governor said, "What do you want?"

"Well, I've come to see you about reversing your decision. I have your letter."

"It's impossible to reverse my decision."

"Well, you've bound our hands. We can't preach, we can't teach the people. We must go to them. They can't all come to us."

"It's quite impossible."

My father continued to talk to him, saying everything he could, but the Governor kept interrupting him, not allowing him to complete a sentence or a thought. Finally, because he was so desperate, my father said, "Mr.

Governor, you interrupt me all the time. You don't give me any chance to say what I want to say. Won't you please just listen for a little while, and let me finish what I want to say."

The Governor looked at my father, possibly recognizing how desperate he was, pulled out a long cigar, jammed it in his mouth, lit up and leaned back in his swivel chair as much as to say, "Go on talking; I'll just enjoy my cigar," but he was quiet.

My father began by telling him how the Dayaks had changed since becoming Christians. The people were buying soap from the Chinese and bathing their bodies, some of them were buying toothbrushes and brushing their teeth, they had stopped chewing the terrible betel nut which rotted their teeth, and they didn't smoke tobacco anymore. The Governor had been quiet up to this point, but now asked,

"Now you tell me, Mr. Mouw, what is wrong with tobacco."

"Mr. Governor, these people were slaves to tobacco. They were so poor they didn't have enough rice to eat, and yet they took the rice and went down to the Chinese merchant and traded that rice that they should have eaten for tobacco. What good is tobacco anyway? All you do is puff in and you puff out."

The Governor laid his cigar over to one side of the table and after a while he said,

"Mr. Mouw, you can go back. You can go back into the jungles. You can travel anywhere you want to travel. You can go anywhere you want to go. I have confidence in you." Then he added, "I'll give you a letter and you can take it into the jungles with you."

"Mr. Governor, you don't need to give me a letter; your word is enough."

"I will give you a letter!"

The Governor called his secretary and dictated a letter in Dutch. When the letters were typed and he had signed all the copies, he gave one to my father. "Here it is, Mr. Mouw. Everything is taken care of."

As the Governor was walking my father to the door he asked, "By the way, did Mrs. Mouw come with you?" My father answered that she had accompanied him. He knew that at that moment she was down on her knees praying for him.

"Do you think Mrs. Mouw could meet my wife tomorrow?"

"Yes, I'm sure she could."

"All right. You be here with Mrs. Mouw, ten o'clock in the morning."

"All right. But are you sure it will be all right with your wife?"

"Oh sure. It will be all right."

The way he said this made my father wonder if he ran his wife the same way he ran his office.

When my father returned to the boat, my mother was praying. He showed her the letter. He had both letters in his hand: one said "you can't" the other said "you can." Together they prayed and thanked the Lord for His help.

Later, my father was talking to the Dutch Minister of Finance, a Christian whom he knew. The Minister looked at the two letters and said,

"This is absolutely a miracle! Never before has that man ever reversed a decision."

"You know, God wouldn't let those dear Dayaks down," my father responded.

The next morning my father was there with my mother at ten o'clock to meet the Governor and his wife. The two women talked together for about twenty minutes apart from their husbands. Then the Governor asked my father to walk to the door with him, and as he ushered him out of the room he said, "We're going to have a conference up in the jungles on a certain date. All the officials will be there, and I'd like you to come. Can you be there?" My father responded, "Of course," thinking to himself that when the Governor asks you to be someplace, of course you can be there! But he was apprehensive about what this might mean.

He went to the boat and waited for my mother who returned after two hours. She described her time with the governor's wife, and said that she was a true Christian. " All we talked about was the Lord. She didn't want to know about styles. She didn't want to know about California or America, but she was so hungry to have some fellowship with a Christian, that that's all we talked about." She had told my mother that the Governor, the son of a preacher in Holland, prided himself on being the black sheep of the family. Then she added, "You know on the outside he appears to be a very hard man, but on the inside he's very soft."

Our family went back up the river to our home with the Governor's letter saying my father was free to travel anywhere he wanted. But when the day came for him to go and meet with the Governor and the other officials, he had misgivings. When he got to the house where the assistant governor was he said, "My heart sort of failed me," and he asked Nawin, a Dayak man who had accompanied him, to pray. "Don't stop praying until I come back." Nawin immediately dropped his head and started to pray.

My father walked for the second time to the house of the same official he had asked to help him, the one who had said, "It's impossible; it's in the

Governor's hands." The moment he entered the door he saw the officials were all sitting around tables. The Governor, who was facing the door, saw my father first and commanded, "Everybody stand up. Mr. Mouw is here." They all stood up. Then the Governor asked my father to sit down and spoke to the other officials. "This man came down to see me. I listened to what he had to say. I didn't believe it all just because he said it. He doesn't know this, but I sent someone into the jungles to investigate whether or not what he said was true. I have a report here in my hand. And he didn't tell me the half of it. We have to help this man. We may not agree with him from the standpoint of religion, but we've got to help him. He's doing good there in the jungles. He's helping the people." Then he turned to my father and asked, "Do you have anything to say, Mr. Mouw?" My father said a few words, got up, thanked them very much and left. When he got to the top of the bank of the river, there was Nawin, still praying.

In 1936, my mother, brother and I went back to the United States eight months earlier than my father. When it was time for him to leave Borneo and join us, on his way he was in Pontianak and stopped by to visit the Governor. He was glad to see my father and asked, "How is it with your passport? Is everything in order? Let me see your passport. I want to make certain that everything is all right so that when you come back in a year's time, you'll have no trouble entering."

My father took out his passport and handed it to the Dutch Governor of West Borneo. He looked at it, said he would be gone for a few moments, walked down a long corridor to an office and returned with the proper stamps in place. "Here it is, Mr. Mouw. It's all in order. We want you to come back."

14 BUILDING THE CHURCHES

In the early days of my parents' ministry among the Dayaks, the people gathered in their longhouses to hear the Gospel story. Sometimes as many as six hundred people came for Sunday services. It was the only place they could meet as there were no other buildings in the jungle. At our home in Balai Sepuak, services were held under the rubber trees with hundreds of people attending. In 1936, two additional national workers came from the Makassar Bible School and joined Patty and Adipatty. These four men also regularly held Sunday services in two or three Dayak villages.

Meeting under the rubber trees

95

and at Dayak long houses before churches were built

But the day came when my father said to those gathered, "I think the time has come when we should build a church, a church building." They asked him what a church looked like and he tried to describe it to them. After he had finished, they shook their heads from left to right and said, "*Tuan*, we could never build anything like that." But when he said he would help them to build it, they thought perhaps it was possible.

On an appointed day about two hundred Dayaks gathered to discuss this building of the first church. Again they asked what a church looked like, and this time my father took a stick and tried to draw a picture of a church in the sand. He drew the under-pinning, the sides, a roof and, finally, a steeple on top and said, "This is what a church looks like." Again they all shook their heads and said, "Ah, we could never build that." But again, with his offer of help they thought they could try.

The next question was, "Where shall we build it?" There were about eleven villages represented among those who were present, and every one of those men wanted it built close to his own longhouse, because they

96

did not want to walk far to church. My father asked a group from one longhouse, "Where do you live?" and then he put a stone on the ground and told them that this stone would represent their village. Each of the groups was asked the same question, in turn. When eleven stones were all arranged on the ground, he asked, "Now is this where you live?" One man said, "No, this isn't where I live," and he took his stone and moved it over about six inches. Then all the others had to shuffle their stones around, and it took another twenty minutes for this process. After they were all finished with the shuffling my father asked again, "Now is that where you live?" They all nodded their heads.

Next my father chose a big stone and as nearly as possible plunked it down in the middle of those eleven stones, saying, "I think that is where we should build the church." They saw the reasonableness of this. Then he asked, "Where is the location of this big stone?" That started a big discussion all over again as they argued among themselves for another twenty minutes about where that particular place was. Finally, they grew quiet and he knew they had reached a decision. "How do you get there from here?" he asked. Various opinions were offered, but all the directions offered were rather circuitous routes.

"Why don't we just make a new trail from here right to that place?" asked my father.

The men agreed, and all two hundred of them started out. Each one grabbed his long knife and hacked a path through the jungle. The first one cut a little bit, the next one cut a little bit more, the next one made it wider, and so forth on down the line. My father was at the end of the line with no knife in his hand, walking over a brand new path.

When they got to the appointed spot, they chopped down a few saplings and in that clearing bowed their heads and dedicated that plot of ground to the Lord. In two weeks they agreed to come back and start the building.

Felling trees for the church site

My father described that first day. "I had asked for only twenty to come the first day, but two hundred and more came. I asked them if they didn't understand. I didn't want to work a hardship on them. I only wanted the people of one village to come one day, and people of another village to come another day, etc. But they explained, '*Tuan,* we have never built a church before, and so we want to see how it is built.' Well, trying to govern over two hundred Dayaks who had never built a church is practically an impossibility!"

Because everyone had worked on it, some of the studs leaned in one direction, some of them leaned in another, but it did have a good roof, very important in a land with up to 175 inches of rain a year. It had no nails for all the timbers and bamboo were bound by rattan. Like all Dayak structures, it was built high off the ground. This church grew and grew until they had to knock out a wall and build on a lean-to, then another other wall and another lean-to, and still another wall and another lean-to. My father described the process:

The church takes shape

Inside the church

"As I say, it wasn't much from the standpoint of architecture when it was first built, but with all of these lean-to's, it looked even worse. But that one church, Bethel, grew and grew until it had a membership of 1,315. … I never sent a picture of that first church back to my father, because if I had, he would have disowned me. He would have said, 'Arthur, couldn't you build a better church building than that?' You see, I had learned the carpenter trade at my father's hand, for he was a builder.

"Some of those studs of that first church building kept on leaning until one day we had to build another church. We took more care in the erection of the new building which was built about three hundred feet from the original place, and that church still stands until this day." (Arthur, taped sermon)

By 1942, when our family left Borneo during World War II, nine churches had been built. "No one else can realize what a thrill comes to a missionary's heart as he walks down a jungle trail and comes to a clearing where stands a new church, hewn from the forest by the Dayaks, with only the aid of their native tools. The building before me stood as a monument to the power of the gospel." (Arthur, *Out of Borneo*)

15 *TEACHING THE DAYAKS TO PRAY AND TO SING*

My father grew up in a family that prayed. Every night when he was growing up, the family—his parents, one brother, six sisters, and he—gathered for worship. His father would reach for the big family Bible, read a chapter, and often his mother would read one too. Then they always had family prayers. Sometimes his father would say, "We're going to pray all around," and my father would groan because he felt he had more important things to do. He wanted to go outside and play ball before it was dark. Describing this time, my father said, "Some of us children sure could pray short prayers, but everyone prayed. And my father would pray for all of us. Sometimes he'd reach over and lay his great, big, callused hand on my head and pray, 'God make an evangelist, Lord make a singer, Lord make a missionary out of one of our children.' And when my dad prayed like that, I was scared to death because I'd seen so many of his prayers answered, and I was afraid that this one was going to be answered. As an ordinary young man, I wanted to grow up, get a good job, make a lot of money, drive the best car; and I knew if I said 'yes' to what my dad was praying about, I probably wouldn't be able to have that." (Arthur, taped sermon)

The power of prayer was a cornerstone of my father's belief. He believed that his change of heart, attending Bible school, becoming a missionary, and going to Borneo had all occurred because of his parents' prayers. In one sermon, speaking about the thousands of Dayaks who had become Christians, he said, "And I think I know as well as anybody that this work that came under God in the land of Borneo did not come by accident, but there were mighty men and mighty women of prayer and of faith that prayed and bombarded this place with prayer, and I was just an instrument with my wife to go in and see what God wanted to do and what He did do."

After the Dayaks became Christians, they would come to him and say, "Tuan, teach us to pray." How would you teach someone to pray who had never prayed before? My father would ask them to bring him two objects—perhaps it would be two pieces of firewood, two sweet potatoes, or two cucumbers. Let it be cucumbers this time. He put one cucumber on the right and one on the left. The people looked at the cucumbers and they wondered what that had to do with learning to pray. They had seen cucumbers all their lives, and they had never learned to pray.

He pointed to the one on his right and said to the people gathered, "When you begin to pray, you say, 'Our father who art in Heaven,'" and asked them to repeat this. Then, turning to the cucumber on the left, he told them, "When you end your prayer, you say, 'We ask this in the name of Jesus Christ, our Savior. Amen.'" Then he asked them to repeat this; once they had, he announced that they knew how to pray. All they needed to know was the beginning and the end, how to start and finish. Pointing to the space in between the cucumbers, he said, "In here you can put anything you want. If you want to praise the Lord, you can praise Him. If you have a burden on your heart, tell the Lord about it. If you are troubled about your rice crops, tell Him about that. If there is someone with whom you are having a problem, just pray for him or her. Tell the Lord all about it."

He taught them to be sure to pray when they first got up in the morning, to pray before they ate their meals, when they were going to take a journey, and when they came home from the fields at night. The Christian Dayaks took this teaching very seriously. My father recounted a time when he was in a Dayak longhouse, sleeping deeply about four o'clock in the morning, when an old man sleeping about ten feet from his bed awakened and started to pray. Since Tuan had taught him to pray when he first got up in the morning, he did so, not silently, but aloud, telling the Lord about this and that. That morning, my father wished the man had waited another hour to pray or not prayed as loudly, so he could have gotten another hour of sleep.

Why was praying so important? The Dayaks didn't know how to read or write, so in the early years of their ministry, my parents couldn't give them a Bible or a New Testament to read. But the Dayaks could pray, and this helped them to grow in their new faith.

When my parents came to Borneo, the Dayaks didn't know how to sing; they knew only rhythm and how to chant. But they had heard my father sing, and some had also heard singing on our wind-up phonograph. When my father came to their longhouses, they would ask him to sing, and he would try to teach them to do the same. He later said of those early efforts, "For the first six months it was the worst music I ever heard in all my life. It didn't make any difference how many people were gathered, there were that many tunes; everybody was singing a different tune." As he continued to travel and hold meetings in the Dayak longhouses, the Dayaks from one longhouse would follow him to the next longhouse and this was repeated until often many hundreds of people were going along the trail with him. They sang as well as they could the choruses that the native workers and my father had taught them. "Though they did not at that time know much about tunes and harmony, when it reached heaven it must have made the angels rejoice with exceeding great joy. ... But one day it just seemed like they sort of shifted gears, and they learned to sing the parts; and in time they were using four-part harmony. And to hear them sing 'Out of my bondage, sorrow, and night, Jesus, I come, Jesus, I come'—people who had been in bondage, sorrow, and night all the days of their lives, and so had their parents—and then to hear a choir singing with all their hearts, they became a real blessing." (Arthur, taped sermon)

I visited the Dayaks in 1991 (see chapter 41) and heard them sing. They sang a cappella, with no piano or other musical instruments to accompany them, and knew all the verses to the hymns. When I first heard a congregation of over four hundred Dayaks lift their voices in song at a Sunday morning worship service, I was so overcome with emotion that I broke down and sobbed. It was some of the most beautiful music I had ever heard; it was a song of faith, a song from the heart.

When my father spoke at churches in the United States during the 1950s and 1960s, he would occasionally end his sermon by singing his favorite missionary hymn, "Throw a Line." He introduced the hymn by saying he had learned it from his mother when he was a young boy; she often sang it while doing housework. He had grown up in a family that sang together, and I remember family parties with my father and his brother and sisters all gathered around the piano singing the great hymns of the church. My father had a beautiful tenor voice, as did his brother, and his sisters joined in with their lovely sopranos.

"Throw a Line" is my father's signature hymn. Here I can only give the words and music, but I am fortunate to have his rendition of this song on tape.

Throw a Line, Arthur's signature hymn

16 *TEACHING THE DAYAKS TO TITHE*

My parents believed in tithing, in giving a portion of one's earnings to God's work. My father had learned this practice from his own parents who, even in very lean times, always set aside a portion of what they had for the church and its ministry.

In the early days of my parents' ministry in Borneo, the two national workers who came to help in the work were not themselves Dayaks but young men who came from other islands in the Dutch East Indies (now Indonesia) and who had attended Bible school in Makassar, Celebes. In those early years, these two men were supported by The Christian and Missionary Alliance under whom my parents served, using money given by American churches. As more national workers came to work in Borneo, my parents used their own tithe to support them, "because we feel it is one of the most worthwhile uses for our money as the national workers can do so much that we could never do. They know the people better than we can ever know them." This was during the mid- to late 1930s when America was in a depression and missionary allowances were often only 50 percent to 60 percent of normal. I include this detail to affirm how important the concept of tithing was to my parents: it made no difference how much or how little one had, a portion belonged to the Lord.

My father had long believed in self-support and had a vision for the future of an indigenous church in this part of West Borneo. He had a strong conviction that an organization could not long exist if founded on sand, the sand of foreign finance. He was convinced that no structure so built could long endure when foreign help ceased to be a reality.

One day in 1935, he spoke to the two national workers (the two from other islands) about the subject of self-support. He was warm and enthusiastic on the subject. "God loveth a cheerful giver. It is more blessed to give than to receive. The laborer is worthy of his hire." These and many other scripture verses he brought to their attention, as they nodded their heads in assent. His concluding argument was from Malachi 3:10 – "Bring ye all the tithes into the storehouse, that there may be meat in mine house, and prove me now herewith, said the Lord of hosts, if I will not open you the windows of heaven and pour you out a blessing, that there shall not be room enough to receive it." My father concluded his talk to these two men: "The reason I have given you this account from the Scriptures is because I believe God wants and intends us to help the Christian Dayaks to become self-supporting. I want you to teach the Dayaks to give to the Lord."

The two men, Patty and Adipatty, were quite skeptical. "It is impossible to teach the Dayaks to give; they are too poor. The Dayaks now go hungry four to six months out of the year; dare we ask them to give and make them hungrier than they are?" They were very poor, that was true. They could put all their earthly belongings in one five-gallon tin can. The response of the two national workers was sound logic. But logic is not faith, and faith cries, "It can be done!"

But as far as the national workers were concerned, there was only one way – the old way – to continue to receive the monthly money from headquarters. Headquarters received it from America; America was rich – why worry? Finally they said, "Tuan, we know it is impossible; we can't teach the people to tithe; they are too poor. But if you believe in it so much, why don't you teach it yourself."

My father began to visit the Christian Dayaks, going from village to village. He admitted, "I must confess that I started out with fear and trembling because I also knew of their poverty." He started by asking them if they knew how he got to Borneo. The answer was simple, of course - "By boat." America is a long distance away and it cost four hundred dollars for boat fare. Where had the money come from? Simple again was the reply - "Tuan, is rich, has lots of money."

Our family had humble enough furnishings in our jungle home, yet to the Dayaks, our table and four chairs, our set of dishes, our cutlery, was wealth that they had never seen before. They believed we were rich and the argument my father had wished to use – that Christian men and women in America provided our fare and support through sacrificial giving - was not working.

That introduction had failed. He began again, holding his large Bible high. "Everything I have taught you has been from this Book. From it you have learned about creation, about the origin of sin, but best of all, you have learned of God's love, redemption and salvation through the Lord Jesus Christ, and you have believed it. Is this book true?"

"It is true," they answered with one voice.

"Although you cannot read this book, has it ever told you a lie?"

"Never a lie, Tuan. Only the truth," they responded.

"Now I will teach you something new."

My father began to teach them the rudiments of tithing. As their alert faces looked at him, he continued. "Tithing really means this: if you have ten chickens, one belongs to the Lord; if ten eggs, one belongs to the Lord; if ten measures of rice (precious to them), one measure belongs to the Lord." Then he added, "Upon the authority of the Word of God I can tell you God says He will bless, will open the windows of heaven, and will rebuke the devourer for your sakes, that He will not destroy the fruits of your ground, neither shall your vine cast her fruit before the time in the field." (Malachi 3:11)

He could say no more. Most of them wore only a loincloth made of the bark of a tree. Many of the women's skirts were made of the same material. He sat down feeling he had utterly failed to get the message across. The perspiration was rolling off his face.

Finally the Dayaks began to talk, some very deliberately, others with haste. After half an hour they were quiet and sat waiting for my father to say the next word. He asked, half-doubting, what they thought about the message from God's Word and the plan He set forth. Very simply they answered, "Tuan, we have decided to accept this plan. God has done so much for us; we have been wondering how we could show a little gratitude to God for giving His Son for us. This is a way."

The speaker continued, "Tuan, we have chosen three men whom we know to be honorable. They will accept our gifts and once each moon, if it will be all right with you, they will bring them to your home."

It was all accomplished in their half-hour of discussion. Would it be all right? My father described his response: "I almost flew through the shake roof and up to the clouds." He continued: "What made the Dayaks so responsive? It was because these people's hearts were still warm, they had only a few months before learned for the first time of a God who loved them, who gave His Son. They were still in their first love, a love pure, trusting, believing."

My father and the two national workers continued to journey from longhouse to longhouse where there were Christians. Their message was the same; so was the response – a great willingness to tithe.

A few weeks later the "new moon" arrived. One morning we awakened to find Dayaks on our front porch; some had traveled for days. A dozen chickens were tied to the railing; there was a high pile of cucumbers, many eggs in a basket, and two or three rattan carrying bags full of rice. With a slight wave of the hand, pointing to all that was on the floor, the three men simply stated, *"Ini, Tuhan Allah punya."* (This is the Lord's portion.) My father's heart was full of praise; his eyes filled with tears. He could hardly see his way around on the porch because of the cucumbers, eggs, chickens, rice, fruit, vegetables - precious food to these Dayak Christians. That morning our front porch became a cathedral. Each month it was so; our front porch was covered with squash, cucumbers, sweet potato roots, rice and chickens. Each month God's portion came. All the produce and chickens were sold to the local Chinese merchant and the money was used to build the churches and a little later to support their pastors.

Bringing the tithe (rice) to Balai Sepuak

Trouble came as well. The Dutch administrator called my father to his office, seventy-eight miles away. He was angry and said, "I understand you are taxing the Dayaks 10 percent. This is unlawful; only the government can tax. I command you to cease teaching this at once."

My father respectfully replied, "It is true we teach the people to tithe and give 10 percent of their produce, but it is not compulsory. It is given freely and of their own volition. It is not for me, but is for the support of their own Christian work." Taking his New Testament from his shirt pocket he held it up and said, "I have never mixed in politics nor do I intend to. I came here to teach God's Word. In God's Word, as you very well know, tithing is taught. I would not tell you how to run the government; please do not tell me how to teach the Word of God." My father never heard from that official again.

Once the churches were built, the people brought their offerings to the church. On the outside of the church was a big crate. People pulled a latch with one hand and shoved a chicken into the crate with the other. At the top of the steps there was a large box, three and a half feet high, two feet wide and eighteen inches deep, with a small hole in the top. In this they poured their precious rice. Mothers would lift their children as they put their cupful into the bin. Close by stood the basket to receive the eggs, and a little further on there was an empty five-pound butter can with a slit in the top for the few coins someone might have. Such was the offering time in a Dayak church in Borneo.

In February 1940, my father wrote in a general letter, "Today more than three thousand Dayak Christians gather in eight different church buildings made by their own hands without one cent coming either from the missionary or from any foreign source. Today they are a healthy, growing, indigenous church having entirely supported ten native Dayak workers. We also have other workers here from other islands to whom the Dayaks contribute much rice, vegetables and chickens."

A treasurer for each church was chosen to keep account of all rice, chickens, produce and money given. At the end of each month the leading board member of each church brought the book and money to Balai Sepuak where it was then divided among the native workers. My mother was the treasurer for the district as none of the older board members knew how to read or write. After each worker was paid and the cost of nails and general running expense of the churches was settled, there was still money left in the treasury. "We praise God that, with the exception of one native school teacher from Makassar, the work here now is entirely self-supporting and this is little less than a miracle when one considers that only six years ago these dear Dayaks had never heard the name of Jesus before. Best of all there are now two native Dayak missionaries going to other tribes with the gospel and they are supported entirely by the Christian Dayak churches." (Arthur, general letter, March 1941)

In 1942, our family fled to America after the Japanese came. For six years these Dayak Christians were without a foreign missionary, but the native pastors carried on. When we returned in 1948, my father was apprehensive about what had happened during the time we were gone, but he soon found that the Church was as strong as ever - stronger, maybe - because the Dayaks had been completely on their own for these six years.

One day my father took Siga, his first Dayak interpreter, aside to learn more fully what had happened during the six years. Siga said that it had been very hard under the Japanese occupation. When the Japanese entered, they had closed every one of the churches. They made the Dayaks nail them up and close the doors; no services were allowed. (The Japanese had closed everything they believed belonged to foreigners.) And from others my father learned more fully of Siga's role at that time. "Siga, a former witch doctor, a killer, the man that God had used more in the jungles than anyone else went right up to the Japanese captain and said, 'You can't close these churches.' The Japanese captain with his sword could have just severed his head from his shoulders, but he didn't. He looked at Siga and said, 'Why can't we close these churches?' Siga answered, 'Because these churches are our churches, and in these churches we worship the Lord. They're really not ours, but they're the Lord's. We built them ourselves; they don't belong to the foreigners, they belong to us. Not one board, not one nail came from the missionary or came from another land. We made the boards. We bought the nails from the Chinese. We built these churches with our own hands. Every one of these churches belongs to us.' The Japanese captain investigated and found out that what Siga had told him was true. He said, 'All right, open the churches.' After the first year of occupation, during all the time that the Japanese were there, the Dayaks were allowed to worship in these churches." (Arthur, taped sermon)

Another result of the Japanese occupation during World War II was that their control of the island brought an end to rice being imported into Borneo, and the island was forced into self-sufficiency. The Christian Dayaks had the reputation among surrounding tribes of always having a surplus of rice. The Iban people of neighboring Sarawak began to travel to these Christian Dayaks, the Mualang people, to work and trade for rice. The Dayaks attributed their ample harvest to their new faith. God was faithfully doing as He had promised in Malachi 3:10: "Bring ye all the tithes into the storehouse, that there may be meat in mine house, and prove me now herewith, said the Lord of hosts, if I will not open you the windows of heaven, and pour you out a blessing, that there shall not be room enough to receive it."

In 1949, an historic conference was called at which time the appointment of the native workers was made by the foreign missionary for the last time. The governing of the church body was surrendered wholly to the native Dayak Church. The property and church buildings were already theirs, for the land belonged to them, and the buildings had been erected by them. It had been just fourteen years since 1935 that the first Dayak in this area had believed.

All these events happened because the Dayaks had learned to tithe, to give a portion of what they had to God.

(Much of this chapter is based on a pamphlet my father wrote in 1948 titled, *We Taught the Dayaks to Tithe.*)

17 SOME ECONOMIC CONSEQUENCES OF CONVERSION

The previous chapter notes that the Christian Dayaks had the reputation among surrounding tribes of always having a surplus of rice. It is a fact that after the Dayaks of this Mualang tribe embraced Christianity, they became more prosperous due to their more abundant rice harvest. They believed this was due to God's blessing and answer to their prayers. But God's blessings are often the result of very practical reasons rather than the miraculous.

The Dayaks' new faith resulted in two lifestyle changes that directly affected their rice production. The first was giving up all the ritual prescriptions and proscriptions involved in their traditional, magically-enhanced approach to agriculture. When a rice crop began to ripen, the Dayaks had to watch their fields – the men took turns throughout the night – as wild pigs, deer, monkeys and smaller animals roamed in search of food. But if on the way to their rice field, the Dayaks saw an unfortunate omen such as a certain bird flying in the wrong direction, their traditional belief required that they immediately return to their longhouse. Otherwise the spirits that inhabited their natural world could be offended and cause harm to the village. Meanwhile, the marauding deer and pigs continued their prowling, often eating and destroying a sizable portion of the rice crop. Other times, an unfavorable omen required that they abandon a field altogether. All these beliefs were replaced by a simple prayer, invoking God's care as they worked in their fields.

A second lifestyle change with economic consequences was the giving up of drinking alcohol. Dr. Allen Drake brought to my attention that in a 1901 geography of Dutch West Borneo Province by J.J. K. Enthoven, there is a characterization of the Mualang tribe of Dayaks that is very unflattering. They are described as the most degenerate of the people of the Sakadau political division, given to drunkenness, compulsive cock fighting, and suffering from poverty as a consequence of these excesses. As Christians, the Dayaks discontinued these rituals. This resulted in improved health and more time for productive activity, because they no longer spent the good part of some days recuperating from these bouts of drunkenness. Most of the Christian Dayaks also gave up smoking and no longer used a portion of their precious rice to purchase tobacco from the Chinese merchants.

The first pictures my parents took of the Dayaks, some included in this book, show the men wearing only a loincloth, the women mostly bare-breasted. My parents did not teach the Dayaks that as Christians they needed to cover their nakedness. However, the Chinese with whom the Dayaks traded for basic necessities (salt, fish hooks, cooking pots) took advantage of the Dayaks' increased prosperity and urged them to buy cloth and ready-made clothing. Perhaps it is a natural tendency of all people to wish to adorn themselves. Be that as it may, as the material means became available, the Dayaks began to purchase material and clothing from these Chinese merchants. This is evident from the later pictures of the Dayaks included in this book showing them more fully dressed.

18 APAI MAMUT, THE MAN WITH THE MUSTACHE

(This chapter is entirely Arthur's words, transcribed from a taped sermon given in 1953.)

One day God led me into a particular area way up in the jungles as far as we could go. Borneo is about 500 miles from east to west, so you can't go more than 250 miles in without starting to go out. As we went from longhouse to longhouse, one day we realized that we weren't going alone, that there was another man that had joined us. He followed us wherever we went. He liked going where we went, because Dayak etiquette requires that they feed anyone who comes to their village, and people always gave us the best food.

He was an unusual character, by nature kind of a clown, and also because he was the only man in the jungles that I ever met who had a goatee and a mustache. He let his mustache grow long and used to twist it around with his hand. And sometimes, right in the middle of a service, he'd stick his chin out and the little children would all giggle. I felt like getting after him because sometimes he really disturbed the meeting just at the wrong time. It troubled me inside. But I'm glad I didn't say anything to him.

Apai Mamut

Then one day in one of the villages, he stopped his clowning and got real serious. The Holy Spirit was making the Gospel real to his heart. When the opportunity was given, he bowed his head and his heart and received the Lord Jesus Christ as his Lord and Saviour.

122

He stayed with us a few days more, and then one day he came to me and said, "Tuan, I have to go. I can't follow you any more. I think I'd better go home."

"Áll right, you had better go home."

"Tuan, I want you to promise me one thing before I leave, that some day you will come and teach my people as you have been teaching the people here."

"What do you mean by my people? Aren't these your people?"

"No. I don't belong to this tribe. I belong to another tribe."

"How does it happen that you are here?"

"I heard that someone was up here in the jungle that was teaching something that we had never heard before, and so I just decided to come."

I found out that he lived a long distance away, but I promised him that just as soon as possible, I would come to see his tribe.

Several months went by. We were so busy in this area and God was certainly working in hearts. It was like a nation being born in a day! I knew it didn't happen by accident; it was because of people who had prayed for the island of Borneo, who mentioned it by name.

Then one day I was traveling down the river in my little boat. I had forgotten the man with the mustache. And about half a mile ahead of me I saw something moving back and forth. I didn't know what it was. I thought perhaps it was monkeys in the trees, jumping from branch to branch. There are thousands of them in those jungles. However, as we drew closer, I recognized the figure of a man. He was waving a palm branch back and forth in an attempt to get us to stop and talk to him. You know by now who that man was. It was none other than Apai Mamut, the clownish fellow with the goatee and mustache.

After we stopped he started to scold us a little. "Tuan, you promised you would come over three and a half moons ago, and you haven't come to our village yet. I heard you were coming down this river, and I have been waiting here three days for you. I thought you would never come, but now that you are here, I told my people I wouldn't come back until I brought you. So get out of your boat and come along with me."

He thought he'd traveled enough with me so he could give me some orders. I said, "I'm sorry I cannot come now. I must go to another place." He asked me where I was going, and when I told him he asked how long ago I had promised them. I was ashamed to tell him. When he found out when we had promised he said, "Tuan, you promised me before you promised them."

Again I told him I was sorry, but I had promised to be there on a certain day and had to go. "I must go, but I'll tell you what I'll do. If you'll be back here in ten days, I'll be right back here."

He reached down on the jungle floor, took a vine and tied it in ten knots. He had his calendar in his hands. He would loosen a knot each day, and the day he loosened the last one, that was the day I would be back. After talking a little more with him and having prayer, I left.

Sure enough, in ten days as we were going around the bend of the river, there was Apai Mamut. He had three carriers with him. They were waving and waving to us having heard the *putt-putt-putt* of the motor, which didn't have a muffler, for a long time.

We pulled up to the bank and he said, "Tuan, we didn't know exactly when you would come, but just to be sure we wouldn't be late, we got here two days ago and we've been waiting for you." I think what happened is that he forgot to unloosen the knots of the vine and he'd lost track of the days, but he was here.

I gave them the few things we were going to take with us and he said, "Aren't you going to take more than that?"

I said, "No, I don't need any more. You know I don't travel with very much."

But he insisted, "No, take some more."

I didn't need anything more; I just knew they'd have to carry it there and carry it back. But they wanted to carry something, so I gave them a few more things and down the trail we went. And as we walked he chattered and told me everything that had happened in the jungles in the last twenty years. He was just like a walking newspaper.

"Tuan, give us something to carry."

Finally, after some hours of walking and talking, we came to his village. The men were gathered on the left-hand side of the trail, and the women on the right. We shook hands with them (Apai Mamut had told them that when I came they were supposed to stick out their hands) and walked up the notched-log ladder into the longhouse.

Going up the notched-log ladder

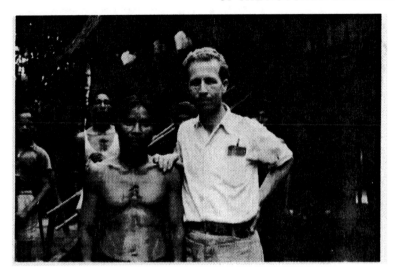

At the longhouse

The chief started giving orders. He could have given out these orders before we got there, but he wanted to let us know he was the chief. I smiled inwardly and thought, "Human nature is the same the world around." He gave orders for the men to get out the coconuts and the women to get out other delicacies. I sat on the floor in front of a brass tray, drinking the coconut water and eating rice balls about the size of a ping pong ball in which there was enclosed about a quarter of an inch square of sugar. I always wished they would make it about half an inch because a quarter of an inch is not enough for my sweet tooth. Then I saw my camp cot leaning against the post and I thought, "Just as soon as we're finished meeting the people and greeting them, I want to unfold that camp cot and have some rest."

But as we sat there and I listened to their conversation I could tell that there was something different about them, and the more I listened, the more my heart was warmed, and I forgot all about that camp cot. Because something was going on in the hearts of these people that ministered to my own heart.

After a while, I couldn't wait any longer, and I said to them, "You don't talk like unbelievers. You talk differently."

They were glad that I had noticed and their faces lit up and they said, "Oh, Tuan, we are people that believe."

"You are people that believe?"

"Yes."

"What do you mean?"

"Tuan, about ten days after Apai Mamut came back, we decided to believe on the Lord, too, for he told us what he'd heard up there, and when we heard it, we, too, wanted to believe. And, Tuan, we are believers. This is what we have wanted all our lives to hear."

I sat there dumb-founded. I didn't know what to say. My heart was warm; there were tears in my eyes. No missionary, no native worker had ever been there before, and yet here were people trusting the Lord the best they knew how.

I asked them, "What did you do on the Lord's day?"

"Tuan, we didn't do anything."

"What do you mean?"

"Well, Apai Mamut said we could only sit on the floor. We just had to stay in the longhouse all day long. We couldn't go anywhere on the Lord's day."

Of course, that was not what I had taught, but that was his interpretation. I went on -

"But what did you do on the Lord's Day. You must have done something."

"Oh, yes, Tuan. We gathered together. We had a meeting."

"Well, what did you do at the meeting?"

"Oh, he stood and he told us everything he had heard and he tried to sing to us. Then we had our noon meal, and in the afternoon he stood up again and told us everything that he knew."

"What did you do the rest of the day?"

"We just sat in the longhouse. And we talked and kept on asking Apai Mamut questions."

"Then what happened?"

"Well, evening came on. We had our evening meal. And then we lighted pitch torches and listened to him until the torches died and we went to sleep."

As I sat there and listened to these people – they had only heard from Apai Mamut – then I realized why Jesus Christ said, "Go ye into all the world and preach the gospel to every creature," and why Paul said, "I am not ashamed of the Gospel of Christ, for it is the power of God unto salvation to everyone that believes." And I'm so glad that you don't have to have a college education or a high school diploma; you don't even have to go to grammar school in order to be able to understand the Gospel. I had the joy of staying with them a few days and of instructing them more perfectly in the ways of the Lord.

God continued to bless, other people were added to these believers, and a church was built in that area. They invited me one day to come and dedicate that church which they built with their own hands. And on the day of the dedication, which was the Lord's day, you would think that Apai Mamut would be right up in front, because he was the man who was more responsible for the Gospel being proclaimed there than anyone else, but he wasn't. Apai Mamut just sat there on the floor with his people, sort of in the back, and as that church was dedicated he just melted in with his people. He didn't become a celebrity or go around with his chin up and his chest out and say, "Look what I have done! Look what's happened because I received the Lord." He just, in his humble way, sat there on the floor and became one with his people.

The people from that village are serving the Lord to this day. From that village came Julak who is now one of the pastors of the twenty-three churches.

19 TROUBLE IN THE JUNGLE

The preaching of the gospel brought hope and peace to the individual hearts of Dayak believers; it also brought trouble to the jungle. There was division between those who wanted to follow this new way and those who did not. Husbands who believed left their wives; wives who believed left their husbands. Longhouses divided because half the people wanted to believe and the other half did not. Those who were not believers were angry and said they could no longer live together with the Christians who had adopted new ways and rejected some of their long-held, traditional beliefs.

In 1935, a man at one longhouse who had recently become a Christian decided he should cut down his *rumah begela*, a little six by eight foot platform he had built to honor the spirits he paid homage to. But chopping down a *rumah begela* meant only one thing in the jungles – that someone was going to lead an insurrection against the Dutch government. When the village chief informed the Dutch officials of this man's actions, he and six other men in the village were imprisoned for three and a half months, because the officials said that the men were planning to start a revolution. The accused man tried to explain that he had torn down his "house of spirits" because, as a Christian, he wished to break entirely with his formerly held beliefs, but the officials said he was lying. One of the men died while in prison. This caused great fear within the village and resulted in about half of the new believers turning back to their old beliefs and customs.

In 1939 my mother wrote the following in a letter to her sister-in-law: "Arthur is kept busy overseeing the work as we have branched out and entered three new districts. Two of these districts are quite a distance from here. ... There are fifteen hundred Dayaks there who have felt moved by the preaching of the gospel which they have heard for the first time. But there is a chief over these fifteen hundred who is very hard-hearted, and the people are so afraid of him they are afraid to confess Christ and put away their old customs. ... It is awfully hard for Dayaks to believe when the strong chiefs do not as their lives are tied up so with the chief's power over them in small details of their lives." In some areas the paramount chiefs, whose jurisdiction covered many longhouses (as opposed to the individual chief of each longhouse), taxed the Christian Dayaks three times each year instead of once. (The tax was usually a cupful of rice.)

Another time about thirty-five Christian Dayaks were compelled by the chief to go to work for the government for five weeks just at rice-planting time. When they returned, the heavy rainy season had begun, and they were unable to burn the brush in their fields, a critical step in the planting process. This was a deliberate attempt by the chief to ruin their harvest and make them renounce their faith. And although most of the villages begged my father to come and visit their longhouse, there were some villages he approached where the chief refused to let him enter.

In those early years, every time my parents heard the *putt, putt, putt* of a motor coming up the river, they feared Dutch officials were coming to settle some new trouble.

The next chapter tells the story of one of those visits.

20 SETTLING THE ISSUE OF BLOOD, THE POWER OF PRAYER

(This chapter is entirely Arthur's words, transcribed from a taped sermon given in 1953.)

We moved into the jungles, right among the people. We were so glad to be there, and, of course, the people were glad to have us there. But every time a boat came up the river, our hearts nearly stopped beating, because no one had boats except the officials. And they had been up there before and had tried to straighten us out, because we were making trouble there in the jungle. Families were divided. The children wanted to believe, the father and mother didn't want to believe; a husband wanted to believe, the wife didn't want to believe, and it was just making trouble and the officials had to come, on occasion, and try to settle this trouble.

One day we heard the *putt, putt, putt* of a motorboat and we wondered, "Is it another official?" And, sure enough, as we waited for it to come around the bend of the river, there we saw the red, white and blue [Dutch] flag, and we watched as the boat came up right in front of our house. Two Dutch officials stepped out, and then there were a few national officials who got out of the boat, too. I walked down the path and met them down at the boat, and we walked up the path together up on our porch. They said, "We've come to settle the trouble once and for all about the business of the blood. That's why we're here."

They ate supper with us that night, but they slept in their boat. They came up the next morning and had breakfast and said, "Now we want you to go along with us because we're going to make a tour of this area. We understand you've started some schools here, and we want to examine those schools."

Having finished breakfast, they wanted to go, and I said, "If you don't mind, I'll be here just a little while." I prayed with my wife and we prayed together, covenanted together, that God would watch over us.

We walked with these men and it took about six hours to get to the first school. They examined the school, but didn't pay much attention to it. I thought they'd be happy because these people were learning how to read and write. They just looked at the crude benches made out of the lumber of the jungle, no sawed boards at all, just raw timber tied together with rattan. In the same way the benches and chairs were made. The blackboard on the wall was kind of a crude affair, but it was black, and the teacher could write some words on there with white chalk. They just glanced at it. I thought they would be happy that these people were being educated, but it didn't seem they were.

We continued on after staying there overnight. We walked through the jungle again to another church. This was our largest church at the time; it had 1325 members. Of course, the members weren't there because we were there on a weekday. But they wanted to stay there overnight. There were two national workers there who had come from other islands. They were the teachers and also the preachers at this particular church, because in those early days we hadn't yet had the opportunity to train the Dayaks. And that night I said to these two national workers, along with some Dayaks who were there, "I don't think we better sleep tonight. We better pray." And those young men and those two national workers and I prayed all night.

The next morning after we had breakfast they said, "Now it's time for us to turn around and go back to your home." And so we'd made a complete circuit and were turning back now and going to where we lived. As we were going down the trail, after a while we caught up with some people, and a little farther there were more people going in the same direction, and farther more people, all kinds of people, more people than usually travel on the trails. I knew that something was different that I didn't know about.

Finally, I turned to one of the officials and said, "Why are these people on the trail?"

He looked at me and said, "You're in trouble."

I said, "What's wrong?"

He said, "We've come once and for all to settle this business about the blood. And you don't know it, but I have sent secret men out into the jungles to call all these people, and we're going to meet, all of them, at your place there along the river." I walked along and, of course, I continued to pray.

When we got to the little town in which we lived, the place was filled with people. It was toward evening then, and again those men slept on their boat and had breakfast with us the next morning. When they finished breakfast I started to walk out of the house with them, and they said, "You'll come." And I said, "Yes, I'll come. But if you don't mind, I'll just stay with my wife a little while." So they went on and they asked for some chairs, and someone carried chairs for them out under the rubber trees.

My wife and I knelt down alongside our davenport – you couldn't really call it a davenport, just a crude something that looked like a davenport - and we knelt there and we prayed. We knew we were in deep trouble. We said, "Lord, if you can find somebody that you can trust with a burden of prayer, don't let them stop praying until this business is settled." We couldn't pray long.

I went out under the rubber trees, and here were the four chairs. Three were occupied and the other one was there for me. The leading official turned to me and said, "Now I want you to tell these people that you call Christians, that they've got to go back and use the blood of the chicken and the blood of the pig again, because if they don't, there isn't peace in this land. They're coming down to our stations all the time, telling of the trouble up in the jungle, because the land is divided. Half of the people use the blood of the pig and the blood of the chicken, but the Christians don't."

What about this business of the blood? Well, when the Dayaks want to plant their rice fields, they chop down the trees and the brush, and when it is all chopped down, they burn the brush, and the burned brush acts as a fertilizer, potash, and they plant their rice fields there. But after the field was burned and there was the potash on the ground, then they killed a pig and caught the blood in a big bowl, and then they went throughout that whole plot of ground, dipping their hand into the blood and sprinkling the blood here and sprinkling the blood there. And they believed that purifies the ground and, of course, they believed that if they didn't use that blood, the seed wouldn't germinate. If the seed didn't germinate, they wouldn't get any rice, and if they didn't get any rice they'd go hungry. And this was the custom of all of the people before we got there. But now the Christians weren't using the blood, and here we were now.

The official said to me, "Now all you have to do to settle this is to tell these people who call themselves Christians, that they have to go back and use the blood of the pig and the blood of the chicken again." And then he said, in the Dutch language, which I had learned and understood a little, "If you don't, that boat there along side the river will take you and your wife downstream, and you'll never get back here again."

I sat there and didn't know what to do, but I was praying, and all of a sudden I said to him, "You know, you must believe that these Dayaks are following the Lord just because of me. But they're not following the Lord just because of me. They have received God's Son, and they are following him with all their hearts. They're not just doing what we're telling them to do. And these people are really changed; they're transformed; they're new creatures." It didn't mean a thing to him.

He said, "It's not possible. Now you go ahead and tell them to use the blood of the pig and chicken again."

I said, "I can't do that; it's impossible."

And he said, "There's the boat."

I was praying, inwardly, asking the Lord to guide. And finally I said to him, "You know, these people wouldn't go back and use the blood of the pig and the blood of the chicken just because I told them to go back and use it. They're not using it because they don't want to use it, and they know they don't need to use it." And I added, "If you don't believe me, why don't you ask one of them?" - because he had said, "Ah, I don't believe that."

Then all of a sudden this Hollander put his finger out and pointed at a man and said, *"Berdiri!"* (Stand up.) And the poor little guy with the finger pointed right at him, he looked around hoping it was someone else, and the official said, "No! You, stand up." The little fellow stood up just scared to death. Just trembling. You could see him shaking all over the place. He didn't say a word. And through the interpreter the official said, "Say something!" He didn't know what to say. The only speech he'd ever made in his life was in church when he was giving his testimony, so he started giving his testimony. "You know, sir, at one time we were all of one heart, following the evil spirits and the birds. We poured the blood on the ground thinking it would purify the ground. We were all of one heart. That man (pointing with his chin) came and he told us about Jesus. How he hung on the cross and shed his precious blood for us so that we might have eternal life. And, sir, we've believed. *Kami turut Tuhan Isa.*"(We follow Jesus Christ.) And Oh, I just praised the Lord for his testimony up to then. But then he said, "You know, sir, we wouldn't go back and use the blood of the pig and the blood of the chicken for anybody. It doesn't make any difference who would tell us to use the blood of the pig and the blood of the chicken, we wouldn't do it. Because we don't believe in that anymore. We just go out into our fields now, and we just stand there and pray and ask God to give us a good crop. We don't have to spread the blood around. We just get a good crop. And, sir, we're getting good crops all the time. And we wouldn't go back and use the blood of the pig or chicken for anybody."

When he said those words, the official became furious, because he knew I hadn't had a chance to coach the Dayak man and tell him what to say; this was all on his own. He started to curse and to swear and take God's name in vain. I was sitting quite close to him, and when he cursed and swore like that, it made me afraid – taking God's name in vain and cursing and swearing at these dear Dayaks. And he was no more finished with that than his head dropped into his hands and his elbows were on his knees, and he sat there for a long time, probably it was five minutes. Well, five minutes is an eternity when no one says anything.

Every eye was on him, and all of a sudden he jumped to his feet and said (in Dutch), "Everything's over!"

The interpreter there said, "*Apa dia bilang?*" (What did he say?)

I said, "*Dia bilang 'Semua sudah habis.'*" (He said, 'Everything is over.')

He asked, "What's over?"

I said, "I don't know."

The leading official got up and walked away, and the other officials followed him. The people crowded around me, wanted to ask me all kinds of questions. I didn't say very much because it wasn't the time to talk. After a while I followed, and here were the two Dutch officials who had come, standing under the mango tree, and one of them said, "You know, we have to be a little diplomatic in settling things like this."

And I nodded my head and said, "Yes, I think we should be diplomatic." I didn't know where there had been any diplomacy, but anyway, they were talking about being diplomatic, and I said, "Yes, I think that's right."

And he said, "I think that we better be going down the river."

I said, "Why my wife is preparing the noon meal and she's expecting you to eat."

They said, "Oh, we can't stay."

I said, "Well, I want you to stay."

They said, " No, we must be going."

The men walked down to the boat, cranked up the engine, and down the river they went. They hadn't settled anything. And the Dayaks who had come, ordered by this man to come – there were hundreds of them – those who were not believers left, but those who were Christians stayed.

We ate our noon meal; they brought their own rice; they ate their noon meal. They were there on the porch and we talked for a while, and finally they all gathered at the bottom of the porch – there were some steps – and they were asking me all kinds of questions. "Tuan, we didn't understand a bit of that language that you were talking to that man in. What'd you say? And then, what'd he say? And what'd you say?" And I tried to tell them what had happened in a nice way, because I didn't want to bring any reproach upon those officials. They were servants of the Lord. They were Dutch; they'd been there for three hundred years. You were safer there in Borneo, any time of the night, than you are in cities in the States. It was well governed, well ruled, and the people were prosperous under the Dutch. I didn't want to say anything against them.

Finally, one Dayak looked up at me – he'd been listening to all the questions and all the answers - and he said, *"Tuan, siapa menang?"* (Who won?) I looked at that dear Dayak, I bowed my head, I bawled. He wanted to be on the winning side, and he just wondered who won. And I said to him, "Don't say anything about who won. If you go back into the jungles and say you won, you'll make more trouble than we've ever had. And we've had enough; we don't need any more. Just go back in the jungles and praise the Lord, thank the Lord that we weren't taken down the river, because that's what they threatened to do. We're not going down the river. We're still here."

They stayed that day and part of the next day, and then they started to go home. We were free to worship in the churches. Those officials never came again.

Some months went by and we received a letter from a man, John DePeu, in Pennsylvania. His letter said, "Mr. Mouw, I don't know what was wrong on a certain day, but I know that everything that was wrong on that day is all right now. A burden of prayer came upon me at a certain hour, and I didn't know for whom I should pray. But I have a prayer list, and I went down my prayer list and finally I came to your name, and as I mentioned your name to the Lord, I knew you were in trouble. And I prayed, and I didn't stop praying until that burden lifted."

After we read the letter, my wife and I traced back as best we could. Pennsylvania is a long way from Borneo and there's a dateline that runs right down through the Pacific and it isn't so easy to determine exactly the time in a city in the States and the time that it would be in the land of Borneo. But as we traced back, as nearly as we could, when we kneeled down at that davenport and prayed and asked for God's help, it was just about that time that this man had a burden of prayer.

I would rather have a man like John DePeu pray for me than I would for a millionaire to back me up. Because in a situation like we found ourselves in Borneo, money wouldn't have helped. There was only one thing that would help, and that was prayer. And God answered his [John

DePeu's] prayer. And as a result of that man's prayer, we were allowed to stay there in the land of Borneo and preach the gospel to these people.

[Some years later, when our family was home during World War II, my father was speaking at a church in Los Angeles and met John DePeu who was attending the service.]

21 A SPECIAL RECEPTION

My father had received a special invitation to come to the village of a chief who had recently become a Christian. The day came for his appointed visit, and as he approached the longhouse, he met the chief who said, "Tuan, we're so glad you've come, but we're not quite ready for you; we weren't expecting you yet."

My father thought this a rather strange reception and wondered whether he was really welcome, but he continued walking with the chief and climbed the notched-log ladder into the longhouse. As soon as they entered, the chief started to give orders to his wife, and within a few minutes my father smelled coffee brewing. The Dayaks were not coffee drinkers; this would be the first time he had been offered coffee in a Dayak longhouse.

Soon the chief came out of a room with a four-legged contraption, something my father could see had been newly made, put it on the floor and declared, "Tuan, we're getting there; we're not quite ready yet, but we will be soon." He went back into the room, came out with a big slab of wood about forty inches in diameter and plunked it on top of the four-legged contraption. With this addition, my father realized that it was to serve as a table. (The Dayaks eat sitting on the floor.) The chief seemed agitated and nervous and again ran into the room and came out with a small, hand-woven cloth to cover the table.

On his next trip he presented the coffee to my father in a bowl that looked as if it had never been washed, set it on the table but said, "Oh, Tuan, just wait a moment; I've forgotten something." This time he came back with a can of sweetened condensed milk, took his long knife out of its sheath, gave the can a couple of whacks to open it, and set it on the table along with a small package of cookies. He seemed, finally, to be a bit more relaxed and said invitingly, "*Minum.*" (Drink)

My father stared at the bowl of coffee that he thought looked something like the water in the Missouri River. The chief directed, "Put some milk in." My father poured some of the thick, sweet milk in, and as he stirred it, all the coffee grounds that were on the bottom came up and mixed with the milk. Again the chief gave instructions.

"Tuan, put in some sugar."

"Oh, this milk will make it sweet enough."

"Tuan, please, put in some sugar."

My father felt he had to put in some sugar, a luxury item for Dayaks, so he put in a spoonful. The chief urged, "Put in another." As he was stirring the coffee my father was thinking, "I'm not only preparing this, I'm going to have to drink it." Finally he raised the bowl to his lips, began to drink the coffee and ate some of the cookies.

Why had the chief done all this? In another village he had heard the Gospel, accepted Christ into his heart and was so thankful that he made my father promise to come to his village. In preparation for my father's

146

visit, he had spoken to Samuel, a young Dayak man who worked with my father.

"When Tuan comes, I want to treat him the right way. What does he drink?"

"He drinks coffee."

"Where does he drink?"

"He sits in a chair at his table."

"What else does he do?"

"Well, sometimes he nibbles on biscuits, and he has milk in his coffee."

"Well, I'll have to get that."

The chief went to the local Chinese merchant and bought some coffee, a can of milk, some sugar and cookies, items the Dayaks would rarely, if ever, buy for themselves. This had cost him a lot of money. The can of milk alone would be the equal to three days labor, as it had cost thirty-five cents and at that time one could hire all the Dayaks one wanted for ten cents a day. Then he had gone into the jungle, cut down a tree to get some wood, and made a table and a chair.

As he sat in the chair that was as wiggly as the table, drinking the coffee, my father's heart was full of thanksgiving. "Do you think I ever regretted the day that I said 'Yes' to Jesus Christ or sang the song, 'I'll go where you want me to go, Dear Lord, over mountain or plain or sea.' God makes up so much more to us; we can't possibly ever repay that which God does for us. And I praise the Lord for being a laborer for him in the land of Borneo." (Arthur, taped sermon)

22 THE MAN IN THE CAGE, THE POWER OF LOVE

"But the fruit of the spirit is love, joy, peace, longsuffering, gentleness, goodness, faith, meekness, temperance; against such there is no law." (Galatians 5:22)

Love is understood everywhere. One of the highest compliments ever paid to my father was about love, said by a man who was once in a cage in a Dayak village. This man had gone berserk, completely out of his mind. Taking a long knife he started to slash everything he could find. He killed some pigs and chickens and the people knew if he were not stopped, he would be killing children next. Before he was put in the cage, the Dayak men of his longhouse had put him in stocks. His legs were encased in an eight foot log about ten inches in diameter. The log had been split down the middle, and in the center two holes had been cut out. The man's legs were put through the holes and the two pieces bound together with rattan. Then they built a cage, because he couldn't continue to stay in the stocks.

One day the people of this village asked my father to come and help get this man, Noe, from the stocks and into the cage. They were afraid because they knew that sometimes people who go out of their mind can have the strength of ten people. My father went up to him and talked to him quietly.

"Do you know who I am?" He nodded his head but didn't say a word.

"Noe, have I ever harmed you or ever done anything to you that I shouldn't have done?" Noe just looked at him and didn't say anything.

"The people of this longhouse are your people; they're of your family. They love you, and they want you to be in a cage instead of in this log. I want to help you."

Continuing to speak quietly he said, "Don't make any trouble. We're going to open this log up and you will be able to get out of it. And when you get out of it, I'm going to take you over to that cage. They made it just for you. Please don't make any trouble."

The rattan that bound the parts of the log together was removed, and Noe could take his feet out of the log. He started to rub his feet, because he had tried his best to get out of that log, and in trying he had bruised his feet around the ankles; they were red and swollen.

My father took him quietly by the elbow and said, "Come with me. We're going over here to help you get into that cage." They walked the few feet to the cage, which was about six feet square and had a small gate, about thirty inches by thirty inches on one side. My father asked him to go in through the gate, but he shook his head; he wouldn't do it.

"Noe, get into the cage. It's all right. Don't worry about it. They're doing it because they love you." He shook his head again. My father continued to talk quietly to him, but he wouldn't move. The Dayaks who were watching grew anxious.

Then my father got down on his hands and knees and crawled into the cage himself. "Noe, come. Come. It's all right. Come in." After some time Noe got down on his hands and knees and crawled through the opening. Now he was at the doorway and my father was at the other end of the cage. Little by little, talking to him quietly, my father made his way to the opening, and exited the cage. The moment he did so, the Dayak men slammed the gate shut and wound it with heavy rattan rope. Noe let out a scream.

He was in the cage for many days. In his travels my father went to this village many times and prayed for Noe, but he wasn't getting better. One night at our home in Balai Sepuak, my father was so burdened for Noe that he couldn't sleep. He asked my mother, "Dear, if there are any Dayaks here, ask them to come into the room where I am. And when you're finished putting the children to bed, please come too, and let us pray." The Dayaks came, knelt on the floor, and that night they prayed only for Noe and asked God to deliver him. At about nine o'clock the atmosphere cleared and they felt everything was all right.

Two mornings later a sampan came down the river. Noe's mother and father were in the sampan with their son sitting between them. They had come to show my father that Noe was in his right mind. Later, Noe became a member of the church, married and had a family.

My father concludes this story: "I ask you which is the greater miracle? That the man was in the cage and then was released in answer to prayer, or is the greater miracle that this man gives testimony that Jesus Christ has come to live in his heart? That is the greatest miracle of all!" (Arthur, taped sermon)

Some time later, when my father was going to return to the United States on furlough, Noe said, "Tuan, we don't want you to go."

"Well I have to go. My wife and children have already gone; they've been gone almost eight months, and I must go home."

"Oh, I don't want you to go."

"Don't worry, Noe. There will be somebody else here to take my place while I'm gone."

"I know. You've told us that several times. But, Tuan, I'm so afraid that the one who comes won't love us like you love us."

The message of love is something people understand the world around.

23 FIRST FURLOUGH IN THE UNITED STATES

From the time my mother moved to Sintang, Borneo, in 1933, she had recurring bouts of malaria. Quinine was the only medication available at that time. It helped with the fever, but could not prevent future occurrences of this disease that is caused by the bite of an infected mosquito.

These bouts of malaria left her in a weakened condition. This had made her life somewhat difficult in Sintang, but there she had the help of the Javanese couple, and her main job was taking care of my brother and me. This changed when we moved to Balai Sepuak in November 1935, because of the constant stream of Dayaks who came to our home, many of whom wanted my mother's attention. And so it was decided that my mother, Burneal and I would go back to the United States a little earlier than planned. At that time, C&MA missionaries in the Dutch East Indies were expected to stay for a term of five years, then have a one-year furlough in the United States.

My mother wrote to her mother-in-law of these plans: "I am not very strong and not strong enough to take care of these big crowds that come. … But Arthur really is the one who feels it is the only thing to do and the

153

best thing to do, for the work here as well as for me. He has so much building to oversee [of the churches] and so much to be done which will keep him traveling all the time, he says he will feel so much better about me if I am home [in the United States] than if I am left alone to take care of the work here. If we are safely home, he can go ahead and work for six months to get the building done and make a tour over the whole district with the native workers. He would never be alone, of course. He would have the four native workers with him part of the time, but always two of them would be with him. Arthur has been blessed with real health and strength so far." (Edna, letter, February 1936)

My father added his comments: "I want Edna to come home in April and I'll stay another year. I'm home so little and it's so hard on her. ... And with the added new territory that we are opening, I will be away more than ever. ... By the time she returns there should be a church nearby, and this will help." (Arthur, letter, January 1936)

The news spread throughout the jungle that my mother was about to leave, and three days before her departure, the Dayaks started to come down the trails from all directions, from up the river and down the river. They came by the hundreds, and finally we had over two thousand people at our home in Balai Sepuak. On the day we were to leave, my mother had my brother by the hand, my father was carrying me, and we were walking down to the river to our little boat that would take us down to the coast. And on each side of the path that we were on were these Dayak people.

"Nyonya, hurry back," they pleaded with my mother.

"I'll come back just as soon as I'm well," she replied.

Some others said, "Nyonya, don't forget us."

She looked at them with love. "I could never forget you dear people."

They handed her eggs and chickens, cucumbers and all kinds of vegetables, because she was going a long way and needed to eat on the way. They gave so much that some young men had to follow with baskets to hold everything.

My father and mother thanked them graciously for all their gifts, knowing they couldn't possibly be refused. (Of course we couldn't take all these things with us, so about half way down the river they were sold and the money received was put into the church treasury.) The people kept telling us to hurry back and again and again asked my mother not to forget them. There was longing in their voices, because no white woman had ever come to the jungle before to live among them, and they knew that she loved them. Again my mother told them she would never forget them and began to cry. And then the Dayaks started to cry.

This is my father's description of that moment: "When she started to cry, she just broke down and wept. And these Dayaks started to cry. The men cried, the women cried, the children cried, the babies cried because they saw everyone else was crying. The Chinese that were there were crying, my children were crying, everybody was crying except myself. And I looked at all these people crying and it just struck me the other way and I got the giggles. And I couldn't stop laughing. I tried to stop, but I couldn't stop. And they looked at me as much as to say, 'You're the hardest-hearted man we've ever seen. It's your wife that's leaving and we're doing the crying.'" (Arthur, taped sermon)

We got in our little boat, went down to the coastal city of Pontianak, crossed the Java Sea over to Singapore where we boarded a boat for America. My father went back to Borneo, and we crossed the Pacific Ocean, arriving in the United States on August 6, 1936. We stayed in Seattle where my mother's mother and one of her sisters lived. My brother's fourth birthday was on August 15, nine days after we arrived. At his birthday celebration, which included ice cream, a new experience for a couple of Borneo kids, he asked if his ice cream could be heated which sent our three cousins into gales of laughter.

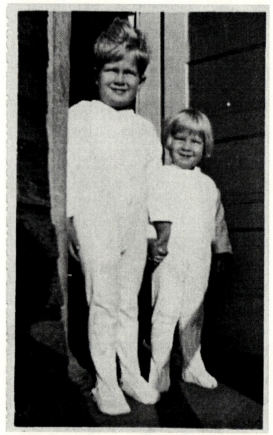

A good morning picture to send to Daddy

While my father was alone in Borneo, he wrote to his parents. "Don't feel sorry for me here as I'm really happy and contented to be here alone. … I am so conscious of Edna's love that it comforts me, and to know that she is where she is getting proper food and care makes me very happy. …

The heat is terrible now – no rain for six weeks. I don't mind it, but the heat almost made Edna drop." And in another letter two weeks later he wrote, "It's a joy to be here even if my dear wife is away. God bless these precious Dayaks; they are as wonderful a people as God ever made, and there is nothing that they wouldn't do for me." (Arthur, letter, September 1936)

Later, he described his own departure: "Previous to my leaving there were three days of shaking hands and shedding tears. More than two thousand people gathered at Balai Sepuak for a farewell service." He left Borneo for the United States in January 1937, and joined us in February. We spent about half our time in southern California where my father's parents, his brother and sisters lived. We lived in a home in a missionary colony, in Glendale. A wealthy woman, Mrs. Suppes, owned about twenty-five small homes that she rented at a very reasonable rate. Mrs. Suppes told this story: She owned property near Long Beach on which oil was discovered. Because of her desire to help missionaries, she prayed and asked God to give her $50,000 to purchase homes she would rent to missionaries who were home on furlough. When the well had produced $50,000 in profits for her, it dried up. "I didn't have enough faith," she said; "I should have asked God for $100,000."

The homes on Mission Road, as our street was named, were completely furnished including dishes, cooking utensils, bedding, and linens. In a letter to her sister, my mother described the layout of the house, the furniture, gas range, and yard. It was a modest house, but compared to our home in Borneo my mother said, "Really, I feel like quite an aristocrat!"

On April 18, 1938, our family boarded the SS *President Cleveland* in San Francisco. We stopped in Honolulu, Yokohama and Kobe, Japan and arrived in Manila in mid-May where we transferred to the SS *President Harrison*. This ship took us to Singapore where we stayed for five days in a Brethren Mission Home. My mother wrote of our stay there, "We are here in this lovely, big mission home. There are no other guests here – just the lady in charge, who is very lovely. We can get a Chinese boy to clean our two rooms and do all of our cooking for sixty or sixty-five cents a day." (Edna, letter, May 1938) From Singapore we took another boat to Pontianak, a smaller river boat up the Kapuas and Belitang rivers, and arrived in Balai Sepuak on May 31.

Announcement of our return to Borneo, April 1938

24 BACK IN BALAI SEPUAK

Our arrival on May 31, 1938, was not the gala affair our initial arrival had been when my mother, brother, and I first moved to Balai Sepuak. No one knew when we were coming, so there were only a few people to greet us. By this time there was a school at Balai Sepuak with one teacher who came from Makassar. He and his twelve students were on the bank to greet us, as were some of the Chinese traders and the missionary couple, John and Ruth Meltzer, who had stayed in our home during our absence. (Soon after our arrival, the Meltzers went on to a new area, the Melawi River district.) The Dayak schoolchildren had learned a song of greeting, and they were singing it lustily as we got off the boat and walked up to our house.

My mother wrote about her reaction to being in her "barn" again: "I still feel that it is like home, but I must admit that the house looked more desolate than I had pictured it. It is just the same, of course, but after being away for so long I had just pictured it as being better looking than it is, and so the building surely did look rough and dirty the next morning. All in all, the house looks awful to me, so crude and dirty, but I'll get used to it again. The big rough boards for the floor, with the holes here and there and the cracks, being able to see the ground below, etc., is what seems so different after coming from the nice homes in America." (Edna, letter, June 1938) Later, on a trip to Pontianak the next year, my parents would buy some bright linoleum. My dad would put new boards over the kitchen floor, cover it with the linoleum, and finally, whitewash the kitchen walls. After this makeover, my mother would write to her mother, "It's the nicest kitchen I've ever had in the Netherlands East Indies." By this, she meant it was the best of three kitchens: one in the early years in Makassar, one in Sintang, and this one in Balai Sepuak.

The first Sunday after our return, there was a meeting at our home attended by many Dayaks because a special mouth-to-mouth edition of the "Jungle Herald" had been issued, telling of our return. They were very glad to have us back, "but not any more so than we were to see them. We sat under the rubber trees facing the best-looking crowd we had looked upon for fifteen months. With a lump in our throats, we praised God for giving us the wonderful privilege of again meeting these dear, faithful Dayaks, whom we love. Special songs were sung, drums were beaten, prayers were offered, hands were clasped, and then, single file, down the several jungle trails they wandered homeward." (Arthur, letter, November 1938)

Several days later, our family was on the trail to visit the first of five established Dayak churches. About an hour's distance away from each church, we were met by native workers and a large delegation of Dayaks, who, while singing and beating drums, escorted us to the church. The pastor's home and a large number of little huts were built close to the church. These huts were for the Dayak families who arrived at the church on Saturday afternoon and spent the night; after the Sunday afternoon service or early Monday morning, they left for their villages again.

In between these weekend visits to the churches, we returned to our home in Balai Sepuak, as traveling over the entire district took some time. One time, the day before we were to leave for one of the churches, my father got malaria. Nevertheless, the next day we spent five hours motoring up the river by boat, then walked another three hours to reach the Immanuel church. The following day, Sunday, my father was too weak to attend the morning service. He went to the afternoon service but just sat and listened. The Dayaks had never seen him sick before, and it surprised them. On Monday, we started on our eight-hour journey home. By the time we got to Balai Sepuak, he was shivering, a common symptom of malaria. He got in bed and my mother piled over him all the blankets she could find. He was sick for about two weeks; some days he got up, other days he stayed down, and then he was fine.

Like all young children, my brother and I had been able to learn the language of the people quickly, but we also forgot it quickly while in the United States. Because the Dayaks did not have this experience with their own children, they were surprised that my brother and I could no longer talk to them as we once had. They also exclaimed over how much bigger we were, especially my brother. We soon picked up the language again, getting the pronunciation perfectly, which led the Dayaks to say we sounded just like them, and my mother to say, "I wish I could talk like they do." Although we would often chatter to each other in Dayak, our parents made us speak English when talking to them. Sometimes we also pretended to mimic our Chinese neighbors. I would say something like "Hwa chee king ho hung," which of course had no meaning whatsoever, and Burneal would answer me.

Playing with our Chinese neighbors

In mid-October, after we had been in Balai Sepuak for almost five months, our family left to attend the annual C&MA missionary conference on the island of Celebes, now called Sulawesi. The conference, which had previously been held in Makassar (where my parents had lived for their first year and a half), had been relocated to a place up into the mountains called Benteng Tinggi, three thousand feet above sea level. This year, twenty-three missionaries and nine children attended. There was a fireplace in the dining-conference room, something we couldn't imagine having or even wanting in Borneo because of the heat, so it was wonderful for us to be in a place where you could want a fireplace. About four miles from the conference location there was a resort town frequented by Dutch people who sought the cooler climate. We could rent small horses from the native people for $1.50 a week, and we MK's, missionary kids, loved this. We went riding for an hour and a half in the morning and again in the afternoon.

The view from Benteng Tinggi was beautiful, especially looking out on the terraced rice fields. I remember this place well, because when our family returned for a third term after World War II, my brother and I stayed there to attend high school while my parents went on to Borneo.

A few months after our return from the missionary conference, my father sent his parents this lovely description of our life in Balai Sepuak: "God is so good and we are so happy here. I have a little boy and a little girl, a sweet, dear wife, and a good roof to keep the rain out. And around us for miles are dear, precious Dayaks who love and worship my Jesus—could anyone ask for more?"

25 DAILY LIFE IN BALAI SEPUAK

Return from the United States

What was it like to grow up in Balai Sepuak? When we first moved there, my mother had been concerned about how differently my brother and I behaved, compared to what we were like in Sintang. She wrote to her mother, "There are so many people here all the time, and the children get so much attention it has made them much harder to train and they don't mind as well. They aren't really so naughty, but they are mischievous; and everybody laughs at the least thing they do, and they will do anything the children ask." She looked forward to going on our first furlough to the United States, where we would no longer be the center of attention.

When we returned from the United States in May 1938, I was four and a half, my brother almost six. We could now compare our life in Borneo to that in the United States, and at first Borneo came out on the short end, mostly because of the heat and skin problems. "Almost everyone who lives here gets a skin disease, so the children have to put up with this too. There is a funny side to it, though. One day Arthur wanted to cut Burneal's fingernails, and he said, 'Oh, Daddy, please leave one fingernail so that I can scratch and open my jackknife.' My, but we laughed, it sounded so pathetic. And Siddy—oh you should hear her. She lifts up her dress or pulls up her shirt and scratches in front of anyone. She will get an expression of contempt on her face and say, 'Borneo!' You have to hear it to know what she thinks." (Edna, letter, October 1938)

Life in Balai Sepuak our second term had new conveniences. Number one on the list was an Electrolux refrigerator made possible by our kerosene-powered generator. The Dayaks who visited us had lived their entire life within one degree of the equator and had little concept of what we think of as cold. The first time my mother made some ice cubes and handed one to a Dayak, he dropped it quickly and said, "Hot!" Another time, she brought a tray of ice cubes to a group of Dayaks sitting on the floor and passed some around. They reacted with loud exclamations and laughs. Some of them placed ice cubes in their mouths and were able to keep them there, but others dropped them immediately.

The electric lights that my father put up in the house were another convenience, but most of the time we used Alladin lamps (kerosene and wicks) because they didn't require starting the generator. And we had a radio. A Philippine station came in very clearly and broadcast in English, so we could listen to world news every evening at 8:30 P.M. We could also get stations in Singapore, London, China, and Australia and several from Java. Programs from the latter were broadcast in Dutch or Malay. The Dutch stations had good classical music, and there was no advertising.

School

My mother had always wanted to be a teacher, but her father died when she was a child and, although she did attend one semester at the University of Washington in Seattle, she had to drop out because she needed to help support her widowed mother. She became a secretary but kept her desire to be a schoolteacher. She got her chance in Borneo, becoming teacher both to my brother and me and to the Dayaks, many of whom she taught to read and write.

We used the Calvert Course from the Calvert School in Baltimore, Maryland. Each year's course contained 160 daily lessons; 5 daily lessons represented a week's work, and 20 lessons a month's work. Each day's lesson covered arithmetic, history, spelling, penmanship, composition, and reading. On some days, the course also incorporated lessons in geography, astronomy, geology, grammar, nature study, art history, and poetry. (According to lesson 5 of year 3, "The aim of the poetry course is to instill in the pupil a love of poetry, and a desire to read more than the assigned poems.") It was a comprehensive, well-organized, and challenging course, and it served us well. My brother and I missed half a year of school in early 1942 when we were escaping the Japanese invasion; nonetheless, we both entered our correct grade level when we started school in the United States in September 1942. Of course, this is also a tribute to my mother's teaching ability. My mother, however, was not so confident of her ability. She wrote in a letter, "You don't know how relieved I am that Siddy and Burneal have actually learned to read and write, for I have never taught before." Later, worried about our level in arithmetic, she asked her sister, whose three children were close in age to ours, to send her samples of the arithmetic done in the third, fourth, and fifth grades. One specific question she asked was "When do they start doing long division with decimal points?" She wasn't worried about our reading level, because, as she noted, "They read everything they can get their hands on."

169

For our schoolroom our father had built a room within the big, central meeting room of our home. First he laid down matting and then linoleum, and he whitewashed the walls. He made a school desk that we both sat at. Seated in our chairs, we faced each other and put our feet on a rest that was part of the desk.

Our custom-made school desk

It was understood that during school hours our mother was the teacher, our father the principal; before and after school they were just mom and dad. Our school hours were generally from 7 to 11 A.M., but there were always interruptions, as an almost constant stream of Dayaks visited our home. The Dayak women would frequently ask my father why his wife didn't travel with him. The women were all so eager for her to come, too, and didn't understand that she had to teach us; they simply didn't realize how important education was for us.

I remember those school days with great fondness. The Calvert Course had a strong classical emphasis. For example, in lesson 128 of the third year, the pupil learns about Leonardo da Vinci and his painting, the Mona Lisa, for art history; writes about Michelangelo or Leonardo for composition; and covers five more pages in "The Gorgon's Head" from Greek mythology for reading. Our history and geography texts were *A Child's History of the World* and *A Child's Geography of the World*, both by V. M. Hillyer. I still have these two wonderful books in my library and would recommend them to any parent.

CALVERT SCHOOL

Sample

DAILY LESSON OUTLINE (Sheet 1 of 2) **YEAR** 2 **No.** 125

ARITHMETIC: <u>Oral:</u> Drill on the 8x table, using the circle
to develop speed.

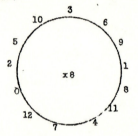

Review reading and writing of numbers. Teach pupil how to
read numbers in the tens of thousands: 10,000 is read "ten
thousand." Show pupil that a comma is placed between hundred's place and thousand's place to make it easy to read
these large numbers. A box will help pupil to read numbers
with as many as 5 or 6 figures in them, like the numbers,
21,006 or 53,024. To read 21,006 put the box over it in this
way:

Thousand	
2 1 , 0 0 6	

See that the comma comes exactly
under the middle of the box. Look at
21. Then read what is over it. Say
21 thousand. Then look at the 6 and
say 6. 21,006 is read "twenty one thousand, six."
53,024 is read "fifty-three thousand, twenty-four"
60,135 is read "sixty thousand, one hundred thirty-five"
75,201 is read "seventy-five thousand, two hundred one"
Write a dozen or more such numbers on paper or blackboard and
have pupil read them. Dictate several more and have the pupil
write them down. <u>Practice daily for five minutes until pupil
has mastered the subject.</u>

Written: 529   1036   1708   33
        x 8   x 6   x 8   54
                                67
8)206   8)496   8)136   7615   29
                        -1658   85
                              + 79

Problem: There were 8 children at my party. Mother gave us
    a dish with 24 cookies on it. How many cookies could each
child have?

Workbook: page 131.

182

CALVERT SCHOOL

DAILY LESSON OUTLINE   (Sheet 2 of 2)   **YEAR** 2 **No.** 125

ART HISTORY: Give pupil picture of The Colosseum, which is
   in Rome and is one of the most famous buildings in the
world. It is a huge open air theatre and held 87,000 people.
It was built not long after Christ died and is now in ruins.
In it used to be held fights between men called gladiators
and wild animals. Also held in the Colosseum was the magnificent celebration of the 1000th Anniversary of Rome's
foundation, 248 A.D.

POETRY: Have pupil learn "The Owl" by Alfred Tennyson.
   Tell him Tennyson was an English poet and was called
"Poet Laureate."

THE OWL

When cats run home and light is come,
   And dew is cold upon the ground,
And the far-off stream is dumb,
   And the whirring sail goes round,
   And the whirring sail goes round;
      Alone and warming his five wits,
      The white owl in the belfry sits.

When merry milkmaids click the latch,
   And rarely smells the new-mown hay,
And the cock hath sung beneath the thatch
   Twice or thrice his roundelay,
   Twice or thrice his roundelay;
      Alone and warming his five wits,
      The white owl in the belfry sits.

Read to pupil "Wynken, Blynken and Nod," p. 40.

SPELLING:

COMPOSITION: Have pupil write a composition on the
   Colosseum and illustrate it with the picture.

READING: Have pupil continue the reading

163

Sample lesson from the Calvert Course

Just as important as our academic work, of course, was learning about God and being taught stories from the Bible. An anecdote my mother wrote about me to her family when I was a little over five years old makes me chuckle: "I am teaching them every morning about the Israelites traveling from Egypt to Canaan and all their experiences along the way. ... They surely enjoyed the story of Jacob, and Joseph, and then of Moses crossing the Red Sea, and so on. When we came to the place where the Israelites asked Aaron to make a god for them, I told them how Aaron made the golden calf and the people worshipped it while Moses was on the mountain. After that lesson, Siddy said she wanted to pray. You should hear her pray. She said for part of her prayer, 'Oh, Lord, we hope that we won't ever want to make a golden calf and say like the children of Israel did, 'This is our God who brought us out of Egypt.' And today I told them about the murmuring and complaining of the Israelites after all God had done for them, and so today she prayed so earnestly, 'Oh God, we hope that we won't ever complain and murmur like the Israelites after you gave them bread from heaven, and we hope, dear Lord, that you will help Burneal and me to obey our parents.' She prays like a little old woman." (Edna, letter, March 1939)

Playtime

We loved living right by the river, and swimming was my brother's and my favorite activity. We especially liked it when, after a heavy rain, the level of the river rose to within a few inches of our front porch. But whether the river was high or low, we would beg our mother at all hours, "May we go swimming now, Mummy?" or "Is it an hour since we ate? Now can we go?"

Swimming, our favorite activity

The river had a strong current, so we needed someone with us at all times. Going for a sampan ride with one of our Dayak helpers was also great fun. When we got a little older, we each had our own sampan and we were allowed to maneuver the river on our own.

Burneal and Sydwell in sampan

When we weren't in school or swimming, we had Tinkertoys, clay, jigsaw puzzles, and coloring books, and we loved the stories our mother told us. "I tell so many stories to them I think I might turn into Mother Goose," she wrote in a letter to her sister. In the schoolroom my father had made for us, we also had a swing attached to the ceiling joists. Sometimes it was a tire swing, an ordinary swing another day, and some days we had rings to swing on. We also regularly walked the pleasant twenty-minute trip to Ebenezer, our district church, built in 1939 by the Dayaks.

Walking to church – Burneal is holding his pet chicken

At our home on the riverbank there was no open space on which to play, but the church had a large soccer field. (When we first came to Borneo, the Dayaks did not play soccer. The young men who went to Bible school in Makassar brought the game back with them.) After a school was established at Ebenezer, my brother and I liked to go there to be with the children and their teacher, Mel, who was not a Dayak but who came from Makassar.

The way Dayaks carry their babies

Pets and Packages

Pets were a big part of our life. We had chickens, ducks, pigeons (my brother's Christmas present one year), rabbits, a dog, and a monkey. My brother would often walk around lovingly carrying a chicken in his arms, kissing it and rubbing his nose against its feathers. Each chicken in our flock had a name, two of which I can still remember: Bungsu and Next-to-Bungsu. (*Bungsu* means 'youngest offspring.') Our pet monkey was a black gibbon, an animal with no tail but very long arms. He lived in the house with us, where he swung among the rafters since our home had no ceiling. After he arrived, our home was free of cobwebs. He liked to play with the dog and made a terrible racket if my brother and I were too noisy or got into an argument. And because my brother liked to tease him, he would scold and run away from him most of the time. He also liked to steal food. He would make a beeline for the kitchen if he saw my mother working at the table. One day she was making a lemon pie, a real treat since we rarely got lemons, and as she poured the filling into the pie shell, the monkey came right down, stuck out his long arm, and scooped up a handful of the lemon filling. It was hot and burned him a little, but he licked his hand off in a hurry and came right back hoping for some more. Then, after my mother had put the pie in the oven, he rushed all over the kitchen trying to find it. Another day as she was mixing cookies, again he came in like a shot and made such pleading noises that she gave him a small piece of the dough.

We regularly received mail and packages from our families in America; this was always a treat for my brother and me. Of course there was no mail delivery to our home. The mail got as far as Sintang and then was sent up the river to us only when a boat came our way; or my father would pick it up on his trips down the river. Telegrams arrived in Pontianak, the coastal city; from there the telegram was telephoned to the next town, then relayed from telephone to telephone until it got to a place that was two days' journey down the river from us. From there it was sent to Balai Sepuak by someone coming up the river in a sampan. Such was the Borneo path of a perhaps urgent message.

The packages we received contained things my mother had asked her family to send her, such as baking powder, gelatin, bobby pins, and elastic, items she couldn't get in Borneo, not even in the coastal city of Pontianak. For my brother and me came books, clothing (some dresses handmade for me by my grandmother), hair clips, crayons, balloons, a rabbit's foot, licorice, gumdrops, marshmallows, and gum. How we loved receiving candy! Sometimes our cousins also sent the Sunday funny papers and comic books. Our favorite comic-book character was Li'l Abner.

Celebrations

My mother did her best to celebrate birthdays and holidays as we would have in the United States. For my sixth birthday she invited Mel, the teacher at Ebenezer, and two young Dayak women who were living with us at the time. The table was decorated with crepe paper (made in China, cheap and available in Pontianak). Also on the table was a can full of gumdrops and licorice, a present from my maternal grandmother. Describing Christmas preparations for 1939, my mother wrote, "I have been teaching the children little Christmas songs every day and telling them the Christmas lessons from the Bible. Now we are cutting little Christmas trees out of green paper and making other cutouts such as rabbits, hens, chickens, and birds. We cut them out of colored paper and stick them all on the whitewashed walls in their own room, so it all looks pretty colorful. We will get a tree soon—not a Christmas tree, but as near the shape of one as we can—and then we'll trim it." (Edna, letter, December 1939)

In October 1940 we received a letter from our American cousins, in which they had enclosed pictures of themselves in Easter outfits and carrying Easter baskets. Burneal and I immediately wanted some baskets, too, and we got one of the young Dayak women to make a couple of baskets out of coconut tree leaves. She wove them easily and deftly. Then we colored eggs with our crayons and paints and had our own Easter baskets just in time for Halloween.

Harvest time was a happy, joyful time for the Dayaks. For many it meant that days of hunger were past. My mother wanted us to join in the fun. "For all it is a time of great rejoicing and merrymaking. Men, women, boys and girls—all take part in harvesting, making it a time of festivity. When the grain is ripe, they work quickly so that all the precious *padi* [unhulled rice] is harvested in time. The rice is all picked by hand here, just the ear or head being taken off, the stalk being left in the field. There are some fine rice fields about two miles from here, so I expect to take

180

Sydwell and Burneal and spend half a day or so with the Dayaks in this happy work. I suppose we'll tie a basket around our waist, too, and try to fill it with the golden grain that means so much to the people out here." (Edna, letter, February 1940)

Helping with the rice harvest

Trips

Taking a trip was a special treat, especially after my father purchased a houseboat. "The dear Lord has given us a lovely houseboat which we purchased at one-fourth the original cost. We have named it *Kabar Senang* which means 'Satisfying News.' We have been very happy as we've traveled in it, and everything is as convenient as in an up-to-date apartment.

Our houseboat, the *Kabar Senang*

Our running water is under the boat! Underneath the front porch is a sturdy little one-cylinder diesel engine which propels us wherever we wish to go." (Arthur, letter, October 1939) My mother liked the houseboat because it was cozy, clean, and attractive compared to her "barn" on the riverbank. But at the end of a houseboat trip, she wrote, "It will be so good to be home again. It always feels good to get back in the bigger house, where we have more room to stretch."

We took trips to Pontianak, the coastal city, to get supplies—medicine, first aid supplies for the Dayaks, clothing, groceries, and hardware. Pontianak also had a much greater variety of food than was available in Balai Sepuak. In 1939 my mother wrote that she hoped we could be there to celebrate my brother's birthday, in August, so we could have some apples and oranges. The apples came from Australia; the oranges were from California and were very expensive. There were also many vegetables—

string beans, carrots, beets, small tomatoes, leaf lettuce, cabbage—as well as beef and pork, none of which was part of our regular menu. We also enjoyed going to the park; its green lawn was an unusual attraction for us.

On one trip to Pontianak, my brother and I (he was seven, I almost six) had quite a little caper. We had just left the houseboat with one of our Dayak helpers when we met a Dutch man whom our family knew well. He was in his car driven by his Javanese chauffeur, and he told us to run back and ask our mother if we could go for a ride. The Dutch man himself would be getting out at his club, but his chauffeur could then drive us around in the car. My mother said we could go. She described what happened next: "When they got in the car, the Dayak boy was afraid to get in an auto, so he came back; but I didn't think anything of it, for I knew they would just ride around a little and return. But the little monkeys can talk Malay like a native, so they just sat in the back and asked the chauffeur to take them to the park and he did. When they got to the park, they told him he could go, and they played in the park for about forty-five minutes and then walked home, all by themselves. It's good I didn't know it until they returned. I asked them how they enjoyed the ride and what they saw, and they said, 'Oh, we didn't go for a ride; we told him to take us to the park and we've been there all the time.' Then I said, 'Did you come home yourselves?' When they said 'yes,' I could have fallen over, but it was too late to worry, as they were back safely." (Edna, letter, November 1939)

Some trips took us into the jungles. We went with our parents to the dedication of a new church, going part way by boat and then walking for four hours. My father carried us over the hard places, and he carried me at the end of the trail because it was night when we arrived, but otherwise we walked the whole way. My mother described the return trip: "Toward the end of the return walk, my how they [my brother and I] complained. We left the church at 9:00 in the morning and arrived at the boat at 1:40, so it was during the midday heat that we walked. No wonder they complained! I felt like an old woman seventy years old at the end of the trail. You get so hot and sticky but just have to keep on plodding. On the boat we soon forgot our weakness. The river was terribly swift, as it had rained in that section of the headwaters and the river was higher. We couldn't use the motor as we would go too fast and the curves are bad ones, so we floated and, even so, had a nerve-wracking time getting the boat around the bends in the river without wrecking it against trees along the bank and logs sticking out at terrible angles. It was good to get home again, but we enjoyed our trip to the church very much." (Edna, letter, November 1940)

Visitors

Non-Dayak visitors to Balai Sepuak were a rare event. An American geologist looking for oil visited our home in October 1938. Most other visitors were Dutch officials. In the early years, a visit from Dutch officials usually meant trouble, but during our second term in Borneo, official visits were more positive events. My mother described one such visit in April 1939: "We have been busy the past week. The assistant governor of West Borneo and another official came up in the government boat to visit the work here and are out now going from longhouse to longhouse with Arthur. I guess they just want to examine things, but they are going to attend the big Bethel church on Sunday. I think they will be surprised when they see seven hundred or more people sitting in that building on the floor. They will be back here Monday, and I suppose I'll have them for dinner.

It makes me a little nervous, for they are from very luxurious homes and are wealthy and have such well-trained Javanese servants. All of these officials out here live like kings in their realm. They bring lovely furniture and so on. However, they admired our lovely Electrolux [our refrigerator]. That is one thing we have nicer than they. They have them too, but not as nice as American ones. They were surprised at our electric lights." When my father and the officials returned, my mother was pleased to hear that, after the Sunday service, the senior official handed my father ten guilders (about four dollars in 1939) to put in the church offering.

Food

As it was for the Dayaks, rice was our staple food. Occasionally, when we could get potatoes, we would have them instead of rice, but this brought complaints from my brother and me. We wanted rice! (I have continued to love rice my entire life and much prefer it to potatoes.) But, being Americans, we couldn't really do without having bread, too, so my mother tried her hand at baking. She wrote about her bread-making during our first term in Borneo: "I am making bread. I learned how to make a starter from a Dutch lady, so after we had been here [Balai Sepuak] a day, I started the starter and the fourth day could make bread. The first loaf wasn't so good. … But by the fourth day [of bread-making], the loaf was lovely and Arthur praised it highly. I feel a little bit proud of my first efforts. I have to bake it in an oven made out of tin by a Malay tinsmith. I have one of our girls [helpers] light a wood fire in the kitchen. The 'stove' is made of stones, and they cook over three stones with the fire in the middle. I have the girls make a wood fire under the oven, which stands on three legs, then we put some of the burning sticks on top of the oven. Considering this primitive way of baking, I think it's pretty good. I'd better remember, though, that 'pride goeth before a fall.'... Bread doesn't keep so well here, so I make two loaves every day." (Edna, letter, November 1935)

Getting vegetables was the biggest problem. My mother tried her best to have a garden, but everything had to be planted in raised boxes because our yard regularly flooded when the river rose after a hard rain. Added to this problem was the soil, which is generally not good in West Borneo, and in our yard was only hard clay. To get some soil to fill her planter boxes, my mother would hunt around at the foot of cliffs or in low places to scrape together soil that had been washed down by the rain. "But I have to make a pile of wood and leaves and set it on fire, then pile the soil on top and burn it all. That is what everyone in West Borneo does to make a garden." (Edna, letter, July 1939) (The Dayaks practice dry-rice cultivation using the slash and burn method. They cut down trees and underbrush, then when it has dried somewhat, burn it all. The ash provides some enrichment to the soil.)

My mother also started a garden at the church, about a mile from our home, where she planted carrots, turnips, beets, tomatoes, and lettuce. There the soil was a little better, but the problem of bugs remained. "The bugs are awful. We have to pick off worms and bugs every day, or within one week we wouldn't have anything left. We had one meal of turnips from my garden, but the rest didn't turn out. I have just about given up hope for a garden of anything but native vegetables, because the worms and bugs are legion and you just have to keep at it from morning till night." (Edna, letter, April 1940)

When we got tired of the cucumbers or squash that were always available, my mother would open a can of tomatoes or peas. We could buy canned goods like these on our trips to Pontianak, but they were very expensive and my mother used them sparingly. We could also get raw peanuts in Pontianak, which she ground to make peanut butter. It did not cost us much to live in Balai Sepuak; rice and chickens were cheap, as was the rent on our home.

My mother liked to raise chickens. She called it her hobby, and wrote her family, "Arthur laughs at me when I come running in to tell everybody I have so many chickens hatched this morning. I have twenty live chicks now that just hatched during the last few days, and they are so sweet. I have five hens setting." Mother's hens kept us supplied with eggs; she also bought eggs from the Dayaks.

For fruit we regularly had bananas, papayas, and mangoes. We also had durian, a fruit loved by locals, but often abhorred by foreigners. A durian is the size of a large cantaloupe and has strong, sharp spines on the outside and yellow, segmented flesh inside. Each piece is the size of a large egg and contains a large seed similar to that of an avocado. My father learned to like durian almost immediately, but it took my mother a couple of years before she could get past its smell. The naturalist Alfred Russel Wallace, who traveled through the islands of Indonesia from 1855 to 1861, approved of durian: "He [Wallace] ate a durian, and like everyone before and after him he rhapsodized over the taste: 'Its consistence and flavour are indescribable. A rich butter-like custard highly flavoured with almonds gives the best general idea of it, but intermingled with it come wafts of flavour that call to mind cream-cheese, onion-sauce, brown sherry, and other incongruities.' The durian was divine to the palate, but it was not an unmitigated delight. It had a hellish smell, which has been compared by centuries of Westerners to everything from old tennis shoes to open sewers; Wallace called it 'a most disgusting odour to Europeans.'" (Daws and Fujita, *Archipelago: The Islands of Indonesia* [Berkeley: University of California Press, 1999], p. 43). My brother and I also loved durian. (Now I am fortunate to be able to buy this fruit, imported from the Philippines, at a Chinese market a few miles from my home in Palo Alto, California. Most of the shoppers in this market are Asians, and whenever I buy a durian, it usually elicits questions about my background from the produce man, the cashier, or fellow shoppers.)

Writing to his parents, my father said, "Edna surely plans wonderful meals, and Sydwell and I have decided we are going to stick around a while yet, as the 'eats' are getting better all the time. I don't have to mention Burneal, because he can tuck away as many groceries as I can. We have ice cream about four times a week, and, as there are lots of eggs, Edna usually has a custard bowl awaiting me in the icebox. We don't get many fresh vegetables or lettuce or tomatoes, but all in all we fare very well, so don't feel sorry for us." (Arthur, letter, mid-1939) The origin of the ice cream was a little unusual. "Did I tell you we can buy canned ice cream here? I am certainly glad as it is better than any I can make. You just open the can and pour the mixture in the tray and freeze it. It is vanilla flavor and you can add any other flavor you wish. It is not very thick, but is thicker than ordinary milk, and we like it. It is from Holland." (Edna, letter, November 1939) Later my mother made her own ice cream using evaporated milk, egg whites, sugar, and vanilla. She liked it so well that she sent the recipe to her sister.

For our second term in Borneo, my father brought a gun, a rifle that required a permit from the government. He let the native workers use it, and occasionally they would shoot a deer or wild pig and give us some of the meat; it tasted delicious after nothing but chicken for months and months. They also shot monkeys, but we chose not to share this meat.

Sickness

Finally, life in Balai Sepuak as in all of Borneo meant dealing with malaria. Now if we choose to visit a country where there is malaria, we can take a series of pills to prevent this terrible disease; however, in the 1930s and 1940s there was no such medicine. Having malaria was a fact of life if you lived in Borneo.

During our first term, my mother more than anyone had suffered from malaria. But like any mother, she was most anxious when it was her children who fell sick. "Burneal had a high fever and a terrible chill," she wrote when my brother was six. "I put him in bed with me and piled blankets over him, but the poor little fellow just shivered. The following afternoon he was delirious and didn't know me, and my heart was certainly heavy. I had never seen him like this." (Edna, letter, June 1939) And ten months later: "Siddy had malaria today. Burneal just got over it. He acted as though he was going to be terribly sick like he was the other time when I was alone, but this time I gave him quinine right away and he was only in bed one day. He gets malaria very suddenly, that is, it comes on at once with a terribly high fever. He was delirious again for just a little while, as the fever is so high, and that is what frightens me, but the quinine surely does keep the fever from coming back again. Then Siddy got a fever suddenly today and she was burning up, but it only lasted about two hours and then gradually went down. It would come back tomorrow if she didn't take quinine, so I gave it to her right away. Malaria can make you thin and pale in two or three days if you don't take anything for it." (Edna, letter, April 1940)

During our first term in Borneo, my father rarely had malaria. But during the second term he wrote, "I'm not nearly as strong as I was last term—too much malaria. I'm not sick, but just tired, that's all, as the malaria certainly takes one's strength. (Arthur, letter, November 1939) The next year my mother wrote, "This year has been a terrible year here for malaria; literally hundreds of the Dayaks and workers have had severe cases of it. There is always a lot of malaria, but this year it just seemed that nearly 90 percent of the population in our district has had it, and quite severely. Many of the Dayaks boil papaya leaves and drink the juice and eat the leaves and never get malaria, at least not a bad case. I try to drink the water from the leaves, but it is as bitter as quinine and so much harder to take." Generally, however, my mother fared much better during her second term in Borneo (1938–1942) than in her first. The furlough in the United States gave her a good rest, and she didn't have as many responsibilities during the second term. The Ebenezer church was built in 1939 about a mile from our home; this meant we no longer had the huge crowds of people coming to our house every weekend as they had before the church was built.

In May 1940, when I was six and a half years old, I got diphtheria. At first my mother thought it was malaria, then tonsillitis, but when my tonsils became terribly swollen and covered with a white membrane, she realized I had diphtheria. Adding to her distress was the fact that my father was away. I had become sick on Thursday, and he wasn't expected home until Tuesday. How thankful my mother was when she heard the *putt-putt-putt* of his motorboat on Sunday night instead.

I was getting worse, and it was difficult for me to breathe. My father anointed me with oil and prayed for me. By Thursday my uvula was so swollen and covered with the white membrane that I could hardly swallow. My mother knew that this membrane could cover the windpipe, and when this happened a doctor would have to insert a tube in the patient's throat to enable him or her to breathe. I hadn't eaten for eight days and didn't even want to drink anything; my mother had to force a little water down me.

As the news of my illness was heralded through the jungle, the Dayaks began to arrive at our home and the nearby Ebenezer church, especially the women. As my father described it, "They wanted to be with us in our trouble. They didn't say much, didn't ask any questions. They just gave us their hand and sat down on the floor. And the whole night through, they just sat and prayed."

On Friday my parents were planning to take me to the doctor in Sintang. This would be a trip down the river of at least two day's time on our boat. But my mother later wrote to her family, "I didn't feel right about it. There were hundreds of Dayaks at the place praying for Siddy, and we thought it wasn't a very good testimony to them to run to the doctor now. When their babies get sick, they can't do that. So I felt we just must pray and trust God to touch her. Arthur really felt the assurance that the Lord had heard prayer for her, but I had been up so much and sat with her so much, my faith began to waver. Saturday she began to improve and could breathe a little more easily, and from then on she began to improve. By that time over two thousand Dayaks were up at the church, and they were all praying; and it was a greater testimony certainly to them than if we had gone off to Sintang." (Edna, letter, May 1940)

I am crying as I write these words. My mother, the loveliest and most gentle person I have ever known, had a faith stronger than steel. I am now both a parent and grandparent and can't imagine what it would have been like to go into the interior of Borneo so many years ago and raise children, knowing there was no doctor nearby, no way to communicate with one, and only a very slow, several-day trip to reach a doctor or hospital.

A small postscript: In a letter she wrote to her sister some months later, my mother said, "This evening Siddy said to me, 'Mother, the nicest thing about having diphtheria was that you sat by my bed all the time and fed me, watched me, read stories to me, bathed me, and gave me drinks and did anything I asked for; it was so nice to have sweet Mummy by me all the time.'" (Edna, letter, September 1940) How fortunate I am to have had such a mother and father.

26 MY MOTHER'S MINISTRY TO THE DAYAKS

Many of the stories I tell in this book center on my father, his travels from village to village, and his ministry to the Dayaks. Although my mother was not able to participate in the same way as he because she had primary responsibility for child raising, which kept her at Balai Sepuak, she nevertheless played a very important role as a missionary. First and foremost, she supported my father's daily life and ministry. There is no question in my mind that my father could not have worked as he did in Borneo over the years if he had not had my mother's support emotionally and spiritually. And it was my mother's wish to be a missionary that had first sparked my father's interest in missions when they met and fell in love in Bible school.

My father had a strong will, a characteristic that served him well in his early years in Borneo. I take after my father and generally have strong opinions of my own. This caused occasional clashes in our relationship when I was a teenager and young adult. I remember so well something he would say to me on almost every visit I made to their home, once I no longer lived there: "Siddy, we may have had our disagreements, but something we both agree on is that the best decision I ever made in my life was to marry your mother. She's the sweetest, dearest woman in all the world." And he was right; we absolutely did agree on this point.

I'm sure it was not always easy for my mother to play a supporting rather than a more active role. Her wish to move from Sintang to our home in Balai Sepuak, for example, was fueled by her desire to be closer to the Dayaks and to relate to them directly and personally. She made a revealing comment about being a missionary in a letter she wrote to my father's parents in November 1935, just two weeks after we had moved to Balai Sepuak: "If you would follow me all day, you'd see me trot into the kitchen and mix up the bread or show the girls [her helpers] how to do something, then back to meet a new group of Dayaks and play the organ for them and sing about ten minutes, then take Burneal or Siddy to the bathroom, then maybe I'll sweep the bedrooms and make our beds and try to get some things unpacked. Then cut to meet some Dayaks and put the rice away, which they have brought, or the coconut or the chicken, and talk to them a little while. They follow us all over, watch us eat, pull the curtains aside to see what I'm doing in the bedroom when I take the children there, watch me cook, and so on all day long. I am getting used to it now, although at first I felt a little funny to have them stand in the doors leading to our dining room and watch us eat. ... I am learning Dayak little by little, and today when a group of women, children, and men were going to leave, they asked me to play the organ and sing with them a while; and when they were ready to go, they asked me to pray. They pray when they get up, when they go to bed, when they leave to go somewhere, and when they are ready to return. ... They are so in earnest. ... We haven't a very nice house, but I don't mind that at all. I am so glad to be here. *I feel like a missionary for the first time now,* and as soon as I can talk without using the interpreter, I'll have women all day long and every day in the week to teach whenever I have time"(my emphasis).

None of the Dayaks could read or write when my parents first came to their area. The Dutch government had tried to open schools but failed because the Dayaks refused to send their children. However, after the Dayaks had been Christians for a time, many said to my parents, "Teach us to read so that we can read God's book, which you always carry with you and read to us." My mother did what the government officials could not do—she started classes in the evenings in our own home and taught reading and writing in Malay at a beginner's level. The school consisted of a bench or two, a blackboard, slates, and pencils. Her first students were the young people who helped our family, and others who visited us dropped in on the class too.

My mother wrote that there was "a real epidemic of Dayaks wanting to learn to read and write," an epidemic that pleased my parents very much. In order to open a more formal school, they had to get permission from the Dutch officials. When the Dutch learned of this change in the Dayaks and later of other schools that were started, they were astounded. The Gospel, of course, had made the difference. The Dutch government helped out by providing reading books. These texts were written in the Malay language, not Dayak, as the government had stipulated that all classes had to be taught in Malay.

As the churches were built, a school was usually established at the same time. At first the pastors were the teachers. Most of them had been taught to read and write by my mother and then had continued their education at the Bible school in Makassar. In the early years, not only children but also some young adults attended the schools. Those who lived close enough to walk back and forth each day did so; those who lived farther away built small shelters in the church area, where they cooked their own meals and slept; they went home to their longhouses on weekends. Once the Dayaks had learned to read, there was a great demand for Bibles and New Testaments.

My mother played an active role in these schools even though she did not teach in them. "I am so busy since we returned [from our first furlough in the United States]. I try to get in some school with the children, but it is a pretty hard job, with the Dayaks coming and going. I will just be in the midst of teaching when some schoolboys will come from one of the four schools we have, and I have to take care of them. We keep all the school supplies here, and the teachers send for things about once a week or so. We have over two hundred pupils in school altogether. They learn reading, writing, arithmetic, a little history and geography, and study the Bible every day too." (Edna, letter, October 1940)

Many Dayaks came to our home for first-aid treatment or medicine— such as remedies for diarrhea, dysentery, or malaria—and most often it was my mother who attended to these needs. In the early years, by far the greatest number came to get medicine for a terrible skin disease. "I wash my hands a hundred times a day, it seems, as I shake hands so much, and if you could see the horrible sores and skin diseases here you would know why. It makes their skin rough and it begins to peel and looks awful. Some have it over their entire body, some only in spots. Arthur has some medicine from the doctor in Sintang, which is good for this. Whenever they come here, they can have one application free, but if they want a bottle, they buy it. [One chicken covered the cost of two bottles of the skin medicine, enough to clear up the disease.] They come by the hundreds for this medicine. ... They won't go to Sintang to the hospital to be treated, but they surely are tickled for Arthur to bring a supply here where they can get it. We have to sell that medicine, but we get so tired of selling it as it takes so much time, and yet it seems impossible not to help them this way, as no one else sells it." (Edna, letter, November 1935)

Dayaks on our front porch who came with a variety of requests

On rare occasions, the Dayaks did reap health benefits from the Dutch government. In March 1940, the government doctor was at Balai Sepuak to give injections for "a terrible tropical disease that caused awful sores and split feet. Three to five hundred people have been here for three days getting injections." (Edna, letter, March 1940)

Occasionally, my mother played a more active health role. One day a Dayak woman who had had the hiccups for three months came to our house. She had seen a doctor—a rare occasion for any Dayak at that time—

a visiting Javanese doctor, but he had told her he could do nothing. My mother remembered how my father had once been able to help a man who could not stop vomiting even though he had nothing left in his stomach. My father thought it had just become an involuntary habit and tied a cloth around the man's abdomen very tightly, so that he could not vomit. This action stopped the involuntary movements, and when he took the cloth off, it didn't start again. Using the same logic, my mother put one hand on the woman's diaphragm and one on her back and pressed very hard against her diaphragm, so that the woman was unable to hiccup. She held it there as long as she could, about five minutes, and when she let go, the hiccups didn't start again.

There was also administrative work required by mission headquarters in Makassar and some data collection required by government officials. It helped that my mother was an able typist. I have a copy of her *Statistical Report for 1941,* which lists the population of the district, the number of organized churches and their membership, the number of schools, the amount of offerings given at the churches, the number of baptisms, the number of inquirers ready for baptism, and other data. Knowing my father's personality, I am quite certain that the gathering and keeping of such statistics was primarily my mother's responsibility.

She also took an active role in the churches. "I have some little songbooks I want to make and get ready for the Sunday school children. I am teaching them some new songs, and as we haven't books, I will type the words and put colored paper on the outside for a cover, with a picture pasted to it. ... I will not have to make so terribly many, as only about half of the children in our Sunday school can read—perhaps not half, but that is wonderful, considering that no one could read when we came."

(Edna, letter, August 1941) By 1940 my mother was also busy getting out a mimeographed newsletter given to the Dayak Christians; by that time, so many schoolchildren could read, and they read the newsletter to the ones who couldn't. It contained general news from the eight churches, any necessary announcements, a little Bible teaching, and some Bible verses to memorize.

The Dayaks loved to receive Bible pictures like those regularly used in American Sunday schools. My mother collected many of these during our first furlough in the United States. Church people also gave her their used calendars and Christmas cards depicting biblical scenes. In February 1940 she wrote in a general letter, "I am sure you can't realize what joy the pictures you have given us are bringing to Dayak children, but not only the children—grownup folks too! In December the children, Arthur, and I made a trip up the Belitang River, and I left many scripture calendar pictures and Sunday school pictures to be given to the children who learned five Bible verses. I left some of the pictures with a chief of a village who can read, and he promised to teach the children the verses. ... Before giving them out, I paste the pictures on cardboard so that they will not tear, and the Dayaks are so proud to hang them on the walls of their rooms. I am giving them out as fast as I can get them ready."

Ebenezer, the church closest to our home, was about a mile away. We always left our home for church early on Sunday morning and carried our lunch, but we didn't have any regular place to eat it or to rest in between meetings. In June 1941, my father and some of the students built a little "Sunday cabin" for our family. My mother described it as "really nice looking," with its windows that were just holes in the wall, and which were covered with a few sticks to keep out chickens and dogs. Within the little cabin, we cooked over a wood fire on the hard clay floor; a three-legged stand over the fire held a pan in which we could boil water. There was also a camp cot in the cabin, because, as my mother put it, "it feels pretty nice to lie down for fifteen minutes after a long meeting and all the hand shaking."

Our Sunday cabin

During the week the church became the schoolhouse. Surrounding it were other little huts where a few of the schoolchildren lived during the week and where the church members who came on Saturday stayed for the weekend, until Sunday evening or Monday morning. It was quite a little community. Most of the time, my father wasn't with us on Sundays because he was visiting other churches in the area.

In June 1941, my mother wrote, "I am going to try and start next week to have a class or two a week in the school [at Ebenezer], so I guess we'll take our lunch along then too. I am so busy as it is, I don't know how I can squeeze these classes in, but I think I should try even if I have to give the children [my brother and I] a little less schoolwork."

When my mother visited the Dayak women in their longhouses, she enjoyed watching them in their creative endeavors and encouraged them to continue the weaving of their traditional Dayak skirts. With their increasing ability to buy ready-made clothing and material from the Chinese merchants, this practice had begun to decline.

Dayak woman weaving a basket

Weaving a traditional skirt

The women who came to our home in Balai Sepuak would regularly ask to visit with my mother. She actively helped these women in some very personal ways. One time, she did a great deal to help save a baby whose mother died very soon after she was born.

Edna with Dayak woman

There were no women in the village who would nurse the baby. A woman from another village had nursed the baby twice, but in eight days she had had only these two feedings, so my mother told the woman who wanted to adopt the baby to bring her to our home. The Dayaks have no formal adoption procedures; the father said the woman could take the baby, and that was all there was to it.

As was common practice, the baby had been bathed in the river since she was three days old. This baby was so little and thin that my mother told its adoptive mother that strong babies might be able to stand this, but that a weak baby couldn't; she helped to bathe her in a small tub of lukewarm water.

Dayak babies being bathed in the river

"The first two days I gave her baths and fed her during the day. We have to feed her six or seven times because she is so little and can just take a little bit at a time. [The adoptive mother] feeds her at night. I fix rice water for her at night, for I am afraid milk might sour. I boil the rice quite a while with a lot of water and then strain it through cheesecloth, and some of the soft rice goes through the cloth so she gets that nourishment. In the daytime I mix milk with the rice gruel." (Edna, letter, October 1940) My mother had learned this feeding method from a woman in Pontianak who had had seven children and hadn't nursed any of them. All Dayak women, however, nursed their children as there was no alternative. There was no canned or powdered milk.

As I described earlier, my mother's moving to Balai Sepuak to live among the Dayaks had a profound effect on them. For the Dayaks, her presence and status as an equal partner to my father confirmed that this new religion was for women as much as for men, an important concept in their egalitarian society. And her willingness to be there with them, the first white woman ever to come into their jungle, assured the Dayaks of her love for and commitment to them.

Every day, as a parade of thirty to two hundred Dayaks came to our home, she handed out medicine and school supplies, played the organ, taught classes in reading and writing, listened to their problems, and gave counsel. And much of the time she did this by herself, because my father's travels took him away for days and weeks at a time. I think there were probably times when, rather than saying, as she did at the beginning, "I feel like a missionary for the first time," she wished she had a little more time just to be Edna Mouw and to take care of her two children.

27 THREE DAYAK MEN WHO BECAME PASTORS

Before there were Dayaks who had received Bible school training, my parents relied on national workers who came from other islands within the Dutch East Indies. The first of these workers, Patty and Adipatty, came in 1935. A year later two more men, Wattimuri and Sampe Ali, arrived. All four were graduates of the Bible School in Makassar on the neighboring island of Celebes. They were fine young men. My mother wrote lovingly of Patty: "He is a fine evangelist; all of the Dayaks think so much of Patty." He became quite ill in June 1939 while traveling with my father and had to be hospitalized in Pontianak, where he was diagnosed with tuberculosis. By April 1940, he was much better, but he left Borneo and went back to his own island of Ambon.

The first Dayak men to graduate from the Bible school – Lombok, Yapet and Surah – returned from Makassar in December 1938, after completing just two years of school, because of the great need for Dayak pastors for the newly established churches.

Lombok

Before the churches were built, meetings were held every Saturday night and Sunday at our home in Balai Sepuak. One young man, Lombok, used to come every Saturday afternoon. In the evening he would stand in the doorway, leaning against the jamb, and listen to the Gospel message. This went on for several weeks.

One day he came to my father and said, "Tuan, I want to work for you. I want to follow you; I want to go wherever you go." He began to accompany my father up the rivers, down the trails, from longhouse to longhouse. He listened intently as my father taught the people from the Bible, and after several months he told my father that he wanted to attend the Bible School in Makassar. He left his wife there in the jungles, because she had not yet become a Christian and did not want to go. My parents didn't think it was right for him to leave his wife, yet there was no doubt that Lombok felt the call of God on his life.

Lombok was away at Bible school for two years; when he returned, he learned that his wife had been unfaithful to him. He wanted a divorce, but my father talked to him, reminding him how the Lord had forgiven him, and advised him to forgive his wife, and he did. Until this time, Lombok and his wife hadn't been able to have children, although they had been married many years. When Lombok took back his wife, God gave them a child whom they named Musa (Moses).

Lombok and Marta

Lombok became a pastor of one of the Dayak churches and later became district superintendent of all the churches. He had twenty-six churches under his supervision and went from church to church, encouraging the people. When a Bible School was eventually established in West Borneo, he became one of the teachers.

When I was fifteen years old and visiting my parents in Borneo for two months (my brother and I had been attending high school at our mission school in French Indo China, now Vietnam), I took a week-long trip on my own, accompanied only by Dayaks, and visited Lombok's church, staying two days with him and his family. They were very gracious and loving hosts. I remember thinking how good looking Lombok was, a rather typical observation of a teen-age girl.

Yafet

One day there came to our yard in Balai Sepuak a young man named Yafet. He met my father by the mango tree at the side of our house and said, "Tuan, I want to work for you." My father thought to himself that he didn't want Yafet to work for him as he knew this young man didn't know how to turn a wrench, he didn't know how to pound a nail. He knew how to shinny up trees and paddle and go down rapids, but my father didn't need these skills. He was just about to send Yafet away and suggest that he go back to his village and help his father and mother grow rice when he remembered a prayer he had made to God -"Lord, send us laborers"- meaning laborers for the church. So my father looked at him again and thought that maybe my mother could use him. He took Yafet up the steps and into the house.

"Dear, Yafet wants to work for us. Can you use him?"

"I surely can!"

"He's all yours."

Yafet had come because the call of God was upon his heart. He faithfully helped my mother, and when my father was gone, visiting longhouses and the few churches, Yafet would anxiously await his return. "While you were gone, your wife and I prayed for you," he told my father and wanted to know how many people had become believers. Yafet was eager to learn how to read and write, and with the able teaching of my mother, he accomplished this goal within six months.

After Yafet had been with our family about eight months, my mother, brother and I went back to the United States early because of my mother's poor health. (My father came eight months later.) Three weeks before our departure, my mother took Yafet aside and told him of our plan to leave.

208

"I'm concerned about Tuan because he isn't a very good cook. When he's alone, he doesn't eat very well. Yapet, will you cook for Tuan while I'm gone?"

"Oh sure! I'll cook for him."

"I'll teach you everything I can in the next three weeks before I leave. And I want you to really pay attention. Will you do it and take care of Tuan?"

"Yes, I'll take care of him."

My father took us down to the coast and over to Singapore and then returned to Balai Sepuak by himself. "I got inside that house which was only a house now, it was no longer a home, because those who had made it a home were gone. ... But Yafet was right on the job and brought me some coffee to drink at 5:30 in the morning. At seven o'clock he had my breakfast on the table which was rice and something else. At noon he had my noon meal on the table which was something else and rice. And at night it was a repeat performance. He was an expert rice cooker before he ever came to our place. My wife didn't teach him how to cook rice. He knew I liked rice so he just gave it to me three times a day, and I ate it. He was supposed to dust the furniture and sweep the floor; he always had a broom in his hand and a dust cloth over his arm, but he wasn't using them. He was a happy young man and he used to sing as he worked around the house." (Arthur, taped sermon)

In time, Yafet attended Bible school, became a faithful worker, married, had children and pastored a church with over four hundred members. On his own he went to another area 125 river miles away where the people had not heard the Gospel. He took his family, built a hut in which to live and began to preach in that area. Much later Yafet sent my father a letter telling him there were more than six hundred believers, and they had a built a church.

"Here's the dear boy who stood under the mango tree, and I almost sent him away. My friends, this is the building of the church of Jesus Christ, and 'Upon this rock,' the Lord has said, 'I will build my church, and the gates of hell shall not prevail against it.'" (Arthur, taped sermon)

Surah

My father met Surah in his early travels as he went from longhouse to longhouse. One night my father decided he should return to a village from which he had just come, about a four-hour walk. It was after six o'clock and dark; would he and those who were accompanying him be able to find their way back? A young lad who had accompanied him on this journey stepped forward and volunteered to lead them back to his own village. "I know the way, Tuan. I can take you there," he said. Step by step this young man, Surah, who knew every twist and turn in the trail, led them back to his village. (This story is told more fully in Chapter 9, "Preaching to Hungry Hearts at Midnight.")

Some months later, Surah came unannounced to our home in Balai Sepuak and told my father he would like to work for him. As he had felt about Yafet, my father had some reservations about Surah's abilities to help him in the way he needed, so he again asked my mother if she could use him to help. My mother, who was kept busy much of every day tending to the needs of the constant stream of Dayaks who came to our home, was pleased to have another helper. Surah came into our home along with Yafet.

When my father returned from his trips both Surah and Yapet eagerly asked, "Did any more of our people believe?" Then they would tell him how, along with my mother, they had prayed for him the entire time he was gone. While Surah stayed with us in Balai Sepuak my mother taught him how to read and write. He was an able pupil, learning quickly, and as he matured in his Christian faith and his ability to read the Bible, he expressed a desire to go to Bible School.

Surah attended the Bible school in Makassar for two years. When he returned, the national workers who had come from other islands to minister to the Dayaks had returned to their own islands. The Bethel church, which had grown in membership to 1315 people, needed a pastor, and Surah became the pastor of that church. He had told my father years ago that he could show him the way back to his village; his feet would show the way. Now he was showing the way of Christ to his own people: "How beautiful are the feet of them that preach the gospel of peace and bring glad tidings of good things!" (Romans 10:15)

Surah and Nyalin

In 1991, I received a letter from Surah inviting me to visit his village of Dampak. I joyfully met both Yapet and Surah during my visit . On my tape recorder, they each recorded a loving message to my mother.

These three Dayak men - Lombok, Yafet and Surah - are now gone, but the fruit of their labor – new generations of Dayak Christians and a strong, indigenous church – remain.

Surah (standing), Lombok, Yafet, Dawan

28 RAIN, NO RAIN

Our home in Balai Sepuak was 246 miles inland from the major coastal town of Pontianak, where my father would go every three or four months to get provisions. He set out on the Belitang River until it joined the bigger Kapuas River, then continued on for another 210 miles. One day he got into the *Kabar Baik*, tied a little barge alongside, and with some Dayak helpers started down river for Pontianak. The trip was relatively quick because the river was high and they went down on a flood tide. We were never certain of the level of the Belitang River that ran in front of our home. It could be only three feet deep at four o'clock in the afternoon and my brother and I could stand in the river with our chins just above the water. Then we would get a tropical downpour during the night, and the next morning when we got up, the water was within a foot of our front porch. The water had come up twenty-six feet during the night.

My father was gone about a week traveling and getting the things he needed in Pontiank. When he had all the provisions in his boat and barge, he started back up the big Kapuas River. It was the month of August, the only dry month that we had in that part of Borneo. There was not much water in the big river, but certainly enough for his little twenty-two foot boat. It took four days to get to the place where he turned off into the much smaller Belitang River, and he still had thirty-six miles to go. As he looked up the river, he could see rocks protruding, and he knew that around the bend there would be sandbars. The Dayak young men who had accompanied my father saw it, too, and they said, "Tuan, we'll have to be here a month before the rains will come and the river will come up."

My father didn't respond to this, but thought to himself, "I'm not going to sit here a month." Then he commented, to his church audience listening to this sermon, "You know, Americans, they're in overdrive, in hydromatic, but those people over there are in compound low. They're not even in low gear yet. So it would be all right for them to sit at the mouth of this river and wait a month for the water level to come up. But not an American!"

The next morning, after breakfast, my father said, "Let's start out," and within a short distance they encountered the rocks. They had to take everything out of the boat, everything out of the barge, put in on the bank, pull the boat over the rocks, then put everything back in the boat. About four hundred feet up the river there was a sandbar, and they had to do the same thing all over again. All day long they worked like this. My father said that sometimes the Dayaks looked at him "and they wondered whether I had all my marbles," but they kept going on. That afternoon they came to a place where there was quite a stretch of water, not very deep, and the rudder and the keel would drag, but if they got in the back and pushed the boat, they could keep it going and make a little progress. But soon there were more rocks and sandbars and they were lifting and pulling and groaning, working as hard as they could. The thought came to my father, "If someone was over on the bank now, taking pictures with a

16mm movie camera, and they would come back to Prairie Bible Institute [where he was giving this sermon] and show the pictures, people would think, 'This is real pioneer missionary stuff!' But there was no one there with a camera."

By the end of the day, if the river had been straight, they could have looked back and seen the place where they had eaten breakfast that morning. The entire next day they worked the same way and were only about half way home. At five o'clock they pulled over to a sandbar and my father said, "I can't go on anymore; I'm all in."

The Dayak helpers answered, "We're half dead ourselves."

"Let's spend the night here," my father suggested, to which they readily agreed.

"Cook some rice and we'll eat, then we'll start out again tomorrow." He sat in the boat and thought about the remainder of the trip. As they went further up the river there would be more rocks, more sandbars protruding, more logs that had fallen across the river. At the rate they were going, perhaps in three days they would be home. Home seemed a long ways away, though it was less than eighteen miles.

While my father was sitting in the boat, another young Dayak man came down the river paddling his eight-foot long sampan. He came up alongside the boat, looked over the situation, got out of his sampan, went over and talked to the other Dayaks who were cooking the rice, then came back, sat in his sampan and said to my father,

"Tuan, I understand it's taken you two whole days to come this far."

"That's right."

"You're not making much progress, are you?"

"No, we're not."

"Tuan, you're working too hard. Why don't you pray?"

"What do you mean?"

"Tuan, if you would pray and ask the Lord to send a little bit of rain, the river would come up, and you wouldn't have to work so hard."

Reason took over in my father's mind and he said, "You know, this is the dry time of the year, the time that the people need to burn their brush. If they don't have dry weather, then they can't burn their brush, and if they can't burn their brush they can't plant their rice field, and if they can't plant their rice field, they go hungry."

"I know. Tuan, all you have to do is pray and ask the Lord to send a little bit of rain. That wouldn't hurt. It would fall on the dry brush but the sun will be out tomorrow, and people will still be able to burn. The river would come up and you wouldn't have to work so hard." Then he looked right at my father and said, "Tuan, why don't you pray?"

My father said, "Let's pray," and because this Dayak man had a lot more faith than he had, he said, "You pray."

This Dayak man prayed, telling God all about my father, how hard he was working and that he wasn't making much progress. "Lord, if you'll just send a little bit of rain, the river will come up and Tuan won't have to work so hard. Amen."

My father didn't pray at first, but he had taught the Dayaks to bring all their needs to God in prayer, so felt he had to pray. "I didn't have any faith and the Lord knew it, but I didn't know whether this Dayak man knew it, and I tried to say things in a way that he wouldn't catch on, so I prayed, 'Lord, let it be according to the prayer of this Dayak man.'" Their prayers finished, the man said he had to be going and shook hands with my father.

216

Then he dipped his paddle into the water and down the river he went, easily maneuvering his sampan in the shallow water.

Soon the Dayak helpers on the bank called and told my father the rice was ready. They ate dinner together, then got in the boat ready to go to sleep. Just as they lay down, in the distance they saw lightning flash and heard the thunder roar, but only a few drops of rain fell on the roof of the little boat. Because they were completely exhausted from their day's work, they slept soundly the entire night.

When they awakened at dawn, the first thing they did was to look at the bank of the river to see whether the water level had come up or gone down. During the night it had come up about thirty inches. After a quick breakfast, on their own motor power, up the river they went and were home in just a few hours.

I continue with my father's words: "You say, 'Mr. Mouw, would the Lord raise a river just to help a missionary get up the river?' Yes, I think the Lord would. The Lord is concerned about you; He's concerned about me. He was concerned about that Dayak. God cared enough about Elisha to have ravens bring meat to him; God does care. ... But when God is answering our prayers, He may be doing something else for somebody else, something that we don't even know about. God is an economist; He can answer prayer for you and for someone else at the same time."

About three weeks later a Dayak man named Jong came to the front porch of our home, shook hands with my father, and asked him to sit down on the bench with him. They talked for about fifteen minutes about the weather, his crops and his people. My father felt Jong must have something he wanted to say, but Dayaks often take some time to say what is on their mind. After awhile he said, "Tuan, I have something that I want to tell you. You know where I live, way up the river?"

"Yes, I know where you live. When you paddle up the river to your place, it takes a day, but when you come down the river, it only takes half a day."

"Yes, that's right. The other day I was burning my brush. I had chopped down my trees and the brush. I chopped it well because I wanted a good rice crop. And I waited until I thought it was the proper time to burn it. I burned it, and, Tuan, it was a hot fire; it was really eating up the wood. And I rejoiced that there were good flames, because I knew as the fire consumed the wood it would create a lot of potash, and the potash would fertilize the soil, and I'd have a good rice crop. But, Tuan, the wind came suddenly and blew the fire in the wrong direction; the fire started toward our longhouse! I rushed ahead of the fire and tried to beat it out, but it was too hot and I couldn't put it out. It was on its way to the longhouse, and I was helpless; there wasn't a thing I could do. You know the worst crime we can commit in the jungle is to let the fire get out of control and burn our longhouse down. It takes three years to build one; it can be burned down in half an hour. I was afraid. Suddenly in my complete helplessness, I remembered that I was a follower of Jesus Christ. I bowed my head in my helplessness and I asked the Lord to help. Tuan, I didn't pray very long; I didn't have long to pray. And, Tuan, I had no more closed my prayer and said 'Amen' when the lightning flashed and the thunder roared, and the rain came down and put the fire out."

My father responded, "Why, Jong, that's wonderful! I'm glad that you came to tell me." After a short pause he suddenly asked, "Jong, when did that happen?"

When Jong answered this question, my father realized that at the time Jong was way, way up the river burning his brush, he was way down that same river trying to come home. And the rain that put the fire out was the rain that came down in the night and caused the river to come up. "God knows exactly where to send the rain. For if He had sent the rain where we were in the boat, it wouldn't have done us any good; it would have just gone downstream to the big river. But way, way up in the jungle, the rain came down, and silently, in the night, it came down the river and raised the river where we were." (Arthur, taped sermon)

29 ON THE PORCH

At our home in Balai Sepuak, from thirty to two hundred Dayaks came to visit every day. One day when my father was home, he decided to set aside the entire day to answer letters, because the next day someone was going down the river, and mail could be sent with him. By 7 A.M. he was busy at his desk writing letters and also some reports that were required by the mission board. About nine o'clock he decided to take a short break and went out on the porch; it was almost empty which was unusual.

But there was one man about seventy-three years of age sitting on a bench. When my father came out, he jumped to his feet, stuck out his hand and said, "Hello, Tuan."

My father returned the greeting and wondered how long he had been there.

He asked, "You've come from your village?"

"Yes."

"When did you come? When did you start?"

" I started at the break of dawn."

My father thought he must have something really important on his mind to have left so early and come so far. He sat down with him and they had a good time of conversation. About twenty minutes had gone by and the man still had said nothing about why he had come. My father told him about the mail going down the river the next day and the letters he had to write. The man responded, "That's all right, Tuan. You go in and write those letters. I'll just sit here and wait."

My father went back to his room and wrote letters for about an hour. He couldn't concentrate the way he wanted to, because he kept thinking of the man sitting out on the porch, so after an hour he again went out. Again the man jumped to his feet and greeted my father as he had done earlier. They sat down on the bench together and talked for a little while. My father thought surely this time he would say why he had come, but he didn't.

At that moment, some women came up on the porch. They asked where my mother was, and my father told them that she was inside being a schoolteacher to my brother and me. "Oh, yes," they said, "we know. But we'd like to see her for a little while. Please call her."

My father called to her and when she came out these women jumped to their feet and stuck out their hands to greet her. She shook hands with them and sat down to talk for a little while. Soon the women said, "Nyonya, we know you're busy, we know that in the morning you are teaching your children, but we just came to sit for a little while and just talk." They had vegetables they had brought arranged in little piles and after a while one of them said, "Nyonya, we brought these vegetables just for you. Just for thanks."

A Dayak backpack used to carry vegetables

Their faces beamed as my mother told them how lovely the vegetables were and that she could really use them. She talked with the women for fifteen minutes, then said that she had to go in because it was school time and if she wasn't there, my brother and I didn't study as well as we should. The women responded, "We know," even though they had never been to school a day in their life.

"You've brought me these lovely vegetables. What would you like me to give you?"

"Nyonya, if you don't mind, we'd like you to give us some safety pins."

223

The Dayaks wouldn't think of selling the vegetables, neither would my parents think of offering to pay for the vegetables. They gave the vegetables to us, then my mother or father gave them something. The Dayaks liked this system. They also liked the safety pins my mother gave them because they were nickel-plated brass and didn't rust like the nickel-plated steel pins they could buy from the Chinese merchant. They called them, "Mr. Mouw's brand of safety pins." My mother got a box of safety pins and gave each of the women some.

During this time, the man who was sitting beside my father had been watching all that was going on. He got up, went over to my mother, stuck out his hand and said, "Nyonya, if you don't mind, I'd like to have a few safety pins," so she gave him a few and he was very happy. Again my father excused himself saying that he had to write his letters. "That's all right, Tuan. You go in and write letters. I'll just sit here. I'll be here when you come back."

My father went back, wrote for another hour, came back out to the porch and the man was still sitting there. He sat down on the bench and again they talked for a little while and some more women came. They asked where my mother was, although almost all the people knew that my mother was her children's schoolteacher in the morning hours. The women said they were on their way home from trading with the Chinese merchant and asked my father to call my mother so they could see her for just a few minutes.

Graceful carriers

She came out and sat with them for a few minutes, and again there were the piles of vegetables. "We brought these just for thanks." She admired the vegetables, said she needed to go back to her teaching, but first she would like to give them something, too. What would they like to have? "Oh, Nyonya, if you really want to give us something, we'd like to have some fish hooks." My mother brought out a box of fishhooks and gave some to each of the women. Again, the man who was sitting on the bench watching all that was going on got up, came over to my mother, stuck out his hand and said, "Nyonya, if you don't mind, I'd like to have some fish hooks too."

As she was taking a few fishhooks out of the box to give him some, she looked over at my father and their eyes met. They smiled at each other and their smile said volumes: "This man may not know why he's come, but he's sure got the 'gimmes'."

My father sat with the man for a short time until my mother called him to come and eat lunch. He turned to the man. "My wife has called me to

225

eat. Do you have anything to eat? Won't you come and eat with us?" The man replied, "Oh no, Tuan. I brought my own lunch. It's right here," and he pointed to a banana leaf wrapped around some rice. "I'll just sit here and eat my rice. I'll be here when you come back."

During their lunch my parents' conversation turned to the man on the porch. My father didn't understand why he had come such a long way from his village, over three hours walking time. After lunch my father went out to see the man once more, another group of women came, and the same little drama was reenacted, but this time the women asked for quinine pills. When my mother was giving the women the pills, the man came over again and asked if he could have some too. For the fourth time that day my father told the man that he had to go back into the house to write his letters. "That's all right. You go in and write letters; I'll be right here."

About 2:30 P.M. my father was writing and thinking about the man on the porch. He knew the man would have to leave soon if he were to get back to his village before it became dark. He decided he would go out this time and sit with him until he left. They talked for half an hour, both enjoying the conversation, and finally the man stood to his feet and said that he had better be going. He put out his hand to my father and said, "Tuan, I just had a wonderful day. It's been wonderful to be here on your front porch and to just be near you. I've wanted to come to your house for a long, long time, just to come and have fellowship with you, and I kept putting it off. But this morning at the break of dawn I decided that this was the day, and I came. I know you have a lot of things to do and you couldn't sit with me all day, but you've spent time with me, and, Tuan, the time has just been wonderful. And I'm so glad I came." He put out his hand and started to leave.

As they started to walk off the porch, he pointed to a rooster and he said, "Tuan, do you see that rooster? I brought that rooster just for you. Just for thanks." They walked to the edge of the porch and the man said again, "I just came to have fellowship with you." Then he turned and walked down the steps, went over the hill, and on to his village.

My father recalled how he and my mother thought this man had the "gimmes," but he had brought the rooster, tied its leg to a post, and throughout the day knew he was going to give it to them. My father knew the rooster cost about thirty cents whereas the little they had given him cost about four cents. All the time the man had been asking for the safety pins, fishhooks and quinine, he knew he was going to give more than he would receive.

I conclude in my father's own words: "I stood there and looked at that bench where he had been sitting from nine o'clock in the morning until a little bit after three in the afternoon, and why did he come? He came because one day in his longhouse he found Jesus Christ as his Lord and savior, and we meant something to him, because he had found peace in his heart and in his soul. And he just wanted to come and have fellowship. And as I thought of that man walking all that way and sitting those hours, it just made me think of the Lord God. What would happen if some day we just say, 'Lord, today I'm going to take the day off. I'm just going to come and have fellowship with You.' And that wouldn't mean you'd have to go someplace and sit, but maybe you could walk through the woods or over the prairie, and this was a day you were just going to have fellowship with the Lord. What would happen if we would do that? I think it would make the heart of the Lord glad if we would take off hours just to come and have fellowship." (Arthur, taped sermon)

30 VISITORS FROM AMERICA

In September 1939, John R. Turnbull and his wife, Rhoda, visited our family in Balai Sepuak and stayed for five weeks. Mr. Turnbull had been a teacher at the Nyack Bible School in New York when my parents attended this school in 1930-31. After he returned home, he published an account of his Borneo visit in a small pamphlet, *From Headhunting to Christ*, which I excerpt in this chapter. (The pictures are from our family's albums.)

****

Mass Meeting in the Woods

Saturday was a grand time to be at the missionary's front door. People were arriving every few minutes from up and down stream. Instead of coming in Fords and Chevrolets and other good cars, they brought their families in dugout canoes with enough provisions to last until Monday. Dayaks are expert campers and if you watch these folks for an hour, you will learn how to omit much arduous toil on your next vacation in the woods.

Dayaks arriving by sampan

The meeting place is in a grove adjoining the new church of Ebenezer, twenty minutes walk from the river here at Balai Sepuak where I write as I watch the Dayaks. ... As the canoes are emptied, the occupants come with one accord to welcome us newcomers. We shake the hand of every adult, youth, child and baby. ... If you forget to greet the baby slung in a cloth from its mother's neck, she will pull out the infant's hand from its little hammock and hold it towards you. Some of the Dayaks bring us eggs. We are also the recipients of enough chickens to feed a fairly large convention of ministers.

A Dayak family

I was fascinated by the movements of the scores of people all along the bank. Each family had long, light baskets woven to fit the back and secured by rattan harness to head and shoulder. In these they brought rice, cooking utensils and their Sunday clothes, two garments. The women... moved with a grace not often excelled in an American Easter parade.

[After arriving at the church] Three long rows of bamboo booths, built six feet off the ground, serve as quarters for some of the visitors, but most of them make their own nest for the two nights they are in the jungle. Every man carries a long knife in a wooden sheath. He chooses a level spot on the edge of the woods, slashes away the saplings, erects a pole platform four feet off the ground and slings his grass matting cover over a ridge pole for a roof. This matting is waterproof. He has already used it in his dugout canoe. I have sat for three hours in a heavy rain covered by such a canopy as I traveled in dugout and kept snug and dry.

Watch our Dayak campers again. Three thick green stakes are driven into the ground with the tops leaning in. A child brings some water, the fire of twigs from the jungle is soon aglow, the rice pot is put on, and within an hour from when the family came to the camp all are seated on their heels enjoying handfuls of perfectly cooked rice.

On Sunday we all arise before the sun. It will be a long busy day with three services in a sloping, natural amphitheater shaded by well-leafed trees. A platform has been erected six feet off the ground, facing the slope. We thought we had seen many people yesterday but that was not half of them. By land came folks along various trails, some of which had water waist deep. The forest fords witnessed hundreds of people crossing over narrow but swift streams on bridges consisting of one big log. The Dayaks are sure-footed!

When the gong was beaten at 8:30, the service grove was nearly full of people. At nine there were over 2000 present. They always count the congregation in a very simple manner. Bundles of small sticks are tied in bunches of a hundred. As each person enters the service he is given a twig. They know the number of twigs they have in starting and count the number left over. This gives the exact attendance. Silence came over all. Prayer was offered as the crowd rose to their feet, a hymn was begun and the singing that swelled through the forest could easily be heard a mile away as with one accord they worshipped the Lord Jesus.

Before I was to preach [with my father interpreting], Arthur addressed the crowd briefly. You could tell by their animated faces how those Dayaks loved him. Well they might, for he is an ideal missionary – a well-balanced

232

combination of the practical, spiritual, evangelistic and shepherding qualities that one admires. He is tender enough to weep when some weak one errs, strong enough to brave any danger to help those in trouble, and then he beams upon them with true love when they show growth in grace. The days preceding this mass meeting were very trying for him. He had to make a journey in his little launch from dark to sunrise. The day before that he had walked seven hours. No wonder that the missionary was very weary on Sunday in the grove.

In the afternoon when the heat was very oppressive I noticed that Arthur was very pale; he almost fainted away on the platform. His fatiguing trips had brought on an attack of malaria. He sat down and continued to interpret for me. When the last song had been sung in the evening we were happy in the knowledge that God had wrought wonders.

House on Stilts

Rhoda and I started through the forest on foot. Four Dayaks carried the baggage for an extended trip. Arthur had some extra work to do at the mission station and said he would overtake us. He is a very fast walker. … When Arthur went over this same trail a few days previously, the water was waist high. Rhoda and I were spared that. We got wet, of course, as we walked through pools that could not be avoided. It was fun crossing several streams on a one-log bridge and we didn't fall in. Arthur took a short cut and was waiting for us at the junction of two trails. Together we entered the longhouse of Tabu village.

The building was high off the ground and in lieu of a stairway had a steeply pitched log with steps cut in it. In the long open room opposite the living quarters we found a few women, ten small babies and many dogs.

All the folks able to work were in the field planting rice. As we sat on a mat on the floor of the open long room, which is about a city block long, we took in the sights, sounds and smells. Along the length of the building, opposite the community room, was a row of apartments called *bilik.* Each of these rooms is home for a family, and behind their abode is a platform open to the sky, sun and rain.

En route to the next village with Arthur, we stopped to photograph the strange pitcher plant which eats insects. This botanical marvel was about a foot wide and had a dozen little pitcher-shaped receptacles on its branches against the ground. A sweet sticky juice intrigues insects and when they get caught inside, the plant has its breakfast. We reached the longhouse in mid-afternoon and stayed there for the night, a rare experience.

"Welcome to our village!"

A dozen women are pounding rice as I write this sketchy description in this village, once the home of head-hunters, now the home of happy Christians. As the women pound in unison, the swing of their lithe bodies makes the building creak like the tramp of a regiment on a bridge.

Women hulling rice

Dayak rice is very healthy. The Lord has put something extra into it. You will never get beri-beri by eating rice grown in Borneo. It is what is called dry rice. The Dayaks burn off a square mile or so of that magnificent forest. They jab holes in the ground with a sharp stick and throw in a few grains of rice. It rains eleven months in the year at least part of the day. In that warm climate growth is rapid.

Arthur is a true burden bearer. For himself he has no care, but for his flock he has the genuine concern of a true shepherd. This spiritual secret is underneath the fruit and strength of his ministry.

Jungle Life

As we sit with Arthur in the longhouse in Borneo, where my rough notes are written, about eighteen little Dayak children have gathered to watch us. Now they sit on the floor and begin to sing Christian choruses in their dialect. Arthur's kerosene pressure lamp hangs from a beam. Women arrive from the river, carrying gourds and coconut shells filled with water for the evening's culinary supply. Soon we are called to supper in the apartment at the front end of the longhouse. The menu is very appetizing – rice, chicken in the broth, fried spiced chicken, eggplant and tea. A big game cock, tied by the foot with a strip of rattan vine, stands silently in a corner next to the door. Once he was used for gambling, as he fought with other game cocks. That is all gone among the Christians but the old rooster remains as a family pet. They will never eat him. He is now their morning alarm clock.

Several dozen adults quietly gathered and took places on either side of us. They sat on their heels. Six young men thumped with their bare hands on long narrow drums and two more applied strong sticks to big brass gongs. Everybody sang the hymns they used to sing when I was a boy back home. Samuel, bright Dayak of twenty, gave a short message; several gave their testimonies. Then with Arthur to translate, I spoke for about twenty minutes. When I grew sleepy and was ready to seek some repose on my camp cot, Arthur was just "warming up." He said he felt like a shouting Methodist and was ready to go on all night. The people would have stayed indefinitely, but Arthur had mercy on us. We kicked off our shoes, crawled under our cot nets and listened to the jungle noises while the congregation wended their several ways to their rooms in the big longhouse.

At break of day the pet rooster in the room where we had supper emitted his "shrill clarion" and in two seconds he received a resounding response. Dozens of roosters, perched in trees around the building, came straight for the roof, hitting it with a thud, some of them directly over our heads. This was followed by lusty crowing on the part of each chanticler on the roof. Another day had started in Dayakland. Doors of rooms all along the line opened and the household duties were soon in full swing.

Later as I entered the longhouse to get ready for our departure, a Dayak arrived from the fields. The men take turns all through the night in watching their precious rice crops. Wild pigs and deer roam at night in search of food and must be frightened off if they are seen or heard in a field. As we announced our intention to leave, everybody came hurrying to shake hands and away we went in single file through the jungle that begins immediately beyond the longhouse.

Our narrative is resumed at Bethel. We arrived here at noon yesterday. The nearest village is only a mile distant. People from twenty-two villages constitute the congregation. The building, like all Dayak structures, is high off the ground on piles. In a corner of the church is a big wooden bin with a hole in the top. That is the collection box. Instead of money the people bring rice for their offering. The rice is packed in baskets and carried six hours through the forest to the missionary. He sells it to the trader and the proceeds support the native pastor. Bethel church is entirely self-supporting and helps others. American money supports the missionary and makes it possible for him to push on into pioneer territory, of which there is a vast area.

31 TRAVELING BORNEO'S TRAILS AND RIVERS

Traveling was a constant in my father's life. Shortly after our return to Borneo in mid-1938 he wrote, "We are back in Borneo again, chugging up and down the rivers in our same little boat at maximum speed of six miles per hour. It's good to walk the jungle trails again. When we get on to a path that is three feet wide or more, we feel like we are on a highway, but try as we may, we can't make more than three miles per hour stumbling over logs, wading through swamps, etc. Since returning, we cannot help but contrast speeding America with poky Borneo."

Wading through swamps

Leeches were a constant problem. Once a leech attaches itself to the body, it cannot be pulled off, because this can cause excessive bleeding. My father carried a small bottle of iodine on most trips, as he had learned that applying a few drops of the iodine to the leech makes it loosen its grasp on the skin.

In the early days of his ministry, he went from longhouse to longhouse bringing the Christian message to the Dayaks. Once churches were established, he tried to visit each church every few months. And there were always new areas to penetrate where people had not heard the Gospel. In August 1941, for example, he wrote to his parents telling them, "In five days I leave for the Batang Lupar country. Naturally I would like to keep at the house* so we could move into it by Christmas, but I can't wait any longer to go again to these people who have not yet given their hearts to God. … I expect to be away a month or more." During this time he visited twenty-eight Dayak villages.

Eating on the trail

He also received many personal requests from the Dayaks to come and help them with a particular problem. He described some of these requests in a general letter written in March 1941. "As I write these lines seated on this boat, the dirty water of this small jungle river rushes down toward the big river and on to the coast. It seems tireless and restless and is never certain of its level. It portrays the spirit of the age - do, do, keep going, there is so much work to be done. It seems to say you must make that trip,

*The house he referred to is one he had just started to build for our family but which was never completed because we had to leave suddenly in early 1942 due to the Japanese invasion.

241

visit that village, go for provisions, repair the sides of the cook stove that has rusted through, and the roof that leaks. The boat needs painting and the bent propeller needs to be straightened. Djagoet and his wife have had a quarrel and his wife has returned to her parents who are not Christians. 'Tuan, you must come and help me settle this trouble before my wife's parents, according to custom, divorce us. I cannot marry again with God's blessing and to be a single man is very difficult; please hurry Tuan.' But I answer, 'Nawai of Sengkoeboeng, one and a half hours away, is very ill and has asked me to come and pray with him this afternoon. Tomorrow is Saturday and I leave for Shilo to preach in the church there over Sunday. Djoelak, the native worker at Bethany church, has been suffering for three weeks with his teeth. He wrote, Be sure and bring your forceps when you come. In two weeks when I'm on my way to the Bethel church to administer communion, I can go with you, Djagoet, and in the meantime we will pray.'"

Whenever it was possible, my father traveled on his little boat, the *Kabar Baik*. Mr. John Turnbull, a visitor to our home in 1939, described a boat trip. "On the second day from Belitang, we had a real taste of fighting rapids, bucking the current. In four places the jutting strata of rock spanned the entire width of the river, with about a foot of water running over. The stream was swift and the rocks were slippery. At one place Arthur shook his head doubtfully. All of us were in the river, pushing and grunting. Then three strangers appeared and with their added help the boat slid forward ever so slowly into the deeper water beyond the rock barrier. We shouted our pleasure like children at a game. For us visitors this was fun, but for the missionary it becomes a lifelong battle of setbacks and final triumphs." In order to pass over these low places in the river, my father and his helpers often had to remove everything possible from the boat, put the things on shore, push the boat over the rocks or sandbar, reload, and in three hundred feet do it all over again. Later, my father wrote of the Turnbull's visit, "They came at the end of the dry season when the boat had to be pulled, lifted, and pushed up over the rocks, and they left on the flood tide when the river level was beginning to come up and under our house." (Arthur, letter, October 1939)

Unloading the *Kabar Baik,* then pushing it over low spots in the river

Another entry from Mr. Turnbull: "He had to make a journey in his little boat from dark to sunrise, through continuous rain, and for half the way against a swift current. I sat with him through the night but couldn't help in steering the boat as I didn't know the way amid many branch streams that all look alike in the dark. After two hours, when his errand was completed, he started home. The day before that he had walked seven hours through swamps, in places across logs where a false step would mean swimming instead of merely walking through water up to his arm pits." (John Turnbull, *From Headhunting to Christ,* 1940)

How does one steer down a Borneo river in the dark of night? "You don't look to the right, you don't look to the left, you don't look ahead. You look up, and whichever way the river turns, there's just a little lighter path in the sky because the tree branches on the banks don't quite go together. And you turn that steering wheel and follow the path in the sky, the light path; then you know you're in the river." (Arthur, taped sermon)

Boat travel occasionally brought unexpected pleasures. Writing to his parents in December 1934, my father said, "You remember when we were kids in Sioux City how we'd hook on for a ride to a grocer cart with our sleds? Well, as I chug along near the banks, occasionally I throw the rope to a Dayak who is paddling up stream in his sampan and give him a tow. You should see his eyes sparkle and his red teeth shine with gladness." [His teeth are red because he chews betel nut.]

These are some of my father's observations, again while traveling in his boat. "I'm sitting in the back of my little launch, and as it putt, putt, putts along, all the natives turn out to see what's coming up the river. ... The boat is just as stable as can be and rocks very little. The only thing is that we must keep a sharp lookout for rocks hidden under water as well as old trees which have sunk.

"In America not so many of the trees sink in water, but here one can almost say the majority do; even when they are cut into boards, they sink. My boat is made from wood that sinks and should it get full of water, it will not turn belly-up and float but go to the bottom.

"I see monkeys in the trees and wild pig tracks on the muddy banks and at night hear the deer call as they come to the water to drink. The water is too high now so we don't see the crocodiles, but they are here. Now all of this may sound romantic, dangerous or exciting to you, but it has become commonplace to me. Romantic it is not, or dangerous either, unless you consider crossing Colorado Street [in his hometown of Pasadena, California] dangerous. Fact is, I'm much safer in my boat and far too cautious to take any chances going swimming.

"Exciting it is sometimes when we see a little red knob going in a zig-zag fashion from one bank to the other. The little red knob is the head of a deadly poisonous snake that has a turquoise green body or a black body with a red stripe. When we see them, we draw near and strike at them with a long stick. They can't jump up while in the water so we are safe. The large snakes here are constrictors and kill their prey in that manner, but it is very seldom that a man is attacked by one. They are afraid of humans, but deer and pigs they swallow whole. How they get their mouth over a four or five-foot pig or a large deer, I can't understand, but they do. The Dayaks have brought these snakes to Sintang with the pig still in their belly. A snake is wise but he is also dumb. After killing by striking and constricting a pig or deer, he doesn't drag it away but immediately swallows the victim. Now he is powerless as the deer or pig is too heavy for him, and he can't move. It is in this state that Mr. Dayak finds him and with one stroke of his long knife, the serpent is beheaded. It the pig is not too decomposed, they eat the pig and usually some of the snake.

"Concerning these small red-headed snakes, about one to three feet long, fortunately they have very small jaws and if one has leggings or boots on, there is no danger. As hot as it is here, I wear wrap leggings [woolen] because they protect just as well and against leeches they are much better. The leeches crawl under leather leggings. Also at night wrap leggings can be washed and hung up to dry.

Arthur wearing his woolen leggings

"So much for the animals – the gnats and mosquitoes are worse. Right now these little gnats are doing acrobatic stunts on my ankles and hands." (Arthur, letter to his parents, December 1934)

32 AN EXPERIMENT THAT FAILED

The early years of my parents' ministry in Borneo were especially joyful as thousands of Dayaks accepted the Gospel and became Christians. When their numbers became too large to meet for Sunday services in their longhouses or under the rubber trees, they began, with my father's guidance, to build their own churches. They learned how to sing. And, in time, their desire to read God's word for themselves led to the establishment of schools. There was, however, one idea my father proposed that failed.

The Dayaks were very poor and had no tools to work with except for their *parang* (knife) that they took with them everywhere. They didn't have enough money to buy a shovel, an ax, or a saw.

One day my father had what he thought was a great idea: to start a tool co-op through the Shiloh church. He suggested that everyone in the different longhouses who attended this church contribute some rice. The rice would be sold to the local Chinese merchant for money, and when my father went down to the large coastal town of Pontianak, he would buy these tools. They would belong to the Dayaks and be kept at the church.

One week the tools would be available to a certain longhouse, the next week to another, then another, and continue on a rotating basis.

The Dayaks agreed to the plan and gave their rice. My father thought it was a splendid idea, that it would really help them. He bought the tools and brought them to the Shiloh Church. The Dayaks all admired the tools and wanted to try them out right away. They found a log to see how the saw would work and were delighted with the quick results.

The system worked well for a while. But then one village that had borrowed all the tools for one week didn't bring them back in time. The people from another village who planned on having the tools the next week came to church on Sunday, expecting to get the tools and take them to their longhouse. This system was very convenient; they didn't have to make a special trip. But the tools weren't there. It made the people angry and it started trouble in the church.

My father described the situation: "Can a saw and a few axes and some shovels split up a church? Well, there have been smaller things than that that have split up churches here in America. That church was just in a terrible condition, all because we tried to start a coop, and it was all my own doing. I said, 'Lord, I shouldn't have done it; I just thought it was a good idea.' We can't always transfer our western ideas to another culture." (Arthur, taped sermon)

One day my father went to try to settle the trouble that had been brewing for several weeks. Like a snowball, the problem was getting bigger and bigger. But there was such trouble and tension among the people that no matter what he said, it did no good. He didn't know what to do and bowed his head and prayed, "Lord, God, forgive me for ever doing this." The Dayaks heard his prayer.

Then my father began to weep, not because he felt sorry for himself, but because what he had done had brought division to the church. In a while, some of the Dayaks began to weep too. The mood had completely changed. The bickering and fighting stopped and one was going to another asking for forgiveness.

(My father's story ends here and I do not know if they tried to restart the co-op idea of sharing tools. But I do know that the Shiloh Church continued to grow and prosper.)

33 CELEBRATIONS

Before the churches were built, sometimes up to two thousand Dayaks would come to our home at Balai Sepuak for services beneath the rubber trees. But once churches were built, people went to church in their own district and the crowds at Balai Sepuak dropped to 200 or 250 each Sunday. But occasionally there would be a celebration and the Dayaks would come from all over as they used to. On one such celebration day, in February 1939, over three thousand people came, many of whom had walked three days to attend.

Dayak drums

Dayaks listening to our wind-up phonograph

During the day there was a variety of games planned by the native workers. They took a coconut with the thick, outside covering still on it, greased it and mixed blacking from charcoal in the grease. Next they made slits all over it large enough to stick pennies in, but with half of the penny sticking out. Then the coconut was hung from a string and the children, with hands behind their backs, tried to pull the pennies out with their teeth. They could keep the penny, not an insignificant amount to these Dayaks, so they tried with great gusto, their noses, mouth and cheeks becoming black in the process. My brother and I also tried this game, but because the black showed up more on our faces, the watching crowd roared with laughter and we soon quit. There was a greased pole with presents at the top, and whoever could climb the pole got the presents. A third game was a fishing pond for the children. A screen was put up and a child would use a pole to "fish" on the other, hidden side of the screen. Someone on the other side of the screen tied a small bundle containing a present on the line, and the child pulled up his "fish."

What were the presents? My father described them: "For prizes there were beads such as are imported by Woolworths, sold to some of you, discarded and given to us. Well, if you could see some of them run for them you'd think that they came from Tiffany's, New York. But who ever heard of an empty tin can being a prize? They are here, and if it has a lid on it, it is more than valued. Pictures cut from Scripture calendars, though, are what they treasure most and these are given for prizes and for memorizing Scripture verses." (Arthur, general letter, October 1939) My mother also distributed Bible story pictures to each village, enough so every *bilik* (household) would have one picture for their room.

"My brother wanted to come, too!"

My father used the generator, strung up wires to conduct the electricity, connected sixty- watt bulbs and "the darkness was no more." Most of these Dayaks were seeing electric lights for the first time. Then he showed stereopticon pictures of Old and New Testament characters and of the life of Christ in color. "One evening as we were about to turn on the pictures, a heavy tropical shower came and deluged us. The people stood as the rain flowed down, hoping and hoping it would stop so that they could see more. After thirty minutes with no let-up, I made a motion with my hands and the crowd dispersed like the proverbial drowned rats. But hope springs eternal in the human breast, and the following evening the largest crowd ever gathered at one time in these parts (3500) stood or sat under the trees as they looked and listened intently to the Life of Christ by Hoffman, in color. As the story was told no one moved and hearts were drawn with power." (Arthur, general letter, October 1939)

The Christian Dayaks loved to sing and it was always a part of their celebrations and services. "You should have seen them gather to sing in quartets, duets, choirs, etc. They just can't be beat anywhere, not even in the USA. God bless these dear people – many of them walked three days to attend this meeting, old and young alike, even blind people came." (Arthur, letter, February 1939)

A Dayak choir

34 THE PRAYING BOTTLE

My father had arrived at a Dayak longhouse and was going through the usual greeting with the people when he happened to glance at a post. On the post, hanging from a string tied to a peg was a little bottle. When he saw it he said, "My heart just went down." He knew that when the Dayaks became Christians they had discarded their previous fetishes, but when he saw this bottle, he thought they had kept one fetish. He wanted to ask them right then what the meaning of the bottle was, but he felt so bad he knew they would sense his distress. He didn't say anything but walked down to the river to bathe with a heavy heart.

After his bath he came back up the path, up the notched-log ladder and into the longhouse and, of course, he looked first at the post. The bottle was still there. That made him feel a little better because he realized that whatever it was, the people weren't ashamed of it; they hadn't taken it down when he was at the river. But he still said nothing about it to them.

That evening there was a meeting. Finally, at the end of the meeting he said, "I noticed that over there on that post, there's a bottle, and I've been wondering what is the meaning of the bottle? I'd like to have you tell me about it."

One man immediately spoke up and said, "Tuan, that's our praying bottle."

"Your praying bottle?"

"Yes."

"I've never seen one in a longhouse before." My father still thought it was one of their previous fetishes, but he knew they didn't pray before they were Christians.

"What do you mean, that's your praying bottle?"

"Tuan, don't you remember when you have come to our village, if there were any sick among us, we'd ask you to come and pray for them. And you reached down into your pocket and took out a little bottle and you anointed us with oil in the name of the Lord."

"Yes, I remember that."

"Well, that's *our* praying bottle."

With this explanation, all the heaviness left my father's heart. He felt like shouting because his troubled mind and spirit were gone. He asked them, "What do you do with it?"

"Well, when someone is sick, we go get the bottle, we anoint them with oil, and we pray for them just like you did."

Then my father asked them a question he realized he never should have asked: "Well, has the Lord healed anyone?" And the people looked at him as much as to say, "Don't you believe what you've been telling us?" But then their faces lit up and they said, "Oh, of course God has healed."

That evening, after the meeting, a number of Dayaks stood up and one by one told my father how they had been healed because of God's goodness and their praying bottle.

35 MY FATHER'S HANDS

I always loved my father's hands. They were big, strong, capable, callused hands that could fix anything. When our family lived in the United States, not once did a service person such as a plumber, electrician, or general handyman visit our home. When I learned to drive and had my own car, my father became my personal mechanic. This service continued through a succession of cars, none of which ever saw the inside of a repair shop until I was forty years old.

In Borneo, once one leaves the few urban areas, rivers were—and still are—the highways; there are few roads. From 1933 to 1935, while our family lived in Sintang, my father needed a boat, but there were no stores there that sold boats. He went to the coastal town of Pontianak and hired some workers to build a little twenty-two-foot boat. Then he bought a secondhand, six-horsepower, one-cylinder engine from a Japanese trader and installed it himself, first converting it from gasoline to kerosene because kerosene at $.20 per gallon was much cheaper than gas at $.66 per gallon.

If there were boat problems, my father was the only mechanic available. Another entry from our visitor John Turnball, who wrote about his travels on the *Kabar Baik*: "Scores of times, the launch bumped into water-soaked logs. An extra-obstinate log ruined the propeller, but Arthur, practical missionary, had a spare and in half an hour made the change. Then another bump on a rough log pulled the main shaft apart. He thought at first he had lost the propeller, but pulling up the floorboards, he discovered that the main shaft had been unjointed. The key pin was replaced and tightened, and away we chugged again, merrily and smoothly. I pause to remark that prospective missionary candidates would do well to acquire some mechanical experience. When anything goes wrong in Borneo, it will stay wrong unless the missionary can fix it. The nearest repair shop was at Pontianak. He was a whole repair crew in himself." (John Turnbull, *From Head Hunting to Christ, 1940*)

Although Borneo is a land with up to 175 inches of rain a year, lack of water can still, on occasion, be a problem. My mother wrote about my father's activities as a hydrologist: "The little stream of water at the new location of the church here and the school got very low, so that they could not use the water, and they had to come down here [to the river, some distance away] for water and to bathe. Arthur has been trying every week or so to sink that pump, which you must pound into the ground. You have to strike sand before the water will seep through and can be pumped out. He couldn't strike any sand, so he chose a spot and asked the schoolchildren to dig a well. Last week they struck water, and my what celebrating! The Dayaks don't know anything about wells, and when people began coming to church and saw the two wells, they were filled with wonder and amazement. They said, 'How does Tuan know where there is water under the ground, and where does it come from?' As soon as the children struck water in the one well, they dug another one close to where they live. They struck water in a second one, too, and now they have just dug a third one. They are really going sort of wild on wells now; it is such a novelty." (Edna, letter, July 1939)

When my parents first came to Borneo, no Dayaks brushed their teeth, and because so many chewed betel nut (similar to chewing tobacco), tooth decay was endemic. The lack of calcium in their diet also contributed to tooth decay, especially in pregnant and nursing women. When my father visited the churches, in between services he would try to help the people by pulling their damaged teeth. Those who wanted his help would line up and, when it was their turn, come sit on a mat. My father would take his forceps in one hand and place his other hand against his patient's forehead, tell this person to open his or her mouth, reach in for the tooth causing all the trouble, and pull it out.

Usually this was done quite easily, as the tooth was already so decayed it had no strength. He told the story of one tooth-pulling episode witnessed by another missionary, Jack Schisler: "One woman came, and I pulled out about eight teeth. Her teeth were all rotten. The other missionary stood there and shook his head; well, I shook my head, too. She went to the end of the line and came again and said, 'Tuan, take out some more of them; they're no good.' And I knew she was right, so I pulled out some more. She went to the end of the line again and came a third time, and this may sound like a terrible exaggeration, but it's not—twenty-two teeth were pulled all together." He also pulled some teeth of a young woman who was terribly thin and couldn't gain any weight, no matter what she ate. After having her bad teeth pulled, she began to gain weight and was so happy for this change that she advised others who were thin, "You ought to go see Tuan and get your teeth pulled out." (Arthur, taped sermon)

Arthur pulling teeth

"Here's your tooth."

My father also used those capable hands to lance boils. Before he was able to help the Dayaks, they either lived through the painful ordeal of a boil or died. One man came with a carbuncle on his back so large that my father could barely cover it with his hand. He took the man down to the river, washed his own hands with the strongest soap he had, made a lather that he spread all over his hands, and then just squeezed the carbuncle. Of course the putrefaction came out and got all over his hands. He washed them in a bucket of water and did it again and again. Then he told the man to wash his boil two or three times a day with the soap given to him. His carbuncle healed, and every time my father visited this man's longhouse, the man would rush up, put his arms around my father, and hug him. The man was probably thankful for his life but, even more, was also thankful that my father had been willing to touch his terrible boil, something no one else would do.

My father put his carpentry skills to good use when it was time to build the first churches. The Dayaks had never tried to build anything but their own longhouses, and they didn't think they could build the type of church my father described to them. But with his help and oversight, they built the first of many churches.

Surveyor

Finally, our family would have been interned by the Japanese in World War II had we not been able to get out of Borneo when we did in February 1942. We could not use our small boat, the Kabar Baik, on the open ocean, so we made one portion of the journey on a boat that its Chinese owner agreed to let us use if my father could get the engine running. He had never worked on that type of engine before, but, three and a half hours later, he had it working. To replace a faulty gasket, for which, of course, a replacement could not be purchased, he crafted one out of a leather tongue from one of our shoes.

Before he went to Indonesia, my father had attended three Bible schools. During his life he continuously read and studied the Bible; he knew it thoroughly and could quote many passages from memory. However, he was in no sense an academic, and he read few other books, even theological ones. But he was ingenious and physically strong, and he had capable hands, qualities that served him well in Borneo in the 1930s and 1940s, far removed from any modern conveniences, stores, repair shops, telephone service, and mail delivery.

36 OUT OF BORNEO

Before America entered the war after the attack on Pearl Harbor, my parents, probably not unlike other Americans living in the U.S., were very aware of the war but felt that it had little impact on their daily lives. In September 1940, my mother wrote to her family: "The war doesn't affect us at all here, except of course that many prices have gone up. Life goes on as usual and we are all just as free as ever; only Germans have been interned, so you need not worry about us at all. When we hear of the terrible bombing going on in England, it seems like a dream almost, but it is a terrible reality there." Earlier she had told her family, "We are under military rule here and are not allowed to discuss war with any native people."

There was no mail coming from Holland to the Dutch people who lived in the Netherlands East Indies, and my mother expressed sympathy for those who did not hear anything from their own families in Holland. " I feel so sorry for them and so it will make many hearts here happy when the war is over and they hear the news. Of course, I am taking it for granted that England will win and withstand Germany. The Dutch women here have clubs and are knitting sweaters and all sorts of clothing to send to Holland as soon as the war ends." My parents, and it seems the Dutch people as well, were thinking of the day the war would end, not that it would spread and encompass their own lives.

In his own account of this period, *Out of Borneo* (all quotes, unless noted otherwise, are taken from this twenty-page memoir, written in 1942 after we were in the United States), my father writes: "It was December 7, 1941, Saturday in Borneo. War clouds were gathering swiftly, but in the dark jungles of Borneo we were unaware of their nearness. The day was like any other to me, like the twenty or more days each month I spent walking the tangled paths, witnessing to the Dayaks and ministering to the Christians... .

"We slept that night – the night of the memorable December 7 – in a little hut provided for our accommodation and were on our way back to the church the next morning when we were surprised to see something flying overhead which was much more formidable than our largest tropical birds. They were bombers, and as I noticed their direction, a strange foreboding filled me.

"This faint uneasiness was still in my mind on Monday as we took leave of the group of Christians and set off down the trail to the river where our small motor boat, the Kabar Baik, waited to take us the last lap of our journey to our station.

"It was good to round the bend in the river and see our station home at Balai Sepuak. It all looked so peaceful and familiar that war seemed remote and unreal. There stood the large house, a former Chinese trading-post...the dense jungle crowding in, with the river lying wide and quiet in front, and my wife and two children waiting to greet me."

That evening, my father used the generator to get our radio going. We then learned, for the first time, that Pearl Harbor had been attacked by the Japanese and that America was at war with Japan. This meant that the Dutch would doubtless soon be at war with Japan, and we were living in Dutch West Borneo. However, a month later my mother wrote to her family, "I do hope you won't be worrying about us too much. If necessary, you know we could make our own rice field here. If this island is invaded, God can take care of us just as well as on the dangerous seas or anywhere else. ... Arthur feels positively he should stay here through thick and thin, and I would have no other thought either, but staying with him, except for the children. At first, it made me very nervous – the first week of war – because of our sweet little children being here. How I wished they were home in America, but God knows all about it and whatever comes, we know 'He careth for us' and whether we live or die we are His." (Edna, letter, January 1942) All of my parents' letters that I have from this period are stamped "Censored." On one of her postcards my mother explains that she is sending cards as "It will cause less work for the censor."

A period of uncertainty began. No word had come through from our American Consul or Mission headquarters, and at first my parents had no thought that the war would actually come to us or that it would be necessary for us to leave. But my father realized that we might be cut off from communication and for this reason set off down the river to get provisions that we could store against such a possibility. On this short trip he learned that Sarawak and British North Borneo, only sixty miles by airline from our home, had fallen to the Japanese. Still there was no word from those in authority asking us to leave.

267

When my father returned home, there was a letter from one of the Dayak pastors asking him to come to his district for dedication services for the church building just completed. (This letter was hand-delivered by another Dayak who was walking to our home; of course there was no postal service.) Both my mother and father felt he should go, although he was somewhat reluctant to leave us alone there in Balai Sepuak. The day following the dedication of the church, my father was waiting for the afternoon meal when a Dayak messenger from the local official's office suddenly appeared and called out, "Pontianak has been bombed. Twelve hundred people were killed and wounded."

My father's account continues: "I sat still for a moment, wondering what to do. Pontianak was the coastal city of Dutch West Borneo. Swiftly as a bird of prey war had struck – in Dutch territory this time. I thought of my wife alone at our station and I forgot about the rice and chicken. ... I grabbed my canteen and hastened down the trail. In a little over three hours I was climbing up the bank of the river leading to our house.

"The station was unusually quiet, and I soon learned that my wife, the two children, and three Dayaks were the only ones there. My wife looked so calm when she greeted me I thought she could not have heard the news. But she had. ... Thus the days went. Sometimes the news was grave and disquieting. On other days the very lack of news lulled us into a sense of normalcy. ... On Christmas day we listened with aching hearts to the incredible news that Hong Kong had surrendered."

In the days following, my father met with some other missionaries whose station was 156 miles from ours. They, also, had received no message from our Consul or Mission headquarters. They agreed that each family would get to the coast the best way possible in case of invasion of Dutch territory.

"On my return home, I had talked to my wife, but she was not ready to leave. The Dayaks tugged too hard at her heartstrings. Every day from thirty to three hundred of them came to the station. They had their problems and needed counsel and prayer, or perhaps first aid. I was away from the station nearly half of each month; who would help them if she left? Though I was much concerned for her, I had no heart to urge her to leave."

Soon my father left to visit with some missionaries, the Williams family, at another station. He had the only boat in the district and would need to help others if the decision to leave was made. After praying with this family, he and Mr. Williams decided to get the women and children out of Borneo immediately. He left for home, almost dreading to tell my mother of this decision. He arrived home at three in the morning, but my mother had heard the boat's engine and was waiting to greet him. "Dear, I'm taking you and the children to the coast at once to put you on a boat for Java," he said. After a time my mother replied, "If you think I should go, I will."

They started to pack. My mother suggested, "Why don't you take us as far as Java? If everything is all right, you can return to the station here, and if everything isn't all right, you will be there with us." My father agreed that this was, perhaps, the best course. When he told the Dayak workers that he was taking our family to Java, they cried with one voice, "Yes, Tuan, you must get out. We've been wanting to tell you for two or three weeks, but we did not want to influence you. The Japanese won't care anything about us, but they might kill you Americans."

We set out in the small motor boat towing another flat boat without an engine. Two nights later we pulled in at the Williams' station to pick them up. Midnight of the following night found us on the wide river, our flashlights playing over the water to find the landmark that would guide us into the right river to reach Pontianak.

"Pontianak was still with the stillness of death. Heartlessly bombed and machine-gunned, the place seemed like a graveyard as we made our way ashore and over to the steamship company to ask for passage to Java. 'There will be no other boats putting in here,' the manager informed us. 'The last ship left for Java at midnight.' The sound of a siren cut short his words, and we hurried into a sampan and crossed the river to our families. But it was not an air raid, for the approaching plane was a Dutch transport coming to take the last fourteen European civilians from the city. The large plane landed on the river and we went out to the pilot to see if he could take us, too. He shook his head regretfully.

"Never, I think, shall I forget our feelings as we watched the passengers get in, and the plane leave the water and head for Java. Was this our last chance of escape? Had we made a mistake in coming to Pontianak?"

My father went next to the radiogram office to see if it were possible to reach the American Consul in Java to ask if a plane could be sent for us. He waited all day and night.

The next morning the air-raid alarm sounded and from the east came five heavy bombers flying in perfect formation. "Within a few moments, bombs were dropping all around us. We ran for some coconut trees and threw ourselves down in the mud. ... In the midst of the falling bombs and the merciless strafing of the city with machine-gun fire, later, the words of the Psalmist came as a quiet promise: 'A thousand shall fall at thy side, and ten thousand at thy right hand, but it shall not come nigh thee.'"

After the raid was over, my father and Mr. Williams went back to the telegraph office; there was still no word. Suddenly they heard someone shouting as he ran through the streets, "The Japanese are coming!" They both rushed to rejoin us, their families, and make our way to the river where our boat was moored. On the way we passed Dutch soldiers demolishing machinery with heavy sledgehammers. "The Japanese will have this city by midnight. We are destroying it before they get here," the soldiers explained. One soldier, clicking his heels and bowing as he shook hands with my mother said, "Goodbye, Mrs. Mouw. It's goodbye forever." We left them and the soldiers returned to their work, breaking up machinery, dynamiting bridges, and setting fire to ten or twelve storehouses of rubber.

"In just a few minutes, Pontianak was in flames. People were milling up and down the banks of the river, pushing wheelbarrows, on bicycles, carrying packs of their belongings on their backs, hurrying in all directions. The river was full of dugouts, sampans, rowboats, and anything that would float... The glare from the burning city threw an eerie light over the scene, accentuating the desperate fear on the faces of the people as they sought an escape... .

"We walked to our boat, bowed our heads, committed our way to our heavenly Father, knowing not where to go, and started back up the river toward our home. It seemed the only thing to do.

"Suddenly a large motor boat sped toward us, causing waves three feet high to splash into our boat. Only by throwing a trunk and other heavy articles into the river, not stopping to think of their value, did we avert

271

the danger of sinking. We could have reached shore if the boat had gone down, but there would have been no means for us to travel farther. It was impossible to rent a boat. Money meant nothing to anyone. The Japanese were coming; Dutch guilders wouldn't be worth anything then."

We continued upstream. It was just getting dark when I told my father that a man in another boat was waving at us. My father recognized an old friend, a Dutch man he had known for six or seven years. When we told him we were going back to our home he told us not to go. "The Japanese know all about you and they will come up to get you sooner or later." The two of them decided their only chance was to try to go to Ketapang, a coastal city about one hundred miles south of Pontianak. Perhaps there they could send a telegram to the American Consul.

The trip up the river toward Ketapang was not without excitement and even danger. "One night we smelled gasoline, but could find no leak. Then I discovered the gasoline was on the river. Rounding a bend in the river, later, we came upon Dutch soldiers dumping hundreds of sixty-gallon drums of aviation gasoline from a large barge into the river. After we passed this, we breathed a sigh of relief and thanked God for protecting us. Had there been a spark from the engine or a match struck, the river would have flamed and we would have been traveling through a river of fire. Isaiah 43:2 came to me with peculiar force: 'When thou passest through the waters, I will be with thee; and through the rivers, they shall not overflow thee; when thou walkest through the fire, thou shalt not be burned; neither shall the flame kindle upon thee.'"

One morning we stopped along the river as we were nearing the coast and dangerous waters. My father and the Dutch man went ashore to send a message to be phoned to Ketapang, and from there go by radiogram to the

American Consul in Batavia (now Jakarta), Java. When he rejoined our family, my mother told him of the prayer meeting we had had while they were gone. She told him of my prayer: "Dear Jesus, here we are. We don't know what to do. If you want us to go back, if you want us to get out, it is all right. If you want us to stop here, it is all right, too."

We waited a few days, but no plane came. Then my father tried to make arrangements with a Chinese man to rent a motor boat to take us to Sukadana, a city along the coast. We couldn't use our own little boat, as we had to cross twenty miles of open ocean and the waves were too high. The man was reluctant to let us have the boat but finally agreed to our using it if my father could get the engine running. He had never worked on an engine like that one before, and asked God to help him. When he realized he needed a gasket and, of course, could not purchase it, he fashioned one out of the tongue of one of our shoes. In three hours and a half, he had the boat running.

That evening, with deep emotion, we said goodbye to the three young Dayak men who had come with us this far and who would, the next morning, start back to Balai Sepuak in our little boat, the *Kabar Baik*. One of these young men was Samuel, who had a keen mechanical aptitude, and had worked closely with my father for many years. Later, he attended Bible school and became the pastor of one of the Dayak churches.

Samuel, who took the *Kabar Baik* back to Balai Sepuak

We started down the river toward Sukadana and arrived there the next morning at five o'clock. After much bargaining with two taxi drivers, we were driven the final seventy-six kilometers to Ketapang, though we had to abandon some of our luggage. The jungle was behind us, the Java Sea before us. There was still no word from the American consul. How were we to cross the Java Sea?

There was a Chinese junk at anchor in the middle of the river. This was incredible as Chinese junks never came to this place. My father learned that the owner, a Chinese man, had escaped and started south from French Indochina (now Vietnam). He had been in Ketapang three months. Two weeks before, government officials had asked him to take a load of rubber to Java. The junk had been loaded with rubber, but he waited. There wasn't enough wind, he said. "We knew it was not the wind the captain had waited for but for passengers, though he knew nothing about them. Surely God had kept him there until we got on board. There was no more wind then than there had been, but as soon as we were all on board, he began to get the sails ready."

The next morning, about nine o'clock, we started off across the Java Sea.

Chinese junk crossing the Java Sea

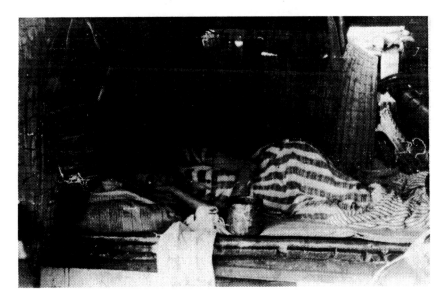

Edna, seasick for most of the trip

As we moved out to sea, we saw what we knew were Japanese boats coming in. Later, after we reached Java, we learned that Ketapang had been taken at 11:30 that morning, just two and a half hours after we left. Four days later we arrived in Tegal, on the island of Java. The officials who came to meet us were none too friendly at first, thinking we might be an advance party of the Japanese.

We had not had proper food for days, the men were unshaven, and we all needed baths. Our passport pictures looked less like us than ever so it is little wonder the Dutch official was suspicious. But he was soon his gracious self, offering us money and sending us to his own home for food and baths.

A little later we left by train for Batavia (now Jakarta). There were ten air raids while we were there seeking a boat to take us to Australia, but there was no boat. My mother suggested we call Surabaya, a large city on the eastern end of Java. We called the American Consul there. He told us a boat would soon be leaving for Australia, and we should get there as quickly as possible. In a few minutes we had paid our bill, taken a taxi to the train station and within a few hours were in Surabaya. Before we sailed, we learned that Bali had fallen, Borneo was gone, Celebes had fallen, and Singapore was lost. The entire Dutch East Indies was in Japanese control except the southern part of Sumatra and Java.

Bill for our passage across the Pacific

Nine days later we reached Australia. There were air raids while we were on the ship. We would each grab a small suitcase, by then about all that was left of our luggage, go out to the deck and get under one of the tables. We could see the bombs falling. My memory of this time is not one of fear, although I'm sure there was fear in my parents' hearts. But I was with my parents; they had always taken care of me; they would take care of me now. And we prayed.

Leaving Australia and New Zealand, we zigzagged toward America. We spent sixty-one days on the 16,000-ton Dutch ship on which we and the Williams family had obtained third-class passage. Changing course approximately every eight minutes, we finally reached the Panama Canal, and one memorable day we sailed into the Mississippi River and landed in New Orleans.

Our Java-Pacific Line ship

Our family on board

It had taken us three months to get from Balai Sepuak, our home in Borneo, to New Orleans, "three months of experiencing God's daily leading and protection."

Our family spent the next five and a half years in the United States, most of it in southern California. During this time my father traveled extensively throughout the U.S. speaking at Christian and Missionary Alliance churches as part of a missionary emphasis week; he also spoke at many other Protestant churches.

In August 1946, my father left San Francisco to return to Borneo with three other missionaries also bound for Indonesia. At that time no visas were being granted to women and children. En route my father became quite ill and, once he reached Batavia, returned to the U.S. by air.

In early January 1948, our family sailed together from San Francisco arriving in Indonesia in late February. My brother and I stayed at Benteng Tinggi on the island of Celebes (now Sulawesi) to attend high school, and our parents then continued on to Borneo.

37 FINAL YEARS IN BORNEO

Six years, two months, and fourteen days after we left Balai Sepuak, my parents steered a boat up the Belitang River and, on April 8, 1948, came to what my father called "Number 1 Riverside Drive." They were royally received by the Dayaks, who were happy to meet them face-to-face again (they had been in correspondence with some native pastors since the end of the war), and my parents rejoiced to be back in what felt to them like their real home. Edna's "barn" was not available, however, because a Chinese merchant had bought it and moved in with his family and goods. Another Chinese family living only two hundred yards down the river offered my parents one-third of their home, and my parents quickly accepted. Their part of the house had a kitchen, one large room, a storeroom, and a small porch. Later, my father said of their home: "This house is built six feet off the ground, which means we have the upper berth, six feet above the sixteen pigs."

In his first general letter after their return, my father wrote, "The war years have here, as everywhere, taken their toll—not in lives laid down but in the havoc that followed in its wake." There were problems within the church that he described as having brought it to "a low spiritual ebb," but he added, "I marvel not that so many have fallen but that so many have remained true … waiting to be led on." And lead on he did. He was kept busy overseeing the churches, helping with the Bible school, and teaching the native workers.

Because the Dayak pastors had received some support from outside sources after the war (initiated by the mission headquarters in Makassar), by the time my parents returned, the Dayak Christians were not giving as much to the support of the church as they had previously. This was a real concern for my parents, who believed so fully in self-support. But a year later, in March 1949, my mother wrote, "We praise God for the way our people are giving. We were a little fearful when we returned to self-support again, but there has been ample for all the workers, with quite a surplus in the treasury. The Christians here surely do give liberally to the Lord, and the Lord has honored them, for they are more prosperous than any Dayaks anywhere near us in this part of West Borneo. Even during the war, Dayaks came from all over to this section to buy rice from the Christians. If they grow in other graces as they have in giving, the Lord will be glorified in their midst."

Arthur and Edna in 1949

Establishing a Bible school in West Borneo was a top priority of this third term, because there was a continuing need for many well-trained, Christian pastors and teachers. The Dayak pastors of the existing churches had all received their training at the Bible school on the island of Celebes, but it had been difficult and costly for them to leave their longhouses and families for several years in order to undergo this training. Having a Bible school in West Borneo was a goal my father and other missionaries had talked of for many years, and before our family returned to Indonesia my father had learned that he'd been appointed to assume responsibility for the building of this new school. To aid him in this task, he had the help of another C&MA missionary, Jack Schisler, who, with his wife, Marian, would be in charge of the school once it opened. This Immanuel Bible School, as it was named, opened at Serandjin in May 1949 with twenty-eight adult students, twenty-three of them from the district in which my parents worked. My father had made a tour of the entire Belitang district (the area where my parents worked) to find prospective students. He had consulted the teachers and elders of each church concerning these candidates. "A day was finally set and we started down the river with fifteen students while their parents, grandparents, uncles, aunts, and friends stood on the banks and waved them off. Although the Bible school was only sixty-one miles away, or ten hours downstream, the anxiety shown and the tears shed by the loved ones were as real as if they were going to the ends of the earth, and Serandjin seemed the end to some of them. Three such trips were made, and finally twenty-eight students with their children were under the supervision of Mr. and Mrs. Jack Schisler." (Arthur, *Report for Belitang Area*, January 1949 through March 1950)

The Immanuel Bible School, located on a former rubber plantation 185 miles inland from Pontianak, operated in Serandjin for eight months, until it was moved to a site near Balai Sepuak in January 1950. (In 1964, it was again relocated to Kelansam [close to Sintang], its present site. Kelansam was a more central location for the increasing number of Dayak churches. In 1980, the Ebenezer Bible School was started as a second, district Bible school, situated at the former location of the Immanuel Bible School near Balai Sepuak.)

The eight elementary mission schools were also subject for discussion. These had been established before the war and had continued to operate during my parents' absence. The schools, each of which was located at one of the churches, taught grades one, two, and three; some schools also taught fourth grade. (Many future village chiefs were educated in these schools, and some of them later told with considerable pride the story of how they attended the third grade four times, a subterfuge that enabled them to obtain the equivalent of a sixth-grade education.) The mission schoolteachers were young Dayak men who had received their training in the same schools or, before these schools were established, at our home in Balai Sepuak, with my mother as their teacher. A few of the mission schoolteachers had had supplementary training in urban government schools run by the Dutch. Was it now time for the mission schools to become government schools? My father made several trips to talk with Indonesian government officials (Indonesian since 1945) about this, and my mother prepared typewritten copies of all necessary information on the schools, such as curriculum, number of pupils, and the educational background of the teachers. However, nothing came of these efforts, and all those involved—my parents, mission headquarters in Makassar, the teachers—felt that the eight schools should continue to be mission schools. (It was not until the 1970s that these schools came under government control and financing. All the former mission schools are still located close to the churches, but they are now housed in buildings separate from them.)

Because of these schools, more and more Dayaks were learning to read, and they developed a great hunger for the Bible and biblical literature. At the end of 1948, my parents went to Makassar for the yearly missionary conference. When they returned their front porch was the center of interest and much excitement. Word had gotten around via the "Jungle Herald" that my parents had brought back boxes of books. The greatest demand was for copies of the New Testament, and my mother felt the only fair way to distribute the eighty copies she had was through the district's churches. People begged her to let them have one, saying, "But Nyonya, you know I need one very much!" It was hard for her to say "no," but she sent the books to the churches, where the pastors and elders would know best who should receive them. She did distribute many mimeographed song and chorus booklets to individuals, and these, she said, "disappeared like magic!"

She also had five copies of *Pilgrim's Progress* that had been translated into Malay, which she sent to five of the elementary schools. The pastors and Dayak teachers there read them first, and then, as one of the pastors later told her, each day after school the boys and girls would make a rush for a copy of the book, snatching and grabbing to see who could get it first. She immediately ordered ten more copies and made the fifteen copies into what she called a "traveling library," so that all who wished to do so could read this classic by John Bunyan.

Another, more personal priority for my parents was to move from the home shared with the Chinese family into a place of their own. When they had first arrived in the coastal city of Pontianak on their way to Balai Sepuak, they'd found our old houseboat, half sunken and in bad need of repair. My father examined it thoroughly, decided it was worth salvaging, and then had it raised and towed to Balai Sepuak. He had little time to work on the houseboat, but he did spend every possible spare minute on this task. Finally, in September 1949, after a year and a half in the shared Chinese home, they moved into the renovated houseboat, the *Kabar Sinang*, which means Happy News or Satisfying News. "How we do enjoy it—the clean, painted walls, the nice bathroom, running water, and the handy kitchen. It is larger than the biggest trailer at home and far more commodious. But best of all, Edna's health seems much improved since our move." (Arthur, letter, March 1950)

Edna on the *Kabar Senang*, our home during the final years in Balai Sepuak

My father continued to travel extensively. In a report prepared by my mother for mission headquarters covering their work during 1949, she lists twenty-five trips that he made during the year. The purpose of these trips included visiting the existing churches, establishing the new Immanuel Bible School, and helping other, newer missionaries. He did, occasionally, travel to new areas where the Gospel had not yet been proclaimed. This term, however, he was accompanying Dayak pastors who had taken the initiative to go into these new territories; they had become the missionaries.

38 DAYAK MISSIONARIES

As the Christian Dayaks grew in their faith, so, too, did their desire to spread the Gospel. Teams of Dayaks went out regularly to new areas to bring the message of God's love to other Dayak tribes.

In 1939 my father wrote to his parents, "Next Monday is going to be the biggest day in our lives. On that day down the river I will go taking six native workers entering three brand new districts where the Gospel has never been preached. I will see two native workers settled in the first district, commit them to the Lord, and go on to the second district, three days away by boat, and again commit two who a few years ago knew nothing of the ministry to which God has called them. Then up the river for one and a half days more to place the last two workers."

The remainder of this chapter tells the story of two Dayak pastors who, of their own volition, traveled to another area and Dayak tribe to tell the Gospel story.

In 1948, two of the Dayak pastors, Lombok, pastor of the Pintu Elok church, and Dawan, the song of Siga and pastor of the Immanuel church, came to my father and asked him, "Do you remember that area where you traveled years ago and tried to bring the gospel?" My father did remember for this was the district he had traveled to fourteen years earlier. When he first contacted the Dayaks there, he found them receptive to the Gospel; however, on a subsequent visit he found them cold and unresponsive.

The two native pastors continued, "Tuan, we weren't allowed to travel or leave our area at all during the Japanese occupation, but would it be all right for us to go there now and minister to those people?"

"Go," my father answered. "We can arrange for somebody else to take your place at your church while you're gone."

Lombok and Dawan traveled into that area, staying about a month. When they came back, each of them had lost a lot of weight.

"What's the matter?" my father asked.

"We weren't received. The people didn't like us. They didn't even give us much to eat. They're too hard, Tuan."

The two pastors went back to their churches for some months, but one day they came again to our home.

"Tuan, would it be all right for us to go and visit those people again, because they are on our minds continually."

My father again told them to go. They went a second time and upon returning, reported that the result was just as it had been the first time. But they persisted and wanted to go a third time. This time when they returned they said, "Tuan, some people have believed." My father asked how this had happened and they related their experience.

"One night we were speaking to a group of Dayaks in a longhouse and as we were preaching, we could tell the chief of the village was very, very disturbed. When we made an invitation, no one came, no one wanted to pray. We could tell they wanted to pray, but they wouldn't raise their hand or come. And that night, just as the service was about to close, the chief came to talk.

'I've been listening to you every time you've come. Do you suppose the Lord could save a man like me?'

'Of course He can forgive a man like you.'

'But I am a terrible sinner.'

'The Lord can save the chief of sinners.'

'You don't know what I've done. He couldn't possibly save someone like me.'

This went on for some time and finally one of us asked, 'What is this that's so bad? What is it that you've done, that you feel God cannot forgive?'

The chief answered, 'Do you remember many years ago when there was a large group of people down in a certain area who were just about to follow this new religion, and several villages were just about to turn to the Lord, and then, suddenly, they stopped, and not one of them went over to your way?'

'Yes, we remember that. Of course.'

'Well, I was one of the ring leaders who caused all those people to reject your message, even though they wanted to follow the Lord. Ten of us chiefs here in the jungle had a conference and the Muslim Sultan came up the river and he got us together. No one else was there. He opened some bags and in the bags were silver guilders. He had 1800 guilders all together [at that time a guilder was worth about forty cents], and he laid it out before us and said, 'Do you see this money? I will divide all of this money among you chiefs if you do not accept this new religion and order your people to have nothing to do with. And when a certain white man comes, have nothing to do with him and don't believe the religion he teaches. But you must swear not to tell anybody about this meeting, not even your wives.' I was one who took my share of that money. And I did everything I could to keep people from following the Lord. You know what happened to that Sultan.' [During the Japanese occupation, the Sultan had been imprisoned and eventually executed.]

'Yes, we heard about it.'

'Do you suppose the Lord could save a man like me, a man who did this terrible thing?'

'Of course He can save a man like you.'

And then this chief bowed his head and heart and gave himself to Jesus Christ."

A month later, while my parents were attending the yearly conference in Makassar, Lombok and Dawan with some elders of the churches and a few young men again traveled to this area to witness to the Dayaks there. In most villages they were well received and over a hundred people turned to the Lord. Some weeks later, after my parents had returned from the conference, the two men came to see my father saying they felt like the Apostle Paul - "Let us go again and visit our brethern in every city where we have preached the word of the Lord and see how they do." *(Acts 15:36)* This time, however, they wanted my father to accompany them.

My father had the joy of returning with Lombok and Dawan to the place he had been fourteen years earlier and to see what God had done there through their ministry. They found that those who had become Christians were continuing in their new faith according to all the light they had. After spending some time in these longhouses teaching and questioning the new believers, my father returned to Balai Sepuak, but the two Dayak pastors remained three weeks longer, preaching the Gospel in other longhouses. They found many open hearts and when they returned to Balai Sepuak they told of one hundred Dayaks in this area who were following the Lord. They also spoke of their desire to move into this district so that they could continue to teach these new Christians and reach others in this area.

In April 1949, my mother wrote, "How we do praise God that these Dayak workers who themselves were in darkness not many years ago, are now burdened for their own people and have a great desire to take the gospel to them."

39 MORE VISITORS

My parents had been living in their newly renovated houseboat for just two weeks when, in October 1949, they welcomed Dr. Louis Talbot, accompanied by Dr. Paul Bauman, to Balai Sepuak. Dr. Talbot was pastor of the Church of the Open Door in downtown Los Angeles, where my father had spoken on many occasions while we were home during World War II. The church property also housed the Bible Institute of Los Angeles (BIOLA), which my parents had attended for a year after their marriage in 1930.

In 1949, Dr. Talbot was visiting many of his BIOLA students all over the world. He celebrated his sixtieth birthday while tramping the trails around Balai Sepuak for five days, going from church to church and longhouse to longhouse. "I really put them through the boot camp in condensed style and no one dare call them armchair observers in my presence. They took the trails, the mud, wading in water, sweating, blisters, and mosquitoes and all the rest, like veterans." (Arthur, general letter, March 1950)

My mother also described this time: "I have just about split my sides listening to Dr. Talbot describe the trip. He is just naturally humorous anyhow, and he sees things, of course, we wouldn't see now, and I have laughed until I ached. He was just about ready to drop when he got back to our houseboat."

At the end of the visit, my parents took the two men back to Pontianak, where they would embark for Jakarta and Singapore. As my parents and their two visitors traveled down the river, they saw many monkeys in the trees along the shore. Dr. Talbot had been talking about wanting to eat monkey meat, so my father used his gun to shoot one, and it was retrieved from the river, where it had fallen. My mother made monkey stew using "lots of onions," and they ate it over rice. This was the first time my parents had ever eaten monkey meat. My mother described it as tasting something like venison, "but just the idea makes you feel funny, but we were all game. We laughed so much while eating it that it helped." (Edna, letter, October 1949)

Just one week after Dr. Talbot and Dr. Bauman departed, my brother and I, who had been attending high school in French Indochina, arrived to spend our two-month vacation in Balai Sepuak. The previous year, on our family's return to Indonesia in early 1948, we had stopped in Makassar, Celebes, and from there journeyed to Benteng Tinggi, a two-hour drive by car, to the property owned by the Christian and Missionary Alliance where annual district conferences had been held since the mid-1930s.

A school for children of missionaries had been established there, something that hadn't existed before the war, and my brother, Burneal, and I stayed to attend this school when my parents traveled on to Borneo. At that point, Burneal and I were fifteen and fourteen, high-school age, and it was no longer possible for my mother to teach us in Balai Sepuak.

The school at Benteng Tinggi had only twelve students, seven in elementary school and five in high school. We had an outstanding teacher,

Elizabeth Jackson, who taught all the high school subjects. After six months the only other girl attending the high school returned to the United States, and I was left with the company of my brother and two other boys. We mingled with the local people and quickly learned the Indonesian language. (As in all of Indonesia, the people had their own local dialect but also spoke Indonesian—formerly called Malay—the commercial language of all the islands.) We often walked or hitched a ride to the nearest town, which had a swimming pool, a few shops, and some restaurants. And we spent time with our parents when they came to Benteng Tinggi for the yearly mission conference.

This book is my parent's story, and I don't want to dwell on our school experiences, but I would like to include one anecdote from those years. We were happy with the food we had in Indonesia, but we did miss American food. American magazines would occasionally make their way to our school, and in those days the Curtis Candy Company used to run two-page ads with a huge picture of one of their candy bars, such as Baby Ruth, covering both pages. (I think I saw them in *Life* magazine.) I tore out several of these advertisements and put them up on the walls of my bedroom. Then I had a bright idea: I wrote a letter to the Curtis Candy Company. It went something like this: "I'm a teenage girl living in Indonesia, and how I do miss Baby Ruth bars. I put the pictures of your ads up in my bedroom. I would love to have one to eat occasionally. I'm not writing this to ask for anything; I just thought you'd like to know about some teenage American kids living here in Indonesia who long for your candy." And off went the letter. About two months later I received a package from the Curtis Candy Company with four dozen Baby Ruth bars! Of course I shared them with the entire school.

In May 1949, after a year and a half in Benteng Tinggi, we four high school students transferred to another mission school, because teaching so many different high school subjects had become too much of a burden for our able teacher, Mrs. Jackson. Our new school was located in French Indochina, now called Vietnam. We flew to Saigon, our first airplane trip, and I remember hearing people on the airplane speaking English who were clearly not native English speakers. The globalization of the English language had already begun. From Saigon we traveled by car convoy to Dalat. The Vietnamese war for independence against the French had begun, and it was not safe to travel alone by car. Dalat was a lovely resort city in the mountains. The temperature was relatively cool, and many French people vacationed there.

Dalat, as we called our school, had a total of thirty-two students, ten of us in high school. Our experience there was quite different from that in Indonesia: we behaved more like typical teenagers, caught up in our own group activities, and we learned little about the local Vietnamese people and their culture. I look back on this time, from my adult perspective, as a missed opportunity. But when my brother and I rejoined our parents in Borneo for the months of November and December in1949, we fully immersed ourselves in the Dayak culture.

We shared our parents' living quarters on the new houseboat. My mother found that our coming changed their lives considerably. "Arthur and I had gotten into sort of a middle-age rut, with things all arranged in our lives as far as where our clothes belong, our shoes, my sewing things, Arthur's tools, etc. But when our two arrived, what a change! We realized that it is good to have children around to keep one young and patient!" (Edna, letter, December 1949)

Burneal spent much of his time fishing and hunting and working with my father on engines. One night when he was out in the jungle tracking some hornbills, he lost his sense of direction. When he realized this, he climbed into a tall tree, expecting that he might have to wait there until morning, and fired his gun a few times as a signal to anyone searching for him. My mother said she "suffered agony for about an hour and a half," but my father and some Dayaks found him and he was home by 9 P.M. I passed much of the time with my mother, and I enjoyed helping her with the cooking. My father said, "Our kerosene refrigerator groaned with desserts, which contributed to the bulging of my waist." Burneal and I spent many hours swimming in the river, and I was surprised at the force of the current, something I hadn't remembered from my childhood. We also explored for miles up and down the river in our sampans.

In early December there was a *gawai* to honor my brother and me. A *gawai* is a celebration of a socially significant event that always includes feasting. About seventeen hundred Dayaks came to Balai Sepuak for this celebration that lasted two days. Several pigs were butchered, roasted, and served with rice and a variety of vegetables. The Dayaks remembered us as small children; now we were taller than they. They couldn't get over the fact that Burneal was now taller than his father.

Siddy and Dayak friend

The best part of this vacation was being with my parents, but the highlight was an extended trip I took to visit several longhouses and two churches. I went alone, unaccompanied by my parents or brother but in the company of several Dayaks. I visited Surah's and Lombok's churches and was graciously hosted by them and their families. These two pastors were both old friends who had shared our daily life in Balai Sepuak in their younger years. The Dayaks were delighted with my visit and surprised that

My hosts, Lombok and Marta

and Surah and Nyalin

I could walk the jungle trails so well, and they wanted to give me anything that I looked at or admired. I came home with deer horns, deer skins, and a hawk's head, but had I accepted all that was offered I would have needed another trunk just to take it all home. One man wanted to give me a baby orangutan, but I had to tell him I couldn't take it with me on the airplane. Burneal also took his own extended trip, and his only disappointment was that he did not get to shoot a large animal like a pig or deer.

Just after Christmas, we returned to our school in Dalat, where my brother was in his final year of high school and I my junior year.

40 LEAVING BORNEO: THE LAST TIME

In their third term, the focus of my parents' ministry had changed. During their first two terms, they had been pioneer missionaries; now the pioneer work became more and more the responsibility of the Dayak pastors and members of their church congregations.

Another big change was that more missionaries were coming to West Borneo. Jack and Marian Schisler were head of the newly established Immanuel Bible School. Later, Margaret Kemp and Lilian Marsh came as teachers. These four were part of the Christian and Missionary Alliance, but new groups of missionaries, serving under the World Evangelism Crusade (WEC) and Go Ye Fellowship, were also entering West Borneo. As the senior missionary in this area, my father helped these new missionaries get settled in their assigned area. To accomplish this, he needed a larger boat.

The *Kabar Baik* had served him well since his early days in Sintang, but it was now sixteen years old. It was too slow and too small for the increased demands of the work. The new boat, the *Kabar Injil* (Gospel News), was forty-six feet long—twice the length of the *Kabar Baik*—diesel powered, and able to haul a ten-ton load. Its speed was seven and a half miles per hour. Again my father installed the engine himself, this time with the help of Jack Schisler. He used the *Kabar Injil* to move the Schislers, Miss Kemp, and Miss Marsh and to take four newly-arrived WEC missionaries and all their belongings to their new location. "And now," my father wrote, "they are settled on the edge of nowhere, the farthest inland of any of the Protestant missionaries." (Arthur, letter, March 1950)

In June 1950, my parents left Balai Sepuak for the last time and traveled to Singapore, where my brother and I met them. Their leaving in mid-1950 corresponded to my brother's completion of high school at Dalat; they wanted to accompany him back to the United States. As we set out on this trip, we traveled not across the Pacific, as we had on our previous trips, but journeyed eastward through the Suez Canal, then crossed the Mediterranean Sea and the Atlantic Ocean, arriving in New York in September 1950. Next, we drove across the country and settled in Glendale, California, where I finished my last year of high school and my brother enrolled in a community college before joining the army.

Once again, my father traveled extensively, speaking in churches throughout the United States and Canada. His sermons from this period, many of them taped and in my possession, provided much of the material for this book.

If my parents had returned to Borneo for a fourth term, they probably would have left sometime in 1952. By then my brother was in the army, I was attending college, and my parents were still relatively young, forty-eight and fifty years old. Why didn't they return for a fourth and even fifth term? A major reason was my mother's health. While in Borneo, she had continued to have bouts of malaria and dysentery that left her in a weakened condition, but a bigger problem was she had developed glaucoma. This disease of the eyes is treatable in the United Sates. With regular checkups and the use of eye drops, my mother kept her vision until well into her nineties. But had she returned to Borneo, there was a real question as to whether she would retain her vision.

In a sermon he gave several years after our return to the United States, my father addressed the question of why they had not returned to Borneo and gave another reason. "The reason I'm home is because I worked myself out of a job. My wife and I taught the Dayaks to tithe, and if you don't want to work yourself out of a job, don't teach people to tithe, because when they learn how to tithe, they become self-supporting. And when they're self-supporting, they have the right to become self-governing. And when they're self-governing, they don't need someone around to tell them what to do. You find yourself, after awhile, on the perimeter, and the Lord just gives you a shove. And he takes care of the people pretty well, by Himself, without us being around. When we left, there were twenty-three churches, and today there are many more. The Dayaks are carrying on, and we praise God for these dear people."

I believe there was another reason, and although I cannot attribute this belief to an actual conversation I had with my parents, I think it is well above the level of conjecture. My father had all the attributes necessary to be a pioneer missionary: he was physically strong, he was an able mechanic and carpenter, and most important, he loved the Dayak people. He loved tramping through the jungle, preaching the word of God to those who had never heard it. He loved teaching them to pray, to sing, to build their churches. But as I described earlier, in his third term the focus of the work had changed. He was more of a teacher and administrator, overseeing and helping the native pastors, churches, and new Bible school. I think he

305

believed his purpose in going to Borneo had been accomplished, and that it was time to turn the reins over to others—to the Dayaks themselves, who were working with the new missionaries who had come.

This change in focus over the years in Borneo has occurred in general in missionary work throughout the world. Most missionaries now work primarily as teachers, translators, or health workers. The Indonesian government, as an example, now issues limited visas only to foreign missionaries working in education and health.

Over the years, my parents corresponded with the Dayak pastors, the Schislers, and other missionaries. And during the 1950s and 1960s, there was often a fifty-five-gallon steel drum in our garage being filled with items requested by the native workers or missionaries, soon to be on its way to Borneo. I know my father worked on and sent at least two generators. In 1984, the Dayak Christians mounted a Silver Jubilee to celebrate the fifty years of work by the Christian and Missionary Alliance in Borneo, and they sent us pictures of this event.

My parents never returned to Borneo, but I did. This trip deserves a chapter of its own.

41 VISITING THE DAYAKS FORTY-ONE YEARS LATER

I never thought much about going back to Indonesia in the four decades after our family left there in 1950. School, marriage, my two children, work, and friends took all my time and energy. But in 1990 I became acquainted with Dr. Allen Drake, an anthropologist who had done fieldwork for his doctorate from 1978 to 1979 in the same Borneo jungles where my parents had worked. He had corresponded with my parents in the early 1980s after returning to the United States, but it took another decade for me to meet him. He visited me in California on his way to Indonesia from his Michigan home, and told me of his experiences living among the Dayaks, describing places and people I had once known well. He said very simply, "Siddy, you should go, and soon, before the people who knew you and your parents best have all died." This meeting was the spark that ignited my interest in returning to Borneo to visit the Dayaks.

Dr. Drake also introduced me to Dudley and Nancy Bolser who have been missionaries with the Christian and Missionary Alliance in West Borneo since 1966, and we began corresponding about the possibility of my visit. Step two was to begin work on my Indonesian language skills.

Everyday, when I took my dog for a walk, I would speak aloud to myself in Indonesian. These were simple sentences: "I am going for a walk with my dog. There are many houses. It is a beautiful day. My dog wants to walk faster than I do." I became aware of what wonderful computers our brains are—forty-one years after returning to the United States, I could still remember enough of the language to carry on a simple conversation.

Next, with the aid of Indonesian language texts, and with tutorials by an Indonesian woman who was teaching at Stanford University, three miles from my home, I pushed my level a bit higher. Step three was to consider what I would say to the Dayaks if I were asked to speak in their churches. I felt I should plan to say more than just a few words about our family, but I certainly did not feel comfortable about trying to give a sermon in any traditional sense. I began to listen to the tapes of my father's sermons, almost all of which are stories about the Dayaks, and decided I would retell some of my father's stories. My dear mother, still the loveliest and most gentle person I have ever known, was eighty-nine years old at the time and excited about and supportive of my trip. My father had died in 1987 at age eighty-three, and I was sure he was cheering me on from above. My mother and brother taped a message in Indonesian for me to play for the Dayaks.

These steps accomplished, I flew on Garuda, the Indonesian airline, leaving from Los Angeles on August 14, 1991, for a three-week stay in Indonesia. I had never taken such a long and distant trip on my own, and I boarded the plane with a mixture of emotions—anxiety and excitement. I arrived in Jakarta twenty-six hours later, then boarded a smaller plane for the trip to Pontianak, the major coastal city of West Borneo. During this flight I was pleased to speak Indonesian to the man sitting next to me, who worked for the Indonesian government. When I told him I was from the San Francisco area, he said "golden bridge" in English. Together we looked at a map of Indonesia in the Garuda in-flight magazine and talked about the different islands. I was also able to converse with the taxi driver who drove me from the airport to my hotel.

In Pontianak

I decided to stay in Pontianak for several days to acclimate myself to the country and language before going on to Sintang, the city of my birth, where I would meet the Bolsers. While in Pontianak, I got to observe the city's celebration of Indonesian Independence Day, August 17. When I turned on the TV in my hotel room, I saw and heard parades, speeches, and throngs of people cheering. I could understand almost nothing. I realized how the students in my ESL (English as a Second Language) class back home must feel. They could easily carry on a conversation with me, but told me they could not understand most American TV shows. Out on the street, however, it was a different story. Here, I could converse with the people I met. Pontianak is not a tourist destination, and everywhere I went people were eager to talk with me when they realized I spoke their language. As I passed one of many food stands lining the streets, the Chinese owners invited me to come around behind the stand, where they were having lunch. Was I by myself? Where was I from? Why did I come? I stayed there talking with them throughout an impromptu three-course lunch of fried bananas, sticky rice and beans wrapped in a banana leaf, and coconut milk with ice and chunks of coconut.

The next day I was hosted by a C&MA missionary couple who gave me a two-hour tour of the city. The following day, I accompanied them to their Indonesian church, where the pastor and most of the other people seemed to know who my parents were, and everyone greeted me with great affection. It was my introduction to the love and kindness that would be showered on me throughout my stay, all because I was the daughter of Arthur and Edna Mouw.

Sintang and Kelansam

The next morning I boarded a fifteen-seat bus bound for Sintang and sat in my assigned seat directly behind the driver. He was playing a music tape full blast, and the speaker was directly over my head. I didn't think I could bear this noise for our long trip, but when he started the bus, the engine made such a racket that it muted the music. Once we left the city, the driver accelerated as if he were on the Indianapolis speedway rather than a narrow, two-lane road, but he skillfully maneuvered around the bicycles and scooters crowding the lane. The bus ride to Sintang took eight hours, including a half-hour stop for lunch—I bought rice and bean sprouts from a local Chinese merchant—and a ninety-minute wait for our turn on a ferry that carried only three or four vehicles at a time. My western mind wondered why a competitive ferry operator hadn't appeared on the scene, as there seemed to be more than enough traffic for two ferries.

In Sintang, Dudley Bolser greeted me at the bus and then taxied us a half hour by boat to his home in Kelansam, where he and Nancy teach at the Immanuel Bible School. I liked them both immediately. Before they moved to Kelansam, the Bolsers had lived in Balai Sepuak for seventeen years. Although they arrived twenty years after my parents left, they came to know and work with many of the Dayak pastors and Christians who had known our family. Now, in addition to teaching at the Immanuel Bible

School, they continue to make regular trips farther into the jungle to visit and teach in the Dayak churches and longhouses.

Dudley and Nancy Bolser at Kelansam

Their comfortable, two-bedroom home was situated in an open, grassy area on the campus along the bank of the Kapuas River, and it had electricity, running water, a telephone, and a computer. How different was life in parts of Borneo in 1991 compared to 1933, when our family first arrived in Sintang! (For the last several years, I have kept in touch with the Bolsers by e-mail.)

The next morning, as I had anticipated, the students asked me to speak at their morning chapel service. I told them my father's story "Preaching to Hungry Hearts at Midnight" (Chapter 9). The young lad in that story, who had guided my father back to his village in the dark of night, was named Surah. He later became one of the first Dayak pastors, married, and had a large family. One of his sons, Pak Seth, was now the director of Immanuel Bible School, and he sat in the audience listening to my words. (*Pak* is a diminutive form of *bapak*, meaning father, and is a respectful form of address for an older man.) Later, Nancy told me that she had seen tears in his eyes as he heard the story about his father. The students attending chapel, who had been born in the years after my parents' ministry, listened with rapt attention. They asked if I would speak again that evening. I was pleased that my decision to retell my father's stories had been a good one.

Mission Aviation Fellowship (MAF), an organization that has been in West Borneo since 1970, was also located in Kelansam, where there is one airplane, a five-passenger Cessna 185, and one pilot who lives on the campus with his family. The Dayaks cut down trees and brush to create the airstrips at Kelansam and twelve other villages. They also maintain these grass-covered airstrips.

For many years the MAF pilot has made regular flights to Dayak villages to deliver teachers from the Immanuel Bible School. These teachers conduct Bible classes at the villages during the day; in the late afternoon the MAF pilot picks them up and flies them back to Kelansam. The plane also delivers medicines and picks up seriously ill people from the villages and delivers them to the hospital in Sintang. (MAF is leaving West Borneo in mid-2004.)

The Bolsers had made plans for me to visit Dayak churches and villages by flying to the small airstrip near the Immanuel Church on one of MAF's weekly flights. The village of Dampak is located close to the Immanuel Church, and this is where Pak Surah lived. He had written me a letter (after getting my address from Allen Darke) and invited me to visit his village. Of course I also wanted to visit Balai Sepuak, where I had grown up, but the MAF plane did not regularly go there. Nancy told me the only way to get to Balai Sepuak from Immanuel was by foot, and she did not see how I could manage the twenty-six-mile walk. I was disappointed by this situation, but there seemed to be no alternative.

When I arrived in Borneo, in August, it was the dry season, and there had been no rain for five weeks. This was the time of year when the Dayaks prepared the land for new rice fields and burned the cleared-out trees and brush. These fires produced a smoky haze over the entire area. On two consecutive days, limited visibility forced cancellation of the MAF flight that was to have taken me to the Immanuel Church. Instead, I was able to get a seat on an emergency flight going to Balai Sepuak to pick up a sick older man. I was delighted that events had transpired to place me in Balai Sepuak where our family had lived for so many years!

Balai Sepuak

No one was expecting me, as they had been told I was going to Immanuel, but Pak Aheng, head of the Ebenezer Bible School, and his wife, Damaris, immediately made me feel welcome. I stayed with them in the same home where the Bolsers had lived, a house with electricity and running water.

313

Balai Sepuak, now the location of a small government station, has about five hundred inhabitants plus several hundred resident junior and senior high school students during the school year. This was quite a contrast to the three Chinese families, our family, and the few Dayak helpers, perhaps a total of twenty people, who had lived there when I was a child.

Pak Aheng and Damaris

I couldn't wait to see our old homestead, so Pak Aheng and I started out on the fifteen-minute walk necessary to reach it. On our way we passed a small hospital and Ebenezer Church, now located closer to Balai Sepuak than when my family lived there. Finally we came to "Edna's barn" and walked up the steps to the front porch. I met the current owner, the granddaughter of Tauke Tua, the Chinese man who had rented us this house in 1935. She lived there with her Dayak husband, Pak Benjamin, who was from Dampak, the village I was to visit.

**Siddy on steps of Edna's Barn with current owner, the
granddaughter of Tauke Tua**

The house had been enlarged, and the big, central room that I
remembered so well had been divided into smaller rooms, but there was
much about this house on the bank of the Belitang River that stirred
my heart. Almost immediately, I was surrounded by a crowd of people.
Everyone seemed to know I was the daughter of Tuan and Nyonya Mouw,
who had lived in this house many years before. I had brought two photo
albums with me filled with pictures my parents had taken of the Dayaks
and Balai Sepuak in the 1930s and 1940s. Everyone gathered around the
books—their curious, intent eyes fixed on these historic photos. Later
I walked down to the river, very low at this time of the year, recalling
the hours my brother and I had spent there swimming and paddling our
sampans.

That evening I shared a delicious dinner—rice, chicken with coconut and spices, two vegetables—with Pak Aheng and his wife. Afterward, people began to arrive, most of them young Bible school students, many with young children. They sat on the floor of the living room and passed the photo albums around. All the pictures predated most of this audience, which was mainly made up of young people in their twenties or early thirties. A large picture of me at age two and a half, standing with some young Dayak boys, provoked giggles. Dressed in their bark loincloths and wearing no shirts, these boys were from another age. Now all Dayaks wear more western-style, ready-made clothes. I talked to a young mother who had named her new baby Dick Cheney after the U.S. Secretary of Defense whose face was seen regularly on television during the Gulf War, even in Balai Sepuak.

I talked with Pak Yafet, age eighty. He was my father's cook and helper when my mother, brother and I went back to the United States in mid-1936, and my father stayed on for another eight months. We looked at the photos together; the memories they evoked brought tears to his eyes. I played the message recorded by my mother and brother, then he recorded his own words for my mother, telling her the events of his life since my parents' departure.

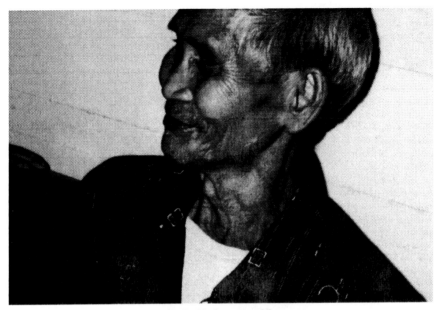

Pak Yafet, age 80

That night, after the generator was turned off, I wrote in my diary by the light of a small kerosene lantern provided by Damaris. I went to bed with a great feeling of contentment: I was in my childhood home, surrounded by the dear Dayaks of my father's stories.

All my conversations with the Dayak people I met were in the Indonesian language, previously called Malay. Unlike the years when my parents were in Borneo, almost all Dayaks now speak Indonesian. The Dutch government had required that the elementary schools established by my parents use the Malay language to teach the students; the Indonesian government continued this requirement. However, when the Dayaks talked to each other, they usually switched to the Dayak dialect, which I no longer understood. They knew this and always spoke to me in Indonesian.

The next morning I toured the Ebenezer Bible School and learned that much of the funding for these buildings had come from German Christians.

Ebenezer Bible School student weaving a belt

(I also learned that the school needed a new generator, and after I returned to the United States, with the contributions of generous friends and family members, was able to raise $1,800 for its purchase and shipping.) Later, Pak Aheng and Pak Yafet escorted me down to the river to show me what remained of our houseboat, the *Kabar Senang*. There on the riverbank lay two fifty-foot wooden keels. Forty-one years after my parents' departure, these two squared timbers remained a part of Dayak memories.

Pak Aheng and Pak Yafet sitting on keel of *Kabar Senang*

Earlier that day I had learned that an airplane might come, and that I might still get a ride to Immanuel, the church close to Dampak, my village destination. But no plane arrived, and at 4 P.M. we set off on foot. Late afternoon may seem like an unusual time to begin a twenty-six-mile journey, but in Borneo one does not travel during midday by choice, when the sun is at its peak. Seven people made up our group—four men, three of whom would help carry my baggage; two women, and me. The two women—Damaris, the wife of Pak Aheng, and Orpa—told me they were coming along so that I wouldn't have to walk alone, but I thought it was also because, according to Dayak custom, it would be improper for me to walk alone with four men. My companions had decided we would walk as far as Kampung Ransa and stay overnight. (*Kampung* means village.)

319

Kampung Ransa

The route was hilly but not difficult for me. I had expected to walk through enchanted forests of bluish green hues, under a towering canopy of trees festooned by vines almost obscuring the sky. I remembered a description from one of my mother's letters: "We didn't have to worry much about the sun as the jungle is so dense in most places." Instead, for most of our journey, we walked through secondary forests, mostly in yellows and browns, and then-fallow rice fields. We also passed many still smoldering fields with tiny wisps of flame visible. These and hundreds of fields like them were the source of the smoky haze that canceled the plane flights. Within a few weeks Dayaks would be planting their rice crops here.

At six o'clock my fellow hikers brought out flashlights; by 6:30 it was completely dark. Here on the equator, night falls at the same time every day of the year. We arrived at Kampung Ransa about an hour later. Our group was staying in a *rumah sendiri* (individual dwelling) rather than the longhouse. After greeting our hosts and depositing our belongings, Damaris, Orpa, and I went to the river to bathe. Dayak style, I removed my clothes while, at the same time, wrapping a sarong around my body and securing it just above my chest by folding over the top few inches several times. Dayak women make this change easily and gracefully; I was an awkward novice. There was not much water, but enough to slosh around, scoop up with our hands, and pour over our bodies. When we returned, we were served very sweet tea while the others passed around the photo albums. I talked with two older women who had known my parents. A short time later, I had my fourth almost identical meal of "rice and something else," as my father used to call it.

We walked a short distance to the longhouse after dinner, and there the entire village was gathered in the long, common veranda, about two hundred people, men and women sitting separately, with children in front. A young man holding the village's only songbook led the people in song; he would start a verse and everyone, including the children, would join in. They knew *all* the words and sang joyfully. Then someone introduced me and I said a few words; after that, we joined in a long prayer. The next event was a pleasant surprise. Several young men began beating drums as two others danced, one at a time, while resting a ceramic plate on the palm of each hand. Each dancer wore rings on the middle fingers of his hands, and, while standing, kneeling, or lying on the floor, he turned and twisted his limbs and torso gracefully to the beat of the drums and the beat of his rings against the dishes. The evening ended at midnight, and I shared a mat on the floor with Damaris. The Dayaks do not have beds, and once we left Balai Sepuak, we entered a world with no roads, electricity, running water, or bathrooms. I was thankful Nancy Bolser had given me a roll of toilet paper to take along.

At 5 A.M. the chickens began their crowing and cackling, and it was impossible to sleep any longer. I needed to use the "bathroom," and Damaris accompanied me outside to the bushes to shoo off the pigs that tend to accompany such functions. After a breakfast, again of "rice and something else," we travelers were on our way.

Children of Kampung Ransa

Damaris and Orpa were returning to Balai Sepuak, and so they introduced me to Marianna, who would accompany me for the remainder of this journey to Immanuel. Damaris mentioned that Marianna was not yet married. (The Dayaks rarely say "isn't," preferring to say "not yet.") Marianna was about forty years old, so I thought it was unlikely she would ever marry. If she had lived in the United States, she would probably have had her own apartment and job and be self-sufficient. Here, without a husband, she was completely dependent on her village, but she lived within a community of caring people. I wondered which was preferable— independence or a sense of community? Dayaks would most certainly choose community. I don't think they could imagine living like most Americans, often strangers within our own neighborhoods.

At Immanuel

Our morning journey took us through a lusher jungle landscape, and we arrived at Immanuel at 9:30 A.M. on Sunday. Pak Surah, now in his seventies, and I greeted one another in a joyous and emotional meeting, for he was one of two people I remembered best from my childhood.

The trail between Ransa and Immanuel

After I washed up a bit at the pastor's home, we walked the short distance to the church. When I saw it, I recalled my father's story about the first time he suggested that the Dayaks build a church and trying to describe to them what a church looked like. And they had responded, "Tuan, we could never build anything like that." But there in front of me stood the Immanuel Church, an impressive building, one of the many Dayak churches in this area, buildings my father called "a monument to the power of the Gospel."

The Immanuel Church

I entered the church where the people were already gathered, walked up the aisle and sat in the front row next to a group of small boys. The congregation began the first hymn, a cappella, their voices so beautiful that I was overcome with emotion and began to sob. I missed my father and so wished he could be there with me. I was also thinking of the sweetness, generosity, and deep faith of all these people surrounding me. When it was time for me to speak, I walked to the pulpit, still crying. I explained that I was crying because my heart was full, and then played the taped message from my mother and brother, which, fortunately, gave me a little time to compose myself. There were 389 Dayaks listening.

I spoke for almost thirty minutes, giving them information about our family, telling about my meeting with Allen Drake, whom many of them knew, and about listening to my father's sermons on tape. Then I retold several of his stories. One was the story of Api Mamut (chapter 18), whose grandson, I found out later, was in the congregation. After the service, almost everyone wanted to shake my hand, and I was reminded of my father's stories about handshaking. When I met people who had personally known my parents, they wanted to be certain that I was aware of this; it was, for them, a badge of honor. Many of the people also remembered me personally, yet I hadn't lived in Borneo since 1942, when I was eight years old, except for a two-month visit during my high school years. Most of the people I met that day had been born after we left Borneo, forty-one years earlier, but a depth of feeling and reverence for my parents and the work they had done there had been passed down to these new generations. I felt their love and affection encompassing me, and this feeling pervaded my entire time among the Dayaks.

I spent the next six days living with Pak Yosafat, the *pendeta* (pastor) of the Immanuel Church, his wife, Ester, and their four children. Their small

Pendeta Yosafat, Ester and their four children, my hosts for six days

home was close to the church. Part of Pak Yosafat's function as *pendeta*, and that of his wife, is to entertain guests. When Dudley and Nancy Bolser come to Immanuel, they also stay in their home. I had thought I would be staying at Dampak, the village about half a mile from the church, where Pak Surah lived, because he was the one who had written to me and invited me to come. But before I arrived it had been decided that I should stay in the *pendeta's* home, where I would more fully "belong" to all the people, since they feel free to visit their pastor's house. Another reason may have been that the *pendeta* gets a small allowance to help with food for guests; if I had stayed with Pak Surah and his family the entire time, it might have been a financial burden. (Of course I made a donation to the church offering to help pay for costs incurred as a result of my visit.)

For the rest of that Sunday, people flowed in and out of Yosafat and Ester's small front room. There were a number of benches in this room, but Dayak style, everyone sat on the floor. They all wanted to look at the photograph albums and again listen to the tape of my mother and brother.

That afternoon I met Pak Samuel, my most direct link to this land of my childhood, as he had worked closely with my father for many years. When my family lived at Balai Sepuak together, Samuel had shown an aptitude for mechanics and had quickly learned how to help keep the boat and generator in good repair. After working with my father for many years, he went to Bible school and became a pastor. He was one of two Dayaks who accompanied our family to Pontianak in 1942 when we fled Borneo and the approaching Japanese army, and it was he who took our boat, the *Kabar Baik,* back to Balai Sepuak afterward. During this visit, he told me that later he was physically beaten by the Japanese who questioned him about where our family had gone. All Americans and Europeans found by the Japanese were interned during the war. As a result of this beating, he suffered from headaches and had had to leave the ministry early. Pak

Samuel lived at a village some distance away and had walked to Immanuel especially to greet me.

I spent several hours talking with Pak Samuel and Pak Surah. I remembered both of them as strong, energetic young men. Now they were in their early seventies, were very thin (most Dayaks are thin), and were missing many of their upper teeth. But as they talked about their memories of being with my family, I saw a light in their eyes and flashes of their brilliant smiles. Pak Samuel's face especially lit up when he talked about my brother. Our conversation was a time of delightful, mutual discovery. I wished for the past to return, if only for an hour, so that my parents, brother, and I could be there together talking with these two dear friends. I asked them to speak into my tape recorder to convey a message to my mother and brother, and they were eager to do so, both speaking for several minutes. Samuel had brought me a beautiful handwoven basket made by his wife, Carolina. In one of my photo albums, he and Surah found a picture of their wives, Carolina and Nyalin, two beautiful young women in their twenties, standing together in the river bathing their two babies. (see photo, page 203 - "Dayak babies bathed in the river") Their babies now had families of their own.

Three old friends meet – Pak Surah, Siddy and Pak Samuel

Pak Yosafat and Ester were a lovely, handsome couple in their midthirties who joyfully welcomed me into their home and spent the next six days catering to my every need. Sunday night when it was time for a bath, Ester and I walked about half a mile to find a spot with some water. Water was a problem here, because no rain had fallen for five weeks. I realized during our walk what a sweet gift she had given me when I first arrived, when she let me bathe on her back porch, as all the water I had used had had to be hand carried for some distance. We walked through a grove of rubber trees, almost all with a groove cut in the bark and a small half coconut-shell attached to catch the dripping rubber, the standard way of collecting rubber. Village law gave Ester the right to collect the rubber from this grove of trees.

We arrived at our bathing place, several whiskey-colored pools. Ester told me not to step into the water but to dip it out with a small bucket, because when the water was this low there was a danger of leeches. It was very humid and the cool water felt wonderful.

That evening after the church crowds were gone, Pak Elisa and his wife came to visit. The youngest son of Pak Surah, he was an extremely good-looking, even beguiling, young man in his early thirties and the principal of the elementary school near Immanuel, which served about 250 students. Because we were both teachers, we talked of school and education. His training allowed him to teach any subject, whereas some teachers were more limited in what they could teach. Seven people taught at this school: one married couple, the rest men. Elisa told me the government had a hard time finding teachers for places such as Immanuel, deep in the jungle, far away from cities. I could understand this because, once the necessities of life— obtaining food, cooking, washing, cleaning, —were taken care of, there wasn't much else to turn to. Aside from the school, church, their own homes, and the nearby village of Dampak, there was only the jungle. School hours were from 7 A.M. to 12:15 P.M., and, allowing for several hours of preparation and correcting papers, a teacher would still have a good deal of free time.

The Schoolchildren

After Elisa and his wife left, a group of six children arrived to visit with Ibu Siddy. *Ibu* means mother and is a term of respect used to address an older woman. These children attended the elementary school but lived too far away to walk back and forth from their villages each day. (The Indonesian government policy has determined that all children will eventually live within one and a half hours' walking distance of their assigned schools.) These children lived by themselves, with no adult supervision, in small rooms near the church for the six days of the school week. They were responsible for their own meals, bringing rice from their village and searching for vegetables in the surrounding forest. They did live close to the pastor's home and could count on this family and the teachers who lived nearby for emergencies. After school on Saturdays, they walked home to their village, often returning on Sunday mornings for church.

The resident schoolchildren

I had brought several small wind-up water toys and sat down with these children and a pan of water; they were absolutely delighted with the swimming toys, and we played together for about forty-five minutes. On another evening, using pages from my diary notebook, I cut forty-eight equal pieces of paper and on them drew twenty-four pairs of pictures (two sailboats, two stars, two dogs, etc.) to create cards for a game of concentration. They caught on quickly, loved the game, and played it repeatedly. It was fun for me to create these activities for them, to enliven their afternoons or evenings, but it made me a little sad to realize how different their regular schedule was, as these children were on their own for six days a week from a little after noon, when school was over, until bedtime. They had little to do, but I realized that "having something to do" is probably a very American or Western concept, and that I should not judge the quality of their life using my standards.

On three mornings I visited classes at the elementary school, eager to observe the Dayak teachers and their students. All government schools are now taught in the Indonesian language. However, when these children first come to school, they speak only Dayak, which is quite different from Indonesian despite some overlap of vocabulary. Their teacher begins the year by teaching them in Dayak, gradually includes more Indonesian, and eventually switches over to that language completely. As I watched the bright, happy faces of the children, I wanted to jump in and offer suggestions, particularly on individualizing instruction, but overall I was impressed with the quality of this school so deep in the heart of a Borneo jungle. In all the classes I observed, the students had no textbooks. The teacher stood at the blackboard and wrote the day's lesson on the board. If told to do so, the students would copy this in their own small notebooks.

In one class the children were having a Bible lesson. The principal told me that this designated religion teacher was a Christian because these children came from a Christian area. If the school were in a Moslem area, the religion teacher would be a Muslim. In none of the classes was there a hint of a discipline problem; the students were well behaved and sat quietly at all times, quite a contrast to the junior high school students I encountered in my twenty years of teaching in California! The rooms were bare except for the blackboards, a few windows (no glass, just openings), and pictures of Sukarno, Indonesia's first president, and Suharto, its current president (in 1991).

Classroom, Immanuel elementary school

As I visited the classes, I thought of my dear mother, the first teacher of these Dayaks, how my parents had started schools in this area so many years before, and the incredulity of Dutch government officials when they learned of the Dayaks' desire for schooling, an idea they had previously rejected. It was the Gospel that had made the difference: the Dayaks wanted to learn to read the Bible.

On Monday, after visiting the elementary school, I said good-bye to Pak Samuel, who had to return to his village. It was a sad parting, and we both cried. Because of his age and the state of his health, I knew I would never see him again. After I returned to the United States, I did send him my father's pocket watch, something he had asked for.

Kampung **Dampak**

Kampung Dampak

My next visit was to Dampak, the village where Pak Surah lived and where I had expected to be staying. As I walked up the notched-log ladder and into the veranda of the longhouse, I saw two women, their slender bodies swaying rhythmically as they pounded rice, each using a smooth, five-foot ironwood pestle to hull it, and other women who were removing the chaff from the hulled rice by flapping it in a flat, wide basket.

333

Two women hulling rice in the longhouse

Surah escorted me to his *bilik* (an individual family room located on one side of the longhouse), where people quickly gathered around us. The photo albums, as usual, were a big hit. For the children, I had brought balloons, which most of them had never seen before. They were enchanted and soon started to play balloon games.

I had let my hosts know that I wanted to see and take part in the activities of their daily life, and so, because they were going to offer me coconut milk to drink, they suggested after a while that we go watch the young men gather coconuts. After we exited the longhouse, I watched as one of them climbed up a very tall coconut tree. The Dayaks are so adept at climbing that it looks as if they are walking, not climbing, up the tree. At the top, he cut off the coconuts, which fell to the ground. With their ever-present *parang* (knives), others cut them open, and we had a small party while drinking the sweet coconut milk and eating its tasty white meat.

When we returned to the longhouse, we went to the *bilik* of Pak Alex, the chief of this village. He was in his late fifties, and his *bilik* showed evidence of higher status: there was a small, low couch and many pictures of women in alluring poses on the wall. One picture was very American, but modest by our standards; others were Chinese pinups, also quite modest, that probably came from calendars. I was reminded of my mother's stories of how the Dayaks prized Bible pictures, which they put up in their *bilik,* and how she collected these from calendars donated by American churches to give out at celebrations. The chief, my companions, and I sat on the floor and ate a kind of split-pea soup; the small couch was unused.

We embarked on a short tour specifically designed to show me facets of the villagers' daily life. First, I watched people hunt for *ubi*, a sweet-potato-like vegetable that grows wild in the jungle. When the plant is tall, three or four large *ubi* will be attached to it underground, each about a foot in length. The *ubi*-hunters also picked the plant's leaves to eat as a green vegetable.

We passed an area of small, unfinished individual homes that would eventually replace the longhouse. The government was urging the Dayak people to move out of their longhouses because it said that disease and fire spread too rapidly within a longhouse. Pak Surah and his wife, who were in their early seventies, did not plan to abandon the longhouse. They said they would die there; they were too old to start over. But the younger families were expected to build their own dwellings and move out. Pak Alex, the head of the village, was still living in the longhouse, but his *rumah sendiri* was almost complete and he expected to live in it by the end of the year. (A few Dayak villages, not ones I visited, had already made the transition from longhouse to individual homes.)

After the *ubi* hunt, I watched them crush sugarcane, the juice of which would later be boiled into syrup. Next my companions conducted me to a small swamp, where a few of them proceeded to fish. It was hard for me to believe they would find anything in the foul-looking water. The women removed some logs and brush, scooped up some gunk from the swamp bottom in a low, wide basket, and searched through it for fish. Within fifteen minutes they had found six small crabs and eight small fish that looked like catfish. I was served these fish that evening for dinner, and they were absolutely delicious!

After fishing, we heard the roar of a chain saw in the distance and walked toward it. We saw a large tree, already felled, being sawed into boards. The tree had been cut in half lengthwise, and a man was maneuvering a portable saw powered by gasoline through the trunk in long, parallel cuts to create boards. It was an ingenious and workable method for people who could not buy lumber, in a place where there were no mills to prepare the wood. This was their lumber mill in the forest.

Sawmill in the jungle

I learned that anyone in the village was allowed to cut down any tree standing on the land that belonged to the village, except for the ironwood trees, highly prized because they do not rot. All the ironwood trees are "owned." Some of them had already been cut down and were lying on the forest floor, but everyone knew who owned them, and if they were not used by the current generation, they would be passed down to the next generation.

At the *Pendeta's* Home

That evening I ate dinner with Yosafat, Ester, and their four children, named Harry, Heppie, Hennie, and Henry. Ester told me a story about Harry, who was three. The boy had kept hearing that *anak Tuan* Mouw, the child of Mr. Mouw, was coming, and he had been anticipating playing

337

with this *anak*. No one had bothered to tell him that this child was fifty-seven years old!

A young woman, Konnie, lived with Yosafat and Ester and helped in the kitchen. I enjoyed watching the two women prepare meals. All cooking was done over an open fire. On two different days I saw Ester grab a chicken from her flock that scampered here and there in the yard, and later I had that chicken as part of my dinner. Ester was also raising a small pig she kept in a pen near the house. It would be slaughtered when it reached an adequate weight. How different was her world of meal preparation from mine! She used no canned goods, no packaged or refrigerated foods, and the entire time I was there she did not go to the store, because there was no store.

After dinner Pak Surah came over to the *pendeta's* home, and I played one of my father's tapes for him, interpreting it into Indonesian. It was the story of Rasa Terbang, Surah's natal village, and how, in the dark of night, he had guided my father back to his village using his "jungle feet." When my father spoke, he would occasionally use Dayak words, and these as well as the sound of his voice, not heard for so many years, delighted Surah. Many others sat in the room and listened with us.

The resident schoolchildren were grouped on the floor, their eager little faces pointed upward, listening, but also waiting for Ibu Siddy, who had invited them to come visit again. Their numbers had grown to twelve. I brought out coloring books, tore out pages, gave them each one, and put crayons out for them to use. They also wanted to see the water toys again. I told them the story "The Three Pigs" and taught them how to count to ten in English. Later that night I lay awake and recalled the laughter and excitement in the faces of these precious, semi-orphaned children. They had found a place in my heart.

Kampung Sepauh

The next morning Yosafat, Ester, a few others, and I set off for another village, Kampung Sepauh, about an hour away. When we arrived, many people gathered in the common veranda of the longhouse as sweet tea was served and the photo albums were passed around.

Kampung **Sepauh**

By this time the albums had been handled so much that the pages had separated from the binding, and each was passed around individually. People shrieked and laughed when they saw someone they knew. One woman recognized her mother who, in the picture, was the daughter's age. Two older men recognized themselves in a photo of two young men holding a large bat by its wings.

Dayaks at Sepauh enjoy pages of the photo albums

Two Dayak men recognize themselves in a picture – second row, far right – holding a bat by its wings

I asked about an old woman sitting with her head slightly bowed and was told she was blind and over ninety years old. I gazed at her lovely, calm face as she sat, silently listening, surrounded by others, cared for by this village where she lived in her daughter's *bilik*. A child of about eleven (perhaps a great granddaughter?) sat with her arm around the old woman's shoulder. I thought to myself about her, "You live here in the interior of Borneo, in a longhouse with no electricity or running water, almost no furniture, no medical system, no transportation. And yet you have everything you need. You are surrounded by people who love and care for you, who are here to help you and guide your steps. If you lived in my country, you might spend much of the day by yourself, feel lonely, and you might live in a nursing home. You have so little, and yet you have so much."

Two older women, one the daughter of the blind woman, told me they had known my parents, a statement of pride. They asked, "Would you like to go bamboo shoot gathering?" Of course I would! So off we went, the two older women, Ester, a young woman in her early twenties, and me.

We walked through the jungle on a wide path strewn with leaves, a canopy of trees overhead, some of them old-growth, gnarled, and enormous. This was more like the landscape I had anticipated. Soon we came to a bamboo grove, and one woman spotted a bamboo shoot emerging from the leaf litter on the forest floor. These women could see a bamboo shoot fifteen to twenty feet away; I couldn't spot one when it was right in front of me. A half hour later, when their baskets were full, we headed back home, stopping first at a small river. There, the women cut off the inedible hard part of the bamboo, washed the shoots in the river, and put them back in their baskets.

Gathering bamboo shoots

I found one of the women particularly appealing. She was in her midsixties with a little wisp of a body (weighing maybe a hundred pounds), wearing a black skirt and plain T-shirt, both of them very old and worn, and slip-on rubber shoes. She laughed, talked, wielded her knife with incredibly deft hands, and walked easily and energetically through the jungle. This was my day for reverie, and I mused, "She may not read or write, has never been to a city or watched TV, doesn't own a car, can't drive, doesn't have a job, knows little about world events, and has few possessions, but she seems so content, so mentally healthy. Who is to say what is the good life? Why should anyone wish a different life for her? Her world is too small for me. I couldn't trade places with her and be content, but I'm not at all certain that I have a better life."

A Party at Dampak

That night at Dampak, I had dinner with Pak Surah and his extended family in their *bilik*.

Pak Surah and his wife, Nyalin, in their *bilik* at Dampak

Afterward, there was a gathering in my honor in the communal room of the longhouse. As usual, everyone sat on the floor, Dayak style. Because Dampak was a Christian village, we began with hymns, a prayer, and a short sermon by Pendeta Yosafat. People asked to hear the tape of my mother and brother again. I also played a tape of my father singing "Throw a Line." Eight little girls sang a song they had practiced especially for this occasion, which I recorded and then played back to them. They giggled with delight to hear themselves, probably for the first time.

A young woman played a tune on her guitar, then offered it to me, and I sang and played "Home on the Range," "She'll Be Coming Round the Mountain," and "Billy Boy," all songs that I sing with my ESL classes at home. They wanted to learn a song in English, and I chose, "She'll Be Coming Round the Mountain" because of its repetitive lyrics. No success. English was *very* difficult for them to pronounce. *Lulun* was served, a traditional Dayak cake of rice flour with brown sugar and coconut, some other rice flour cakes, and sweet tea. Next there was an attempt to get people to dance. One older man danced briefly, but when I snapped a flash photo he immediately stopped. In an effort to promote more dancing, a few men literally dragged several women from where they were sitting to a more central location, but they refused to dance and continued to sit where they were. Finally, the youngest one stood up and began to turn gracefully and move her slender arms. The crowd responded with hooting and clapping, and the two older women joined in. I was sitting cross-legged on the floor, watching them, and began to move with the music. Someone quickly pressed me to dance. Why not? I love to dance. I stood and joined the three women, doing a basic rock 'n' roll step—swaying, feet beating time, body and arms moving. The crowd responded enthusiastically. The man who had stopped dancing started again. His gyrations were more precise, long sweeping movements of his arms and legs. I mimicked his moves with my own and the crowd went wild! The other women sat down and we two—

man and woman—danced. I wondered if this was OK by Dayak standards, since they have conservative ideas about relationships between men and women. Dudley Bolser had told me that unmarried men and women were never allowed to be alone together, even when they were quite old. These restrictions predated the Dayaks' embrace of Christianity.

Later that evening, back in my little room at the *pendeta's* home, I thought about this day that had been like no other in my life, full of rich and rewarding experiences. We had not returned home until 11:30 P.M.; nevertheless, we arose the next morning at 5:30. It was impossible to sleep longer, because each morning the chickens made such a racket. I stayed in my room a while to write in my diary, and as usual, Ester brought me a little tray with presweetened hot tea and deep-fried *ubi* (sweet potato). When I came out, Yosafat was sitting at the table studying the Bible, perhaps in preparation for that evening's service.

Kampung Lumut

Soon Yosafat, Ester, one other woman, and I were on our way to visit another village, Kampung Lumut. On the trail, we ran into eight men, four of whom were carrying a sick man on a makeshift stretcher. The other four were probably along for the next shift. They were taking the man to Immanuel, where I was staying, to put him on the airplane arriving the next day, which would fly him to Sintang, where there was a hospital. I, too, was planning to board this plane, but it didn't come, and I never learned what happened to this man. Perhaps they carried him the full twenty-six miles to Balai Sepuak, where there was a doctor.

I visited the chief of Kampung Lumut, a village that had already been converted to the individual dwellings the government prefers. He told me

345

that he used to help my mother do laundry. Many pictures of Christ from bygone calendars adorned his walls. In the kitchen, women were making *lulun*, rice cakes with brown sugar and coconut, and I sat down to help them.

A *rumah sendiri*, **individual family dwelling**

Roll a bit of flour into a little ball, punch a hole, fill it with brown sugar mixture, close the hole, and wrap it up in a banana leaf. The women were pleased that I could do this easily and quickly, and it seemed to surprise them. Perhaps they didn't see me as someone who regularly engaged in household chores. The *lulun* cakes were steamed in a large kettle for a few minutes. A half hour later we ate these delicious creations, and I was urged by the lady of the house to eat as many as I wanted; I managed five, along with half a coconut and its milk. This little meal of "rice and something else" was a perfect lunch. I recalled one of my father's stories in which

346

he described how much he enjoyed *lulun*, saying that each little cake had about a quarter teaspoon of brown sugar inside, and how he wished the Dayak women would put in a half teaspoon of sugar to more fully satisfy his sweet tooth.

My traveling host, Yosafat, knew everyone at this village—not just their names but also their parents, where they were from, whether they had come from another village, how many children were in the family, and what the children were doing. And he had shown this same familiarity with people at the village we had visited the previous day. Yosafat's knowledge of people, while perhaps somewhat more extensive than others' because he was a pastor, was not unusual. The Mualang tribe, which encompassed all the people I visited, and whose members occupied all the villages I saw, including Balai Sepuak, numbered about fifteen thousand people and was like one large extended family. Anyone was welcome to visit any other village at any time and, if traveling, would automatically be offered food. Upon our arrival at Lumut, the women who had accompanied me immediately went to the kitchen, sat on the floor, and began to help the wife of the chief, who, I'm quite certain, did not know we were coming. (You can't phone ahead!) And the women who had accompanied me to Kampung Ransa and Sepauh had helped the women of those villages just as naturally as if they were visiting daughters or sisters.

After our lunch, we walked back to Immanuel, arriving at the home of Pak Elisa, the school principal, about 4 P.M. He and his wife had a large house compared to others I had seen. The house had several rooms but, as usual, no furniture. We ate in the "dining room" sitting on the floor. Whether Elisa, as principal, could not afford furniture or, as a Dayak, saw no need for it, was not a question I felt comfortable asking.

A Good-bye Service

I was to leave the next day, and that evening there was a service held at Immanuel so people could say good-bye to Ibu Siddy. Dayaks came from several villages, some from a distance of three or more miles. The service began about eight o'clock, and after it was over, at ten, these people had to walk home to their villages. I wondered why they didn't start the service earlier to accommodate them, but, as I was learning, the Dayak concepts of time and schedules are completely different from Western ones.

A woman led the service until it was time for Pak Yosafat to speak. This was not uncommon, as the Dayaks have an egalitarian society. Their singing of hymns, almost four hundred voices joined in harmony a cappella, can not be matched for beauty, and I remembered my father's words, "When their singing reached heaven, it must have made the angels rejoice with exceeding great joy." Four groups presented special music, and I sang "Amazing Grace," my favorite hymn, accompanying myself with the loaned guitar.

When the brief worship service was over, I was presented with a handmade purse woven of plant fiber. My childhood name, "Noni," the date of my expected arrival, "August 22, 1991," and "Immanuel" were all woven into the basket's pattern. These words and the pattern in red, blue, and natural colors were so perfect and symmetrical that I was amazed to know it was handmade. Someone placed the strap, festooned with paper flowers, around my neck as everyone clapped enthusiastically. Pak Yosafat talked for a few minutes about how glad they were that I had come, and how the people lovingly remembered my family. I spoke only a few minutes, giving my thanks for the purse, for Surah's invitation, for my warm welcome in Balai Sepuak and all the villages I had visited, and of course, for the hospitality of my special hosts, Pak Yosafat and Ester. I told them I loved their singing, their prayers, and this night's service, all evidence of their enduring faith, and that I would share all this with my mother, Ibu Mouw, when I returned home.

After these words, people removed the chairs and pulpit from the front platform of the church, drumming began, and a young man performed the plate dance. Many came up to me individually to say good-bye, some lingered to talk, and later there was the usual group of people in the front room of Yosafat's house looking at the photo albums. We finally broke up at 2:30 A.M. Rising time was, of course, still 5:30 A.M. I had come to believe the Dayaks did not need as much sleep as I.

An Extra Day

The next morning I awakened after my three hours of sleep and began to prepare for my trip back to Kelansam on the Mission Aviation Fellowship plane. (The Bolsers had originally planned for me to arrive on this regular, weekly flight: I was to have landed at Immanuel on a Thursday and departed a week later.) I was ready to depart. I had been to Balai Sepuak, walked twenty-six miles from there to Immanuel, visited four villages, and had a longhouse party and special church service in my honor—wonderful, peak experiences all packed into seven days.

At midmorning I was able to take a short nap. I got up feeling anxious that the plane still hadn't come, but soon a procession arrived with drums pounding and bells jingling. A group of Dayak women dressed in their old traditional *kabayas* (blouses) and handwoven skirts, which the women no longer made, danced outside the house. Some of the *kabayas* were very old and had coins sewn into the bottom, which jangled as the women moved. I asked, "How old?" "About seventy years," one replied. I was invited to don a similar *kabaya* and skirt and join in. We danced together. I learned they had planned to have this procession as a farewell event at the airstrip, about ten minutes away, when the plane arrived. But the plane hadn't arrived. The smoke from burning rice fields had again conspired to alter my schedule. I felt frustrated; there was no way for me to make contact with the Bolsers in Kelansam.

Later that afternoon Yosafat and Ester's children and the resident schoolchildren played games in the yard, just in front of the *pendeta's* house. I captured these circular, singing, you're-it type of games on my video camera. Ester told me later that the children didn't often do this, but they had been inspired by me because they saw that I liked to play. This was a lovely compliment, but I also found it a little sad; I wanted them to play like this on a regular basis. That afternoon I taught them Hungarian baseball, a mixer game played with a kickball that I had learned in college, with no similarity to baseball. One of the elementary schoolteachers helped me to explain the rules, and once the children understood it, the game was a big hit. I spent that evening with them, once again engrossed in the concentration game.

The following morning I visited the elementary school. It was Friday, the day all the school children work from 7 to 8 A.M. to clean the school and schoolyard. (Classes usually began at 7 A.M.) Today's job was to cut the grass, so each child had brought his or her *parang* (knife). The children were swarming over the grass, cutting it from a squatting position that they could easily maintain for a long period of time. I visited two classes where the students were doing reading and arithmetic lessons. Again, the teacher in me longed to jump in and suggest teaching the children in groups, since clearly not all were operating at the same proficiency level.

Walking Back to Balai Sepuak

By noon I was certain the airplane again would not arrive. I had decided that if it didn't come, I would have to walk back to Balai Sepuak. I couldn't just wait to see what might happen; the plane might not arrive for a week or two, and I had a flight to catch in Jakarta. Being in Balai Sepuak would offer me a few options: if there were no plane, perhaps I could travel on the Belitang River by sampan. I told Yosafat and Ester of my decision, and by 3:30 P.M. I was on my way, walking back to Balai Sepuak with a few friends.

Our group was made up of Yosafat, Selitonga (another one of Surah's sons, who would help Yosafat carry my baggage), two young women, and me. Ester and I cried when we hugged each other good-bye. The schoolchildren I had come to know so well followed us for a short distance. I knew they would miss me and my games. Elisa, Surah's son and principal of the elementary school, accompanied us for about half an hour, then bid farewell. Ester and Yosafat, Elisa and his wife Deborah, Surah and his wife Nyalin, and Konnie, the young woman who lived with Yosafat and Ester, all had come to feel like my Borneo family.

We arrived at Kampung Pakan about 8 P.M. and stopped to eat dinner. Nothing unusual had happened on our journey, except that a large frog had had the misfortune to be on our path. I, lover of animals, didn't want him killed. It was a particularly big frog that seemed stunned by our flashlights and perhaps disoriented and frightened, because it didn't move. But I restrained my instinct to ask them not to kill it; this was their culture, not mine, and they told me that frog cooked with vegetables was delicious.

No one in the village knew we were coming, but we were welcomed into one of the *rumah sendiri* (individual homes) by a charming man with a wonderful laugh, that punctuated much of what he said. His wife immediately began to cook dinner, although it was well past their own dinner time. A small crowd began to gather. Most of the small houses were dark when we arrived (the Dayaks have no electricity, but they do use kerosene lanterns), indicating they had already retired, but guests, I suppose, always bring people out. Soon the room was full of people. I met a woman who told me she had played with me when I was a child, and that she was one month younger than I. We had our picture taken together that evening.

Siddy and childhood playmate

We were on the trail again by nine o'clock. As we walked, we heard an eerie sound, like the howl of an American coyote, only more ominous. At first we laughed and made fun of it, but the sound persisted. It grew stronger. We walked closer together, looked around, and began to talk to each other. Yosafat tried to light some dry grass by the side of the trail to make a fire, but he couldn't get it going. My four fellow travelers immediately started to sing a hymn with the main refrain "In the name of Jesus." The sound moved closer. I could feel their apprehension growing. I was at the back of the line, which seemed to be the most vulnerable spot, since the sounds were coming from behind. I was surprised, being their guest, that they hadn't moved me farther up the line for safety. The sound steadily grew more menacing and closer. Everyone started running and I followed. Selitonga zoomed to the front of the line.

Then we saw a flashlight and heard the sound of laughter. It was all a joke. A young man in his mid-twenties with a big grin appeared and said he thought we were a group of high school students walking back to Balai Sepuak. He was absolutely gleeful that everyone had been thoroughly frightened. There was much conversation, but all of it in the Dayak dialect, so I couldn't tell if my group expressed resentment, embarrassment, or a sense of humor about his joke. Later at Balai Sepuak, I found out that the creature they thought was following us was a *hantu anak* (ghost child). This is a real animal, now almost extinct, but several in the group had actually heard it in the past. The *hantu* only attacks men, not women, as it is afraid of women. This information was related to me not as conjecture, but as fact. It explained Selitonga's fear and why he ran to get near to the women in our group. It also explained why I was safe at the back of the line.

We arrived in Balai Sepuak about 11:30 P.M. and were warmly welcomed by Pak Aheng and Damaris, my former hosts, even though they didn't know we were coming. After some conversation and hot chocolate, I got to bed at midnight.

On to Kelansam and the Bolsers

The next day, Saturday, August 31, was the most difficult day of my odyssey. There had been no planes in and out of Balai Sepuak, and we decided that I needed to walk from Balai Sepuak to a dirt road that would get me to the Kapuas River near Sintang. I got up at 6 A.M. and ate a good breakfast of rice and vegetables. I had now eaten "rice and something else" every meal for eight days, and this began the ninth day. During this time I had also spoken no English. I said good-bye to my wonderful crew who had brought me to Balai Sepuak. This day I would be accompanied by Pak Aheng and two of the Ebenezer Bible School students.

We left at 8:30 A.M. Much of the walk was through brush country, where the tall old trees were gone and there was little shade. By 10:30 I had less spring in my step, and for the first time I wore my hat to keep off the sun's rays. The road was no more difficult than it had been the previous day, but we were now walking during the heat of the day. We stopped to rest several times, something we had not done on our way to Balai Sepuak.

We arrived at our destination—a small stop on the edge of the jungle where the dirt road began—a little past noon, about the time I thought I couldn't walk much farther. Here, my companions negotiated the cost of hiring two motorbikes and their riders, one for me (I would sit behind the driver) and one for my baggage. The trip would take me to a spot on the Kapuas River, where I could catch a boat to Kelansam. My friends and I loaded up my belongings and said our good-byes, and I gamely eased myself onto the back of one of the motorbikes. My driver started his motorbike, we moved a few feet, and the motor died. This happened at least ten times before we actually got on our way—not an auspicious beginning.

Our bone-rattling, two-hour ride on this dirt road took us across a barren landscape with smoke billowing up in many spots. We had to cross many drainage ditches, our bridge each time only a narrow board slightly wider than the motorbike's tires. Then the motorbike I was on ran out of gas. The two men began to look for some large leaves to use as a container to siphon gas from the other motorbike. Fortunately, in my suitcase I had a small container which they used, and we made it to a gas station. When we reached the Kapuas River, I hired a boat to take me the last leg of my journey, and I arrived at Kelansam at 4 P.M., my clothes covered in dust and smelling of smoke. As I walked up the riverbank to the Bolsers' home, Nancy came down to meet me. Her first words were, "When are you going to write your book?" She and Dudley were relieved to see me. As I'd suspected, the planes hadn't been able to fly because of the smoke. That night Nancy served pizza, salad, and ice cream. It all tasted heavenly.

The next morning it was raining, a welcome event after so many dry weeks. I said good-bye to this lovely missionary couple who had done so much to make my visit possible, then Dudley escorted me to Sintang, where I caught a bus for the all-day trip to Pontianak. Arrangements had been made for me to stay there with a missionary couple, and the bus driver dropped me off at the address I had been given. It was, however, the wrong address, and I stood on the street with no idea where I was.

As darkness fell and I was beginning to feel a little panicky, two young men approached and one asked, "Can I help you?" As I soon learned, he was studying English at the university and welcomed the opportunity to talk with a Westerner. Eventually, with their help and a ride in a van from another good Samaritan, I reached my destination.

Out of Borneo

With the rain keeping the skies clear of smoke, plane service was again on schedule, allowing me to fly to Jakarta the next morning. I took a taxi to the Alliance Guest House, a lovely, gracious home where missionaries and visiting Christian and Missionary Alliance tourists from America may stay. During my two days in Jakarta, I did some shopping, toured the National Monument and adjoining museum, and visited a batik factory. I got around by flagging down a *bajaj,* a two-passenger pedicab with a motor scooter engine.

When I boarded my flight the next day, I felt a sad exhilaration as I reflected on my memorable journey. It had let me see firsthand the impact my parents had had on the lives of the Dayaks. Fifty-eight years had passed since my parents first came to these villagers. They had found a people who believed that spirits inhabited the natural world around them. But the spirits that pervaded their lives were not benign; the Dayaks lived in constant fear of offending these spirits. I saw, instead, people who gather every Sunday to sing in joyous praise to God, who loves them. They pray, invoking the name of Jesus Christ, believing in His redemptive power and care. I thanked God for the presence of His spirit, so evident here among the Dayaks.

Twelve years later, as I write of my visit, the Dayaks' simple way of life, their generosity and deep faith, continue to permeate my thoughts. My life is richer for having made this journey. I am a creature of my culture, a fact that I became intensely aware of during my trip. We think we are individuals, and to some extent we are, but mostly we are shaped by our culture. America is my culture and where I want to live, but I now feel more firmly connected to my Borneo past. My visit has influenced the way I feel about material possessions—something many of us must constantly grapple with in our acquisitive society—because I have met and shared time with a people who have so little, and yet who have so much. My heart is full of love and respect for my parents, Arthur and Edna Mouw, the enduring power of the Gospel, and the Dayaks of Borneo.

EPILOGUE

I visited the Dayaks again in February 2004. During the writing of this book, the Dayaks had been on my mind every day; I simply had to go back to see them once again.

Much has changed in West Kalimantan (Borneo) since I last visited in 1991. The government has put in roads to some of the villages. Because of this, a few of the Dayaks at these villages now own motorbikes, and they can travel more easily to a city like Sintang, something they rarely, if ever, did before. It also means that occasionally commercial trucks come to these villages; for example, trucks pick up the rubber collected by the Dayaks from their groves of rubber trees. The government also supplies electricity at night (from 5:30 P.M. to 5:30 A.M.) to about 15 percent of the villages. A few other villages run their own generators. And a change the government had been advocating—for the Dayaks to build and live in individual homes rather than live collectively in one longhouse—has been accomplished. There are almost no longhouses left; none remained at the five villages I visited.

One thing that hasn't changed is the Dayaks' faith. The churches are strong, vibrant, completely self-supporting and self-governing. There are now about fifty churches in the area where my parents had their ministry, and about three hundred churches in all of West Borneo.

I spent eight days with these wonderful people, again traveling by myself, again having "rice and something else" for all my meals. This time I went to a new area, but one where my father had traveled extensively many years ago. I visited the village of Bethel, where the first Dayak church was built. At Pintu Elok they showed me the Selija River, where my father had baptized many believers. At Kedembak, a third village, there is a large picture of our family prominently displayed in the church. When I saw this, tears came to my eyes and I thought, "What a legacy my parents have left in this land."

This time I met only a few people, perhaps twenty, who had personally known my parents. I again met Pak Seth, a teacher at the Immanuel Bible School (and a son of Surah). During a service when he was speaking to the students, telling them a brief history of my parents' work, Pak Seth told them they were like the great-grandchildren of my parents. And everywhere I went, I was asked, "When are you coming back?" I don't know when, but I do hope I can visit these dear people once more.

Bethel Church in 2004

GLOSSARY

bilik	Individual family apartment within the longhouse.
gawai	A celebration of a socially significant event involving feasting.
ibu	Form of address for an older woman.
kampung	A village.
kabar biak	Good news.
kabar sinang	Satisfying news.
kapala kampung	The village chief.
nyonya	Mrs., Madame – usually reserved for foreigners.
pak	Form of address for an older man.
parang	A knife.
pendeta	Pastor of a church.
rumah sendiri	An individual family dwelling.
tuan	Mr., Sir – usually reserved for foreigners.
tauke	A store-keeper.

BIBLIOGRAPHY

Davenport, William H., ed. *Expedition, Special Issue on Borneo*. The University Museum Magazine of Archaeology/Anthropology, Volume 30, Number 1. Philadelphia, PA: University of Pennsylvania, 1988.

Drake, Richard Allen. *The Material Provisioning of Mualang Society in Hinterland Kalimantan Barat, Indonesia*. Ann Arbor, MI: University Microfilm International, 1983.

Drake, Richard Allen. *The Christian Conversion of the Mualang as a Phase of Messianic Movements Cycle*. Prepared for Presentation to the Second Extraordinary Session of the Borneo Research Council at Kota Kinabalu, Sabah, Malaysia, July 13-17, 1992.

Leibo, Steven A. *East, Southeast Asia, and the Western Pacific 2002*, 35th Edition. Harpers Ferry, WV: Stryker-Post Publications, 2002.

The Central Intelligence Agency. *The World Factbook*. Washington, DC: Brassey's, 2000.

The World Almanac and Book of Facts 2003. New York: World Almanac Books, 2003.

Turnbull, John R. *From Head Hunting To Christ*. Glendale, CA: The Church Press, 1940.

U.S. Bureau of Public Affairs. *Background Notes on the Countries of the World*. Washington, DC: U.S. Department of State, Bureau of Public Affairs, Office of Public Communication, February, 2003.

ACKNOWLEDGMENTS

I wrote this book as a tribute to my parents. I am grateful that my maternal grandmother and paternal grandparents saved all the letters my parents wrote to them from Borneo over the years. I could not have written the book without these letters.

Dr. Allen Drake sparked my interest in returning to Borneo to visit the Dayaks, and, later, he was supportive when I broached the idea of writing this book. He read my first draft in its entirety, contributed significantly to some factual chapters (4, 5, 8, and 17), and always responded with insight to my e-mail inquiries. If we had never met, I doubt this book would have been written.

It is daunting to consider writing your first book at age sixty-eight, so before getting started I took a writing class. The first two sessions were intimidating, as it became clear that most of the other students had been writing for much of their lives, and writing was their passion. But the teacher, Sharon Bray, made all the difference. In an early assignment, she asked us to "write about a house you have lived in, with the house as narrator." I told the story of Edna's "barn" and received enthusiastic and

365

supportive comments from both Sharon and my classmates. After that I couldn't stop writing! And Sharon continued to advise me and cheer me on throughout the writing of this book, for which I am much indebted.

A year before I began writing, I had put together a photographic essay about my family's years in Borneo, which I took with me to my annual weeklong get-together with six college friends. Their enthusiastic response to this essay verified that I had a story worth telling. Later, after I began writing the book, they read some of my chapters, listened to others, and gave suggestions. Thank you Claire Lewis, Joyce Hatfield, Marilyn Boyce, Barbara Meldrum, Joan Weathers, and Phyllis Dow; I am fortunate to have had your aid and encouragement.

Two artist friends, Susan Drake, a writer, and Ann Rinehart, a painter, also gave generously of their time. And Susan Drake introduced me to Bonnie Hurd, who edited many of my chapters. Thank you, Bonnie, for exercising your remarkable skill.

Pat Holt, for many years the book editor for the *San Francisco Chronicle,* read my first draft as part of her Manuscript Express service and responded with eight single-spaced pages of observations and suggestions. I shall forever be grateful for her comment: "I can't tell you how much I came to love Arthur and Edna while working on this book." Since my purpose was to pay tribute to them and their work, she helped me to believe I was succeeding.

Most of all, I thank my husband, Sam Halsted, for his loving encouragement every step of this journey. He urged me to take the trip back to Borneo, was always willing to listen when I needed a sounding board, read all my chapters and offered suggestions, and never complained about my hours and hours at the computer.

About The Author

Sydwell Mouw Flynn was born to missionary parents in Indonesia and spent most of her years there until the age of seventeen. For most of her adult life, she has been a junior high school and English As a Second Language (ESL) teacher. Her trip back to the country of her childhood, in 1991, was the event that led to the writing of this, her first book. She lives in Palo Alto, California with her husband.

She can be reached at sydwell@aol.com.

Printed in the United States
22957LVS00003B/70-219

9 781418 471057